Urban Coffee

Revised Edition

A Quick Note from the Author

I'm excited to share this revised edition of *Urban Coffee* with you! Over the years, I've grown as a writer and as a person, so I went back and updated some of the more intimate scenes to be more respectful and true to the story I want to tell.

This edition still has all the heart and realness of the original, but with a fresh, mature touch. Whether you're a new reader or have been with me since the beginning, thanks for being part of this journey.

— Denitres B.

TABLE OF CONTENTS:

Published by Denitres B

ISBN: 979-8-9910867-3-8

This is a work of fiction. Names, characters, places, and incidents are used fictitiously or are a product of the author's imagination.

Introduction
Revised Edition

Within the vibrant diversity of neighborhoods and communities, the close-knit groups of best friends and family navigate the ups and downs of everyday life. ***Urban Coffee*** is a heartfelt contemporary novel that explores the complexities of personal and professional relationships, the highs and lows of love, the sting of betrayal, and the unwavering comfort of faith.

As life unravels, unexpected truths—both good and bad—emerge. Each chapter brings surprises that evoke joy and heartache, capturing the essence of human connection in its most raw and realistic form.

Urban Coffee is a moving journey through the moments that shape us, celebrating resilience and the transformative power of change. With uniquely developed characters who feel like your friends, family, or neighbors, this narrative will charm, challenge, and devastate. It's a story that lingers long after the final page is turned.

CHAPTER 1

Staying Connected

Malik Nelson stepped off the plane, the familiar weight of the air in his lungs filling him with relief and anticipation. It had been another exhausting two weeks of work and school, and each moment spent on the road added layers to the distance between him and the life he once knew. But now, as his feet touched the ground of his hometown again, a quiet hope stirred within him.

Returning to town always meant something more than just being back home or catching up with friends—it was about the four people he needed to see first: his daughter, Mazo, his parents, and Zora, the mother of his child. The woman he still loved, despite the distance between them—the woman who still held a big part of his heart.

His desire to provide for the people he loves and to build a life with Zora had been his fuel.

****

At 4:30 p.m., Zora's hospital shift was winding down, and her ex, Malik, appeared unexpectedly. The moment he stepped through the hospital doors, his presence was undeniable. Handsome and charming, he carried himself with a warmth that drew people in without him even trying. His genuine and captivating smile instantly softened the room. Nurses greeted him with broad, eager smiles. Even the men on shift couldn't help but admire his flawless style and polished grooming—qualities that seemed as natural to him as breathing.

It wasn't just his good looks that stood out—it was how he made everyone around him feel seen and appreciated, his kindness and charisma shining brighter than any outward appearance.

Approaching the receptionist's desk, Malik found Zora standing alone, attentively working on her tasks to wrap up the day. As she looked up, a hint of surprise flashed across her face.

After processing his sudden appearance, she greeted him with a sarcastic tone and an adoring grin.

"What are you doing here... you lost?"

He scoffed, admiring her curls, which were styled in an updo with a soft yellow linen scarf wrapped around them like a work of art.

"I'm trying to get lost in you," he replied with a touch of finesse. Zora raised her brows as if he needed to elaborate. Malik smirked at her facial expression and moved closer, leaning on her work surface.

"You've known me a long time—no explanation required." She smirked in response to his flirtatious confidence, playfully pushing him on the chest.

To her surprise, he held her hand firmly and locked eyes with her. Zora felt the definition of his chiseled chest muscles, and she began blushing like a schoolgirl with a crush. Her light-honey complexion made it evident.

He took her hand and tenderly kissed the back of it, maintaining a steady gaze and smile for a moment before turning around and walking away. She thought to herself with a smile on her face. *"Oh my goodness, this man!"*

Looking back...

Despite their romantic history, Zora and Malik have maintained a friendship following their breakup, primarily driven by their shared love and, most importantly, their commitment to co-parenting their toddler daughter, Mazo.

When they first got together, Malik took pride in providing for her, reflecting his father's example. He ensured she lacked for nothing, even transportation.

Zora was everything he wanted in a girlfriend and wife: intelligent, educated, family-oriented, and nurturing.

However, once Malik completed his four-year bachelor's in architecture studies and began pursuing his master's and an internship, their relationship crumbled. Zora couldn't handle his demanding schedule and constant travel. Despite his ability to work on finishing his master's in architecture in six years instead of eight, Zora still grew resentful in the long run.

Nonetheless, he excelled as a father, ensuring financial support for his child so that Zora never needed to worry.

Moreover, she had hoped he would return once he established his career, aching for their family to reunite.

Current day...

At 5 p.m., Zora finished her shift and slipped off her short black suit jacket, which matched her form-fitting knee-length pencil skirt. Beneath, she wore a sleeveless, frilly yellow blouse and black heels, ready to head home.

She drove home with a swirl of emotions, her thoughts still lingering on Malik's unexpected visit. She couldn't shake the feeling that their past and all the unresolved feelings between them were now more present than ever.

She pulled up to her house around 5:35 p.m. and observed his car parked in her two-car driveway. Emotions flooded her, as they often did in his presence. Each visit from him carried the hope that he might be there to mend their relationship, possibly indicating a change in his schedule or workload, or some other positive outcome that would bring them back together.

Malik's motivation, however, was rooted in the knowledge that maintaining a connection with Zora was crucial, regardless of the breakup, as he understood the risk of losing her for good.

He had arrived 10 minutes earlier, wearing a charming smile as he approached her side of the car and courteously opened the door. "I missed you," he said.

"Yeah, you only miss me when you want something," she retorted snippily.

"C'mon, that's not true. You don't want me here?" he responded tenderly, wasting no time to ask.

She wanted him there, but she found playing hard to get sometimes was enjoyable. Zora loved seeing how much he cared for her.

Malik offered his hand to guide her out of the car, and together, they walked up the pathway toward her front door.

"So, what's up? Are you ready to come home?" her voice bold and marked with hope.

Malik's brows furrowed as he glanced at her. "I don't know. You tell me."

He desired so much to have what they once had. But the reality of his hectic career, with its demands and constant travel, made it hard to give their relationship the attention it deserved.

Zora was still well aware of his workload, so he couldn't understand why she asked that question.

Before she realized it, he swiftly picked her up. She let out a playful scream while laughing. “Ugh! Put me down, Malik!”

He held her with one arm behind her back and the other one cuffed underneath her legs. She paused when she noticed the look on his handsome face. He gazed into her eyes, leaned in, and kissed her lips twice. Zora returned the soft kisses with pleasure. She missed him just as much but didn’t want it to be so apparent. She is sometimes reserved in expressing her feelings, but he is the complete opposite—open and honest.

After they parted from the kiss, Malik gently let her down and asked about the yard he had noticed earlier.

“What’s up with this grass? The overgrowth is crazy!” Zora chuckled when she turned and saw the look on his face.

“I know, I know. Remember the little young guy you were paying to cut it?”

“Yeah, Thomas,” he answered.

“Well, I haven’t seen him and can’t find his number.”

“It’s all good. I’ll contact Thomas and get my OG by early Saturday morning to hook you up.”

“Aww, thanks, Malik. How much will he charge me?” she enquired.

Malik looked at her as if she were crazy for asking that. “Zo? Your money’s no good with me, baby,” he responded with a firm slap on her butt.

“Ouch! Okay,” she reacted, giggling and rubbing her backside. For a second, their eyes locked. He gave a subtle nod towards the door, nonverbally saying, *‘Let’s take this inside.’*

Zora turned and followed suit, feeling nervous as she approached the front door. She tried to insert the key into the lock, but her movements hesitated when Malik wrapped his hands around her waist. He tenderly embraced her, his hands trailing up to her breasts as he placed gentle kisses on her neck.

With each intimate touch, her heart raced faster. The skill of his touch, the way his body pressed against hers, ignited feelings she couldn't entirely control.

Gently, he turned her around to face him and kissed her softly. Pulling away just enough to speak, he teased with a smirk, "What are you doing with that key? Or do you want the neighbors to have a front-row seat?"

She paused, slowly looking up at him, a wave of embarrassment taking over her. She chuckled at his sarcasm, trying to brush it off.

Malik flashed a subtle smile and a wink, his gaze lingering on her for a moment before she turned to open the door. The moment it swung wide, he quickly stepped forward, his hand gripping her waist as he spun her back toward him. With a swift move, he used his foot to nudge the door shut.

They began kissing intensely, their hands eradicating each other's clothing. Their love and attraction fueled every touch and caress as they moved close to the sofa. She was lost in his gentle aggression and loved it.

As their kiss deepened, Zora whispered, "Babe, what about Mazo? I have to pick her up from daycare at 6:30."

He, gently lowering her onto the couch, whispered against her lips. "Don't worry. I took care of it."

Malik was six feet of mocha-brown smooth masculinity. His biceps and six-pack were sculpted, made for a fitness magazine. His hair was neatly trimmed in a tapered, low-cut fade, reminiscent of the Caesar style, with a dark, wavy texture. His manhood had expanded noticeably.

He gently repositioned her on his lap, entering her tightness, guiding her down slowly—their faces close, their hearts racing in unison. Her body fit so perfectly against his. Zora braced herself, placing her hand on his chest, feeling the solid strength of his muscles and the steady beat of his heart. They held each other close, their movement slow and tender. Zora's breath heightened as she held him, their connection growing more profound with every moment.

Her body trembled from the overwhelming emotions that passed between them. Tilting her head back, she felt the depth of his love in every kiss he placed on her lips, her neck, and the gentle caresses on her breasts.

Her sighs were soft, filled with the vulnerability of giving herself entirely to him, craving his affection, his love.

Malik whispered in her ear, his voice warm and assured. "I love you so much."

His words resonated with Zora powerfully, a sentiment she recognized all too well. She knew his love was not just words; it was in his actions—how he cared for her, his daughter, his family, and his friends. She reacted instinctively, pulling him closely and kissing him deeply as she felt the connection between them intensify—her breath caught in her chest, her heart racing in time with his. Everything else faded away at that moment, leaving only the raw, unspoken love they shared.

Tears welled in her eyes. The tender moment overwhelmed her with an extreme euphoria, and she breathed more heavily every second.

Malik sighed deeply, completely immersed in her tightness, feeling his presence surrendering to her. They held each other, their bodies pressed close, every unfathomable movement filled with gentleness. As their love came down, their hearts beat in sync.

Zora's body quivered with emotion—Malik holding her closely.

The air was rich with affection, and their quiet, shared breaths filled with the overwhelming power of their bond.

"Oh, my goodness," she whispered breathlessly, resting her head on his shoulder, her arms around his neck. Malik maintained his embrace as they breathed in unison.

After a few moments, he felt her embrace tighten around him. "You okay, baby?" he lovingly asked.

Zora was emotional, desiring him to be back for good. Moments like this feel so real, as if they had never been apart.

"I'm okay," she responded, still resting on his shoulder. Malik heard a tremor in her voice, sensing she was about to cry.

"Hey, look at me," he urged gently. She hesitated but eventually lifted her head to meet his gaze.

"I'm okay, I promise," she whispered, her voice shaky. Zora paused, her mind racing. "I just..."

Before she could finish her thought, Malik gently gripped both sides of her face and kissed her lips softly—her whole body was soon calm.

After their lips parted, he spoke caringly.

"We won't think about anything else except for this moment, okay?" He didn't want to deviate from their connection.

As she lay in his arms, Zora's mind swirled with uncertainty. Could they truly rebuild what they once had, or was it all just a brief fantasy? She still believed in their love, but doubts crept in because of his workload. But in moments like this, she questioned if she could ever forgive herself for not being more patient with him due to his career demands.

****

Some time had passed, and Zora woke up alone on the couch, wrapped in Malik's t-shirt. As she went to get up, she noticed a neatly folded pink, moistened washcloth on the coffee table. The sudden recollection of him wiping her down before they dozed off almost brought tears to her eyes. She reminisced momentarily about his sweet gestures when they were together. The little things left a lasting impression in her heart, forever etched in her mind.

After a long sigh, she stood and walked into the kitchen, settling onto a barstool at the granite island. Malik stood at the stove, wearing only his boxer briefs, sipping a glass of iced coffee. Although he usually drank it on weekends or before flights, he often bought coffee pods in bulk for Zora from a warehouse in the city called Traditional Brew.

As he hustled around the kitchen, preparing his famous shrimp Alfredo pasta, Zora admired that muscular form and his cooking skills. His cooking was truly impressive, and she cherished his passion for it.

"What's up, beautiful?" he greeted, his voice warm as he leaned in to gently kiss her forehead. "I hope you're hungry because you made daddy work for it," he teased with a grin and a sexy wink.

She giggled, her nature cheerful and relaxed. "Yeah, and you worked mama out too, sir," Zora countered, her smile wide.

"I didn't hurt you, did I?" Malik asked, his tone teasing.

"No, honey, it was a good workout... trust me," she said, her voice soft and full of affection.

He chuckled, walking around the counter to place her food in front of her.

"Do you want daddy to kiss it?" he asked, his voice playful as he wrapped his arms around her waist from behind, his lips grazing her neck softly.

"I'll kiss it... just say the word," he murmured, pressing another gentle kiss to her neck, his touch sending a warm sensation through her.

"Malik, stop it," she whispered, pretending to pull away, though her body deceived her. He moved to the other side, his lips placing another gentle kiss on her neck.

"That's what you want... me to stop?" he teased, his voice low with affection. "I'll stop... tell me again," he said, stirring with playful intent.

Her heart racing, Zora reached back, pulling him towards her lips, and they kissed deeply.

When they pulled away, she met his gaze, her voice barely above a whisper.

"No, I don't want you to stop."

Malik smiled but quickly shifted the mood. "Okay, right after you eat this grub. I didn't slave over this stove for nothing, sexy lady," he replied, giving her a playful tap on the thigh.

Zora laughed, covering her face with her hands, feeling embarrassed but completely charmed. "Oh, my goodness... You play too much!" she exclaimed, her laughter filling the room as he strutted back around the island, grabbing his plate to join her.

Sitting beside her, he caught her eye and winked, causing her to blush while plastering a big smile.

He grabbed her hand and bowed his head, and Zora followed suit as he said a prayer over their food before they began eating.

"This is delicious," she exclaimed after the first bite, savoring the flavors with her eyes closed.

Malik, pleased by her satisfaction, smiled as he took another forkful of pasta.

At that moment, he remembered something important. "Oh yeah, you're running low on groceries, and I used the last of the milk," he mentioned casually.

"Yes, payday is coming up, so I'm restocking soon," she reassured him.

"Okay, cool... don't forget the coconut milk and heavy cream. I want you to try my new curry chicken joint," he added eagerly, rubbing his hands together. Zora blushed at his enthusiasm, knowing he wouldn't disappoint.

He noticed her affectionately gazing at him, so he leaned in closer, initiating a kiss, and she responded eagerly, meeting his lips with a tenderness that spoke volumes.

"I love you, too," she whispered after the kiss, her voice full of warmth. Malik gently brushed his finger across her cheek, smiling in return. They continued their meal, chatting and laughing for the next hour.

Later, they were settled on the couch, enjoying some of their favorite TV shows. He silenced his cell phone, focusing entirely on her and savoring each moment, knowing his hectic schedule would soon disrupt her peace. He wanted to protect it, but sometimes, it was inevitable—at least for now. Zora rested contentedly in his arms, laughing as they watched an episode of Martin.

In the early days of their relationship...

After their first year together, Malik surprised Zora with the three-bedroom craftsman-style home, imagining a future where they would raise a family together in that very house. It symbolized their plans for a life built on love, stability, and success.

This home also reflected Malik's journey into house-flipping, a venture he started with his best friend, Brayden, right after high school. Their success in the business led them to focus on obtaining licenses and building their realty company, safeguarding a sustainable future for both.

Over time, their social circles had naturally overlapped; Zora had introduced Brayden to one of her best friends, Brooklyn. The two groups grew closer as the years passed, further cementing the bond between Malik and Zora.

Current day...

After their TV shows ended, Malik reached for his shoes. "Babygirl, I appreciate you letting me spend some time with you."

Zora quickly interrupted, her tone playful yet serious. "Hold on, Malik. What do you mean by *appreciate*? Could you not talk to me like we're strangers? Sounds like you're trying to friend-zone me."

"Whoa, hold up, baby," he replied, raising his hands with a dramatic gesture of surrender. "I didn't mean it like that."

She shot him a half-smile, her voice dripping with exaggerated sarcasm. "Just letting you know."

Despite the teasing, she couldn't shake the anxiety she always felt at this part of their visits—when he'd be leaving, headed back to his place, to work, or somewhere out of town.

"So, where are you off to next?" she asked, reaching for the remote to switch off the TV.

"I'm hitting the gym for an hour, then I've got a conference call with Brayden tonight...

We've got some promising buyers for our recent flips, so we're hoping to finalize a good offer with their agents," he explained, shifting focus to the day ahead.

He reached for Zora's hand, guiding her toward the front door. "We're still on for family day Sunday evening, right?"

"Yes, babe. I wouldn't dream of taking that away from Mazo. She knows that after Sunday church, Daddy takes us out to eat as a family," she affirmed with a smile.

"Can I get a kiss?" Malik asked softly, wrapping his arms around her waist.

She nodded, and they shared a tender kiss. He gently caressed her cheek when they pulled apart, his gaze lingering on her. "I'll see you later?"

"I hope so," she replied, Zora's smile lighting up.

Malik reached into his pocket to retrieve his wallet, then took her hand and placed some money in it. "Buy some groceries for the house, and don't forget the coconut milk and cream," he said, heading toward his car.

"Oh, and I'm calling my OG. He'll be here Saturday morning to tackle this jungle of a yard," he added, grinning.

Zora laughed and shouted after him, "Oh, you got jokes!"

He flashed her the peace sign with one hand while holding his phone to his ear with the other. She watched as he slipped into his silver Mercedes and drove off.

Looking down at the $700 in her hand, Zora counted it twice, a grin spreading across her face. *"Yes, Lord!"* she said to herself, recognizing the urgent need for money to help alleviate some of her medical and credit card debts for this month.

The same went for the mortgage—Malik faithfully pays it by managing to double the payment to $2,400 each month. Zora couldn't help but feel a sense of gratitude, acknowledging how consistently Malik comes through for her. Now, she felt relieved knowing she wouldn't have to dip into her paycheck to cover the inflated grocery expenses for the upcoming pay period.

She reached for her phone with a cheesy smile, ready to call a friend.

CHAPTER 2

Unexpected Circumstances

Working at a high-end clothing store, Devin approved a fifty-percent discount on an outfit she wanted for the outing with her friends the following day.

Devin Davis is forever well-dressed, has no children, and holds a degree in Fashion and Design. She's a risk-taker by nature and is highly intelligent—book smart.

Despite being close to Zora, the two differ significantly in their views on men and relationships. Devin, with a carefree attitude, couldn't care less about commitment. She prioritizes her own pleasure and lives life on the edge, embodying what one might describe as a free spirit running wild.

Devin reached into her pocket to grab her phone, intending to make a call. However, just as she did so, she noticed an incoming call from Zora.

"What's up, Chica? I was just about to call you," she said as she headed towards the empty dressing rooms to talk.

"Hey, girl."

Devin immediately sensed that her friend was hiding something. "Are you okay?... I hear something in your voice."

"Yeah, I'm fine," Zora reassured.

She began to open up, sharing how her day with Malik went and her desire to reestablish their relationship.

"Even though we're not together anymore, I need him to want me back like I want him...

And I wish he would understand that while I support his career goals, it wasn't fair for him to add other projects outside his degree. If he hadn't started the extra stuff, we could've had our family back together by now."

"I'm sorry, Zo. I, too, thought the breakup would bring y'all back together before now. You may have to give him an ultimatum or something; I don't know."

Devin couldn't understand why Zora was making such a big deal about it, though, especially since he was still so active in her life. However, even as a teenager, Devin was aware of her friend's family ambitions. Zora often shared her vision of a stable family dynamic in which her husband would be present at home daily and not consumed by work.

This was indeed Malik and Zora's relationship dynamic until his hectic school and work schedule, just shortly after their daughter, Mazo, was born.

"Zo, maybe you should explore dating other people. I mean, it's been about two years since y'all broke up. On top of that, how do you expect him to change anything, and you still deal with him when he's back in town?"

"If you've experienced being made love to by Malik, you wouldn't ask me that question."

Devin couldn't help but chuckle. "Touché, *heffa*. Touché."

But seriously, Dev, I love him! And when I agreed to the breakup, I thought he would somehow change his mind about working so much. Ugh! What should I do?! Zora expressed frustration and a bit of anger. "And you're right, maybe I should let him see me talking to someone else."

Devin paused, quickly realizing her suggestion to her friend wasn't good. She knew Zora shouldn't play these types of games.

"I don't know, girl–maybe you shouldn't listen to me. Malik seems like the serious type when it comes to the heart. If you play with him like that, you'll regret it."

"Yeah, I know, but something has to change. Everyone has limits," Zora countered.

Urban Coffee

On the other side of town, Brooklyn was working her shift at the fast-food restaurant when she heard **Brayden Colman's** voice through the drive-thru speaker. Her heart skipped a beat.

"Can I get a club sandwich, kid's meal with strawberry juice, please? And add a number two and four meal to that, along with a salad," Brayden's voice rang out, calm and leisurely.

Brooklyn, standing near the counter, froze. She couldn't help but listen to him order more than just for himself and their son, Nathan. As soon as she heard the salad, her pulse quickened. She wasn't prepared for what she knew was coming.

"Is ranch okay for your number two meal, sir?" the employee asked him.

"Yeah, the ranch will be fine."

Brooklyn's mind was racing as she moved toward the window, her stomach a knot of tension. She watched as Brayden pulled up in his black Navigator, Nathan strapped in his car seat in the back.

But it wasn't just the sight of her son that threw Brooklyn into a whirlwind—it was the woman sitting in the passenger seat. The woman's dark caramel skin and golden blonde curly hair caught her eye immediately.

Brooklyn couldn't hold back her emotions any longer. Without thinking, she stepped forward, brushing past the employee at the window.

"I can't believe you brought some slapdash female along with my son to my job, Brayden!" Her voice was sharp with hurt and anger.

"Excuse me, fast-food lady!" the woman shouted, her tone defensive.

Brayden immediately intervened, raising his hand to calm things down.

"Hey, chill," he said to the woman in the front seat before turning back to Brooklyn. "I'm sorry, Brook," he said regretfully.

But Brooklyn didn't want to hear it. Her eyes, filled with hurt and anger, stared back at him. She said nothing, just glared at him as the weight of everything they had been through hung between them.

"I'm sorry," Brayden repeated, his voice softer this time as he drove off.

From the backseat, Brooklyn heard Nathan's small, innocent voice calling, "Mommy..."

Keisha's expression tightened as Brooklyn's words hit her. She hadn't realized that this was Brayden's baby mama's workplace. Still, her curiosity was irked, especially after the insult Brooklyn had thrown her way.

"What does *'slapdash'* mean, Brayden?" she asked, her voice laced with confusion and annoyance.

He stopped at a red light and didn't want to engage. But seeing the anger in Keisha's eyes, he knew he had no choice.

"It means something random, thrown together—out of order...I don't know! he replied reluctantly, glancing at her.

****

After Brayden had pulled away, Brooklyn rushed to the back office, her tears flowing uncontrollably.

She wanted so badly to chase after him, to make him understand the hurt she was feeling.

I can't believe he did this to me, she thought, pacing back and forth, her frustration mounting as she anxiously awaited the next shift manager's arrival. She fumbled through her purse, desperately searching for her cell phone. Without hesitation, she dialed the first person she thought might be able to help—someone who understood her situation better than anyone.

"Let me call you back—Brooklyn's on the other line," Zora told Devin.

"Okay, tell her I said what's up," Devin replied.

Zora switched over just as the phone rang the third time. "Hello?"

"I can't believe he did this to me... right in front of my face!" Brooklyn ranted, her voice trembling with emotion as she sobbed nonstop.

"Hold on... calm down, sweetie," Zora said gently, trying to soothe Brooklyn's frantic outbursts. "Brook, tell me what happened, honey. What's going on?"

Looking back...

Brooklyn Abrams is a restaurant shift manager who lives in a comfortable two-bedroom condo owned by Brayden, her son's father. Despite their deep love, they faced challenges as Brooklyn struggled to appreciate Brayden's qualities as a good man.

When their son, Nathan, was born, Brayden's love for her grew even more. Brooklyn began to recognize how much she relied on his affection, seeing his willingness to support their family–his love was steadfast.

However, instead of reciprocating his thoughtfulness, she took his love for granted, failing to recognize its value. Their relationship became an unstable cycle of breakups and compromises until Brayden decided to move on.

Brooklyn now strives for self-improvement. She is pursuing a degree in Hotel Hospitality and working towards an entrepreneur certification.

She has a shared dream of owning a cozy coffee shop with her friend, Zora. Balancing school, work, and single motherhood, Brooklyn regrets not appreciating Brayden's love sooner.

She realized it was worth it only after it was too late.

Current day...

Brooklyn detailed the incident at the drive-thru window, but only after Zora had managed to calm her down.

"You're the one who introduced me to that man!" Brooklyn jabbed, wiping tears from her face.

"Yep, and you're still crazy about him, too, so don't even try it," Zora shot back. They both laughed softly, the tension easing just a little.

"And don't be causing drama with Brayden. We both know he's the coolest."

"I know," Brooklyn admitted, her voice quiet and apologetic. "That's what makes it hurt so much."

At that moment, it was as if a lightbulb went off inside Brooklyn's mind. She suddenly felt an awakening, a shift in her heart. "You know what? I'm going to his house right now. I can't take this!" she declared.

Zora's eyes widened, a flash of panic in her voice. "Wait a minute, Brooklyn! You know how you can get. Think about this first. You cannot go over there while he is with his girlfriend...

Do not call that man or go to his house, Brook. It won't help anything," Zora cautioned urgently.

"Don't you dare call her his girlfriend again!" Brooklyn snapped, though sadness crept into her thoughts. "And I'm good... I got this," she added, though the confidence in her voice didn't fully match the insecurity bubbling inside her.

"How did I let him slip through my fingers like that?" Brooklyn questioned softly, the weight of her realization heavy on her chest.

There was a brief silence on the phone before Zora finally broke the tension, her voice filled with concern for her friend.

"I know Brayden still loves you. But you need to check your emotions before speaking with him. He's worth fighting for," Zora said gently.

Brooklyn frowned, her tone unsure. "Zo, you always have the best advice for us. Why can't you and Malik work things out? Why can't you two reconcile?"

Zora's lips curled in frustration, feeling Brooklyn's lack of support. "What do you mean? It's not me—it's him!

He changed once he landed that internship and started taking on all those extra projects. We had a regular life, and he walked away from it!"

Brooklyn shook her head, her tone firm. "Zo, the man had to work. He wasn't busy for no reason—he was trying to secure your future. Honestly, you didn't even give him a chance to adjust."

Zora's voice rose in disbelief. "Whose side are you on? Did Brayden tell you Malik said that?"

Brooklyn chuckled, shaking her head at Zora's curiosity. She had undoubtedly discussed this topic with Brayden before Malik and Zora's relationship started falling apart. But now wasn't the time to get into it. There was something more pressing in her life at the moment.

"Zora, calm down—nobody said anything," she replied lightly. "I've got business to handle," Brooklyn continued. "Thanks for letting me vent, though. I'll talk to you later... love you."

With that, Brooklyn ended the call.

Urban Coffee

Brooklyn finished her shift, determination fueling her steps as she headed to her car. She dialed Brayden's number, and he picked up after a few rings.

"Brooklyn, please... I'm sorry," Brayden's voice came through, remorseful.

"Brayden, you were wrong!" she snapped, tears rising to the surface.

He sighed. "I know. I wasn't thinking. Nate wanted food from your job. I chose the drive-thru because I didn't want to flash Keisha in your face like that. It won't happen again, I promise. Please don't cry. I would never intentionally hurt you."

Brooklyn's frustration overflowed. "I can't help but cry," she said, voice shaking. "I know you didn't mean to hurt me, but I just... I can't accept this. I still love you," she admitted boldly.

"I love you, too," he responded, his voice steady. "But we can't keep doing this."

Brooklyn fell silent for a moment, processing his words. Then, her voice sharp, she continued...

"You said you weren't rushing into a relationship, but you did, huh?"

Brayden hesitated. "Brooklyn, not now."

"I have every right to ask," she shot back. "Especially with this *gutter-bird* around my son."

"Don't call her that. You don't know her," he said, his tone calm but firm.

Brooklyn's anger flared, but she held back.

Feeling her frustration, Brayden went ahead and answered. "Fine. I've only been seeing her off and on for about six months—nothing serious."

"Six months... It didn't take you that long, huh?" Brooklyn's voice hesitated with defeat. She fell quiet. The hurt mixed with the weight of her words as they lingered in the air.

"Hello? Brooklyn?" Brayden's voice broke the silence.

"I'm still here," she replied calmly.

"We're both trying to move on..." he started, but she cut him off.

"Don't speak for me!" I'm not trying to move anywhere! And what's so special about her?"

Brayden sighed, running his hand down his face.

"Never mind, don't answer that," she added quickly. "I'm on my way over there right now."

His voice turned panicked. "Wait, what? Brooklyn, don't do that."

"Why not?" she shot back. "I know she's not there. We've been talking too long. I'm on my way." She ended the call with a snap and tossed her phone onto the passenger seat.

****

Brooklyn stopped by her house, quickly freshening up. The hot shower soothed her nerves, but when she slipped into a sexy outfit beneath a long black trench coat, she felt the weight of her decision. She hesitantly grabbed the perfume Brayden had always loved. It had been untouched since their breakup, but she wanted to remind him tonight of what they shared. She sprayed it on, locked up, and was on her way.

As she merged onto the highway, her heart pounded in her chest. It was now or never.

Urban Coffee

Upon reaching Brayden's house, Brooklyn hesitated at the front door, fear of rejection creeping in.

The two-story brick home, trimmed with stylish black shutters, felt overwhelming, but she pushed past the nerves, gathering the courage to knock.

After the third knock, Brayden answered. Seeing her chocolate brown Range Rover parked outside—the one he bought her when she was pregnant with their son—he opened the door.

Brooklyn stepped inside without waiting for an invitation, and Brayden, always honest, didn't waste any time.

"Brooklyn, why are you here?" I just dropped Nathan off at my mom's—she's been asking for him for days."

"Okay, that's good. You know I'm not here to see my son," she replied.

He shook his head, still processing the fact that she really showed up. "I just took Keisha to her house after we grabbed food, but she'll be back here later."

Brooklyn's face scrunched up in annoyance. "I don't care about her! She's not my concern—you are."

Brayden turned, walking toward the couch. He bent down to pick up the remote, probably dropped when he answered the door. "Brooklyn," he started, his tone serious, "we can't do this. It's not the right time for you to be here."

As he picked up the remote and turned back around, Brooklyn stood unyieldingly. She was dressed in a seductive red lace lingerie set paired with four-inch black heels, her purpose evident.

She tossed her coat onto the plush recliner and approached him with a slow, sensual walk, gently pushing him back onto the couch. Grabbing the remote from his hand, she powered on the stereo—a device she knew all too well.

The soulful sound of *'Feenin'* by Jodeci filled the room, coming from his state-of-the-art sound system.

The music set the perfect tone for what she had longed for since the day Brayden ended their relationship. She ached for his touch, kisses, and the comfort and security in his arms.

She treated him to the most sensual dance he had ever witnessed. His eyes locked on her every move, captivated, as though he were in a trance.

Brooklyn swayed her hips slowly and deliberately, drawing Brayden's attention with every gesture. He watched, mesmerized by her grace and confidence.

It had been so long since they shared this kind of intimacy, and the air between them sizzled with unspoken cravings. Brayden looked up at her beautiful face and into her eyes, and in that moment, all the reasons he had fallen in love with her flooded his mind.

Brooklyn's gaze met his, and the world outside them dissolved. She straddled him and was in his arms again—everything felt like it was falling back into place—this connection, this love they shared, despite the distance and time apart. Brayden's hands gently caressed her back, pulling her closer, feeling the heat between them rise.

Brooklyn smiled softly, her eyes shining with both love and remorse. "I miss you, Brayden," she whispered. "I don't ever want to fall out of love with you. I can't."

He leaned in, their lips meeting in a kiss that spoke of everything they hadn't said in a long time.

As their kiss deepened, Brayden felt the weight of all their past moments, good and bad, settle between them. This wasn't just physical but emotional—a reconnection that had been inevitable.

He gently laid her on the couch, removing her bottom. His kiss was deep and slow. There was no denying the chemistry between them or the desire that had always been there.

As he entered her, they made love unhurriedly—their movement natural and overwhelmingly pleasing. It was about their bond, the love that had never truly faded. It felt like a promise that they would never stop loving each other.

He was so gentle, moving within her secret place, her legs wrapped strategically around him. Her body quivered, their eyes locked, both lost in the moment as their love came down instantaneously. Her breath quickened, her body responding instinctively as she closed her eyes, overwhelmed by his passion, their connection.

As the moment lingered, their bodies slowing, the heat between them gradually softened, and the room became serene.

When the quiet before the storm settled, Brayden gently lay beside her, and Brooklyn rested against him, their breathing slow and steady. He held her close, feeling the weight of everything they had shared. There were no words for it, not yet. But there was a knowing, a quiet certainty in their hearts that they'd crossed a threshold they couldn't return from.

As they held each other, Brooklyn whispered, "I don't *wanna* leave."

Brayden kissed her forehead gently. "I don't want you to."

But neither of them was ready to face what would come next.

Brayden slowly removed his arms from around her, allowing Brooklyn to rise from the couch, wearing her nakedness as if it were still an everyday occurrence with him.

She walked over to the stereo, browsing through his playlist. "Do you still have the surround sound set up upstairs?"

Brayden nodded. "Yeah, why?"

She reached for his hand. "Come on, we may not have much time. Aren't you expecting company soon? I have no time to waste," Brooklyn said alluringly.

Brayden stared at her, momentarily caught off guard by her words. But he couldn't resist following her upstairs.

Who is this girl? He wondered, still surprised by how calmly she seemed to dismiss his guest.

As they reached the shower, Lauryn Hill's *Nothing Even Matters*, featuring D'Angelo, began to play from the speakers, filling the room with its soulful sound at the perfect moment.

They kissed passionately, holding each other close as if they were the only two people in the world.

Pulling away from the kiss, Brayden reached for the shower knob and turned it on.

He led Brooklyn into the spacious, steam-filled shower, the warmth enveloping their bodies, deepening their intimacy.

As he gently cupped her face in his hands, he tasted her lips, savoring the sweetness of her kiss. Brooklyn felt a deep sense of belonging—she was his, and he was hers.

A quiet certainty was in her heart, a deep, comforting peace she hadn't felt in a long time. She felt cherished in his arms—for that brief moment, everything was right in the world.

Amid their intimate phase, the sound of the doorbell ringing through the house shattered the silence. Brayden's mood immediately shifted. "Dang!" he muttered softly, his disappointment evident. Brooklyn's chest tightened, a mix of irritation and sadness flooding her.

He turned off the shower, dried himself quickly, and put on the nearest t-shirt and jeans. Clouded with frustration, Brooklyn's face displayed anger and sorrow.

Brayden sensed the old Brooklyn returning—the one who was quick to react—and braced himself.

He reached out, gently taking her arms. "Baby, please, don't freak out on me."

Though she wanted to lash out, Brooklyn paused, their eyes locking. A realization hit her: losing her temper now would erase everything they'd shared tonight. She was trying to win him back. She forced herself to calm down, with effort, though the irritation lingered in her chest.

"I'm sorry. Go. Answer the door. I know it's her. I'll be fine." Brooklyn's voice was laced with hurt.

To avoid looking at him any longer, she turned away, her eyes filled with sorrow as the reality of the situation set in. Brayden gently took her arm, turning her back toward him and lifting her chin to meet his gaze.

"Please don't be upset," he whispered, kissing her forehead softly.

But instantly, panic quickly overtook her. "Brayden, our clothes are downstairs!"

His brow furrowed with concern as he remembered. "You still have some things in our son's closet. I'll take care of the clothes downstairs," he reassured her.

Brooklyn stared at him, surprised by the revelation.

She was momentarily speechless. "I... um... I'll get dressed and come down the back kitchen stairway," she finally managed to say. Brayden hurried downstairs, and Brooklyn moved quickly toward Nathan's room.

She rummaged through his drawers before heading to the closet, where she found exactly what she was looking for.

Four pairs of jeans and a few T-shirts were tucked at the back.

A couple of pairs of sneakers were neatly packed in a small box. She stood there momentarily, confused, wondering why Brayden had never brought these things to her, unlike everything else.

Still, in a rush, Brooklyn dressed quickly and slipped through the back hall entrance, making her way quietly to the kitchen, careful not to draw attention to herself.

Meanwhile, Brayden had already sprang into action, quickly picked up Brooklyn's lingerie from the floor, and discreetly hid it out of sight. As he reached the front door, he saw Keisha just as she closed her car door.

She initially rang the doorbell but stopped, realizing she had left her cell phone in the car. She returned to retrieve it. Brayden took a deep breath and tried to steady himself. He went outside, greeting her with a warm hug and engaging in small talk to delay her entry into the house. He silently prayed this would give Brooklyn enough time to get dressed. It did.

Eventually, Keisha entered the house, her eyes scanning the area.

Upon seeing Brooklyn's car outside, she went into investigation mode. As she made her way toward the kitchen, her gaze landed on Brooklyn sitting at the table, and pure fury flashed across her face.

Brayden quickly intervened, playing it cool despite the thick tension in the air. He needed to distract Keisha before things got worse.

"Brook, uh... We'll talk about Nate's school stuff tomorrow. You should go ahead and schedule the parent-teacher meeting," he said, keeping his voice light, hoping to shift her focus.

Brooklyn shot him a sharp look, but she quickly forced a smile, rising from the kitchen table to play along.

"Okay, I'll take care of it," she replied, her tone tight with restraint.

Before Brooklyn could pass by Keisha to leave, she paused at the fridge to grab a juice. Keisha's reaction was swift—her finger jabbed in Brooklyn's direction, pointing side to side.

"Uh-uhn! What do you think you're doing? This is no longer your territory, boo-boo!" she disputed.

Brayden's eyes widened, then his brows furrowing in confusion.

"Keisha, calm down; it's just juice," he quickly interjected, hoping to defuse the tension.

"Oh, so you're taking her side now, Brayden?" Keisha snapped. "I want her gone. Now!"

Keisha's eyes locked onto Brooklyn again, and in an instant—*SMACK!*

Before anyone could react, Brooklyn slapped Keisha so hard that she stumbled backward, nearly falling to the floor.

"Whoa!" Brayden exclaimed, his hand instinctively covering his mouth in shock. He knew Brooklyn could be lethal when it came to fighting, but the speed and force of that slap caught him entirely off guard. It was like something out of a movie—it happened so fast yet seemed to unfold in slow motion, like a scene from *The Matrix*.

Keisha stood there, wide-eyed, holding her cheek in stunned silence. Brayden rushed to her side, but Keisha, now truly consumed by fury, lunged at Brooklyn.

Like a fight between cats and dogs, the altercation escalated quickly—a chaotic brawl of flailing limbs. Brayden struggled to separate them as Keisha's arms swung wildly.

Despite the frenzy, Brooklyn remained calm, landing quick right and left jabs to Keisha's pretty face.

In the chaos, Keisha managed to grab Brooklyn's hair, and they both tumbled to the floor. Keisha's panties and breasts were exposed as they fought fiercely. The brawl felt like it went on for minutes, though it lasted only seconds. Keisha had a bloody mouth and a small gash under her eye.

Finally, Brayden managed to break them apart, pulling Brooklyn off of her and heading toward the kitchen, pleading with her to leave peacefully.

"Brooklyn, babygirl, please, just go," he begged, his hands clasped together in a praying gesture.

After his plea, Keisha angrily exploded, venting her frustration and embarrassment.

"That's right, hood rat! Get out of our house and leave my man alone! Your time here is over!" she yelled, pulling her skirt down and covering her breasts with what was left of her blouse.

"And we'll pick our son up tomorrow!" she added, shouting after Brooklyn.

At first, Brooklyn was smirking, moving toward the front door, her hair a bit disheveled. But when Keisha made her final comment, Brooklyn's demeanor shifted.

"You just crossed the line!" she snapped, rushing at Keisha to land another jab to her face. Brayden quickly intervened, grabbing Brooklyn from behind and escorting her out the door. Keisha was flailing her arms frantically like a wild woman, scared out of her mind.

Once she realized she was in the clear, she dashed to the front door, shouting victoriously.

"Yeah! You're stupid! Look who gets to stay!" But her victory was short-lived.

"Keisha, shut up! Get back in the house and close my door!" Brayden snapped, his frustration plain.

Keisha, stung by his harsh tone, froze. She had never heard him speak to her like that before.

Shocked, she reluctantly retreated into the house, closing the door behind her.

Outside, Brayden approached Brooklyn, who was pacing restlessly. He could see the tension in her, and the regret over the night's events was intense.

"Brayden, you better school your girl in there!" Brooklyn yelled, still furious.

"Brook, calm down," he urged, trying to soothe her.

He lowered his head, fighting back a smile. Despite the chaos, he appreciated Brooklyn's calmness and warmth during their time earlier. It was a side of her he hadn't seen much—maybe earlier was just an exception, he wondered. But he kept it to himself, though. He didn't want to get her—or himself—hoping for something more right now.

After a few moments, he managed to guide Brooklyn into the car, with him taking the passenger seat. He gently lifted her chin so their eyes met. "I'm so sorry it ended this way," he said softly. "But I'm glad you came by."

The tension between them lingered in the air for a moment, and Brayden took a deep breath, trying to calm the whirlwind of emotions. Still slightly rattled, he gave a playful smile and added, "I'm in shock from that smack, too."

"Shut up, crazy," Brooklyn replied, playfully pushing his arm. Their laughter broke the tension, and Brayden was grateful for the lightness brought to the moment. He knew he had a lot to make up for, but tonight had felt different—and for the first time in a while, it made him think about the future with her.

Brooklyn seized the moment to express her commitment to personal growth and self-improvement. It wasn't just about her love for him, but also about her self-worth. She understood that, whether or not she could win him back, she still needed to prioritize becoming the best version of herself.

"Brayden, you know what my upbringing was like," she began, her voice calm. "My mom was so passive with my dad. He got away with everything because she was determined to keep the peace. He cheated, and she pretended it didn't happen.

Brooklyn paused there, reflecting...

"It wasn't until the end of their marriage that my mom started speaking up, but by then, my dad was already too far gone."

She took a steadying breath before continuing. "Even after the divorce, Mom dated, but Dad couldn't let her move on in peace...

It was like no one else could have her if he couldn't have her...

So, I made it my mission to make sure that didn't happen to me—by any means necessary."

Brayden listened quietly, his gaze thoughtful. "Oh... now I get it," he murmured, his voice low but clear.

"Get what?" Brooklyn asked, seeking clarification.

He hesitated before answering, a hint of mockery in his tone. "By any means necessary, huh? Does that work for you?"

Brooklyn's expression hardened.

"I guess it doesn't," she admitted, her voice soft with resignation. "I inherited more of my dad's selfish side than the part of my mom's I needed but tried to avoid."

She paused, the weight of her words sinking in. "And if it had worked, I wouldn't be sitting out here, being kicked out of what used to be our home."

Brayden sighed and moved a little closer to her. "I'm not kicking you out," he reassured her sincerely.

Brooklyn met his gaze, her eyes filled with emotion, and for a fleeting moment, she found herself wanting to kiss him.

She leaned in, drawn to him, but Brayden gently stopped her. His hand on hers was firm yet kind as he turned slightly away from her.

"Babygirl, we can't. It's already wrong on all levels that I was with you before Keisha came back tonight. But... she's here now. Literally a few feet away. That would be stone cold."

Brooklyn stopped, a tear slipping down her cheek. Brayden's heart sank at the sight. He wanted to hold her, but he had already seen Keisha lurking through the curtains twice.

He leaned back against the headrest with a sigh.

"I think I've done enough damage for tonight," he said, guilt heavy in his voice. "I'll call you tomorrow, okay? Can I do that?"

Brooklyn nodded, her voice plain. "Um... yeah," she replied, her heart aching. The thought of Keisha staying behind, held in Brayden's arms, tore at her. It felt like her chest was being ripped open.

Before leaving, Brayden reached over and gently cupped her face, looking at her with soft eyes.

"Before you go," he said quietly, "I want you to remember something. I know that sexy outfit and dance were meant to get my attention. But you don't have to do that—you're beautiful and sexy to me no matter what." He paused, his voice sincere. "And I'm sorry if I made you feel like you had to do that."

Brooklyn blinked back more tears, touched by his words. "I hear you... And thank you for saying that."

There was a brief silence between them.

"I'll call you. Be careful and text me," he said.

Brayden stepped out of the car, lingering for a second, watching Brooklyn back out of the driveway before she drove away.

Turning towards the house, he prepared for another round of conversation he wasn't ready to engage in. But Brayden understood the importance of facing the consequences like a grown man, preparing to endure every word that awaited him.

As he opened the front door and began to step inside, he was confronted by Keisha, standing there with her arms folded, pain evident in her expression.

"Did you sleep with her?" Keisha's sudden question stunned Brayden, freezing him in place. She repeated the question calmly, her lips tight with tension.

"Did you sleep with her? Brayden, answer me! Did you sleep with your baby's mom?!"

Unable to do anything but gaze at her with guilt in his eyes, he watched as she began to cry, tears flowing.

The pain was intense as she collapsed onto her knees, covering her face in distress.

"You did! Didn't you?!" she cried out, letting out a painful scream into her hands.

Overwhelmed with remorse, Brayden knelt before her, his heart heavy with blame. Yet, Keisha allowed him to pull her closely into his arms.

"I'm sorry. I'm so sorry," Brayden whispered contritely. "This was not my intention."

He hated to see anyone he cared for shed tears, especially if he was the cause of it.

"Keisha, look at me," he humbly begged.

Reluctantly, she looked up at him, and he gently touched her face.

"I'm sorry," he whispered, his gaze mesmerizing. His apology was so sincere that it was difficult for her to stay angry as she had anticipated. However, she couldn't help but express the pain she felt as tears continued to flow.

"Brayden, you hurt me! I never thought I would go through this with you! You were supposed to be different!" she cried out.

"I know, and I'm sorry. We can work this out... I didn't mean for it to happen," he reassured her.

Keisha fell deeper into his arms, feeling weak and injured. Yet, she couldn't help but feel reassured by the firm caress of his strong hands and the sincerity in his voice as he held her tightly and apologized.

She knew Brayden was a good man, the kind she thought she would never meet. She understood that entering the relationship would be challenging, especially with his small child and the love he still has for his son's mother.

She knew there might be baby-mama drama, but she didn't care. She was willing to face every challenge, focusing on the bigger picture—staying with Brayden.

Right after Brayden & Brooklyn's breakup...

Early on, Brooklyn consistently created challenges for Brayden following their breakup. Upon hearing about his interaction with another woman, she would promptly contact him by phone or appear at his doorstep as if it were urgent.

Brooklyn's behavior displayed a lack of emotional stability during this time.

However, **Keisha King** stood out as the one with lasting commitment. She recognized Brayden as a genuinely good guy and was determined not to let him slip away easily.

In her experience, most of the good men were married, and others were either players, in jail, homosexuals, or all of the above. So, she valued the uncommonness of finding someone like Brayden.

From the start, her sole objective was to satisfy him in every conceivable manner, appreciating his admirable Southern qualities. He opened doors, pulled out chairs, and held hands. His gestures of kindness seemed endless, making him an example of the ideal man.

Keisha set her sights on Brayden from the first day he walked into the bank, even though she was aware of his existing relationship and child. When Brayden visited the bank with Brooklyn and little Nathan, she remained confident in her pursuit.

When Brooklyn wasn't with him, she took every opportunity to engage him in conversation, even tracking his deposit days and scheduling her lunch breaks accordingly. She took her efforts further by leaving anonymous notes on his car window during his visits and orchestrating a deceptive house showing to learn more about him. She even told lies about her relationship troubles to gain his sympathy and trust.

Keisha works as a bank teller, striving to build a life different from her upbringing, and pursuing an associate's degree in banking and finance.

Despite residing in a comfortable one-bedroom apartment in a neighborhood with possibly unsafe conditions after dark, she manages her life well. She presents an attractive package, with her stability and the fact that she has no children.

Current day...

Brayden held her in his arms, where she felt safe and comforted despite what he had done earlier. After finding relief in his embrace, Keisha forgave him. However, she couldn't shake the lingering sense of threat to Brooklyn's existence.

"I can't stand that tramp!" she blurted out, unable to contain her frustration any longer.

Brayden responded swiftly.

"Listen, I understand you're upset, but I won't tolerate disrespect towards her from you. She's still the mother of my child."

"Brayden? Are you defending her?" she questioned.

"It's not about defending her, Keisha. Just keep the negative comments to yourself... I'd do the same for you if the situation were reversed."

He has always been honest with Keisha about his feelings for Brooklyn. From the beginning, he made it clear that he still had love for the mother of his son.

CHAPTER 3

Consequences

Meanwhile, Brooklyn drove home, tears streaming down her face. Her thoughts were a whirlwind of emotions, and the song *"Have You Ever"* by Brandy only intensified her sadness. She cried, wishing nothing would ruin the precious memories she hoped to rebuild with Brayden.

But as the car's audio system filled with the melancholy lyrics, her mind drifted to their earlier conversation. Brayden cared for Keisha, and that thought struck her like a cold wind. She knew Brayden's commitment ran deep—it was all in when he dedicated himself to something. She had taken that for granted, and that realization hit her harder than ever tonight.

You don't usually miss what you have until you see someone else reaping the benefits, she thought to herself.

Brooklyn had taken the long route home, finally pulling into her condo's parking lot. Her phone rang—frantically digging through her purse to find it...hoping it was Brayden.

"Hello? Hello?" she answered, out of breath.

"What the?! Why are you answering the phone like you're running for your life?!" Amina teased.

"Oh, hey, Mina. I thought you were someone else," Brooklyn admitted.

"Who, honey, Brayden?" Amina asked sarcastically, chuckling. "Yeah, you know you can't hide anything in this circle, boo," she added with a giggle.

But despite the playful jab, Amina was one of the most loyal people to her friends. **Amina Anderson**, the youngest of the group, was 22 years old and enrolled part-time at a local college, focusing on general studies. She hadn't decided what she wanted to do with her life yet—no children and no pressing worries. Amina enjoyed financial support from her father, who was sporadically present—often only when he had the means to help with necessities. Amina had a girly-girl demeanor but wasn't afraid to get rowdy when necessary.

"But seriously, Brooklyn, I spoke to Zora earlier and got the *deets*. I'll meet you at Brayden's right now. What's up?"

Brooklyn chuckled. "Classic Amina Anderson—always ready for a brawl."

She could relate to Amina's energy, but the old Brooklyn didn't want things to escalate.

"You know you want to—don't fake the funk," Amina teased, smacking her gum in Brooklyn's ear. They both laughed.

"I said, no... You menace to society," Brooklyn replied, shaking her head. "I'm good, Mina... for real. No more *drama-queening*. I'm a grown woman, so I should act like it."

"I feel you, girl. Do your thang!" Amina sang lazily.

Brooklyn's eyes widened. "Mina? Are you drunk? You seem hyped for just a Thursday night—and we don't even drink like that or at all!"

"I am, but girl, I'm a little horny. I think I'm going to call my big daddy." Brooklyn frowned. "Mina, ew! You still dealing with that old man?"

"Yeah, girl! He's got some mean tongue action!"

Brooklyn was disgusted. "La, la, la, la, la, la, la!" she responded loudly, not wanting to hear another word.

"Bahahaha!" Amina burst into laughter. "You are hilarious, Brook. I was playing, stupid girl! I don't have time for old ding-a-lings! I only hang out with him occasionally. He wants some arm candy at his little shindigs sometimes, that's all."

Brooklyn kept the same frown. "Mina, he may be looking for something more in the future, foolish girl!"

Amina pursed her lips, unfazed by Brooklyn's words.

"He can look all he wants. He knows what's up!"

Brooklyn, shaking her head. "Honey, you can have those short-lived relationships. I'm looking for something genuine and long-lasting."

"I hear you, girl, but Roccorio messed that up for me."

Brooklyn smacked her lips. "One man doesn't stop the show. You're 22 and beautiful, Mina. Don't underestimate yourself."

"Yeah, yeah. Alright, girl! You've ruined my night by making me mention Roc's name."

"Why, Mina? What's up with y'all lately?"

"Ugh! There's no y'all!" she shouted. "He just started calling me out of the blue again a few weeks ago, wanting to hook up. This is him texting me right now! It's like he's had this epiphany or something and wants me to trust him again instantly."

"Well, you never know. Just hear what Rocco has to say."

"No, no, Brook. Don't even try it. There's still too much pain. Look, I'll get up with you guys tomorrow night. I don't wanna have this conversation anymore."

"Okay, sweetie," Brooklyn respectfully digressed, and they ended the call.

****

Brooklyn entered her condo, tossing her cell and purse onto the couch before plopping beside them and kicking off her shoes. Her condo was always clean, with a sweet apple pie aroma from her scented plug-ins.

Sitting on her soft gray sectional sofa in the dark, with just a hint of light filtering through the draperies from the outside lamppost, she felt overwhelmed by everything that had happened earlier.

She couldn't shake Brayden from her mind. The mere thought of his hands caressing her, his sensuous kisses on her lips, and his seductive voice whispering in her ear, saying how good it felt to hold her. Her body shivered at the thought, and her mind raced relentlessly.

She began tearing up again, prompting her to rise and head to the refrigerator for a bottle of fruity wine cooler.

She wasn't a drinker, so the 4-pack had been sitting in the fridge for weeks. Just one half of a bottle would do—make her tipsy enough to fall asleep.

She was determined to keep the troubling thoughts of Keisha being with Brayden tonight at bay.

She reclined on her couch, turned on the 55-inch flat-screen TV mounted on her wall, and sipped her fruity drink until she was halfway through it. Eventually, she drifted off to sleep.

Urban Coffee

The following morning, Keisha was awakened by Brayden showering in his main bathroom. She hadn't slept much; something felt different. He hadn't held her close as they slept last night. And it didn't take him long to fall asleep, which was different from the last time.

The one other time she stayed over, Brayden held her, and she was the first to drift off. That's just who he was—incredibly selfless.

But last night, she didn't receive the same treatment, which made her uneasy. She lay in bed, tears forming in her eyes as she rolled over onto her side, allowing them to trickle down her face silently.

"Oh, my goodness, what am I supposed to do? He still loves her. I can't compete with this. They are his family. No, no, no, no! She's not his family! Little Nate is his family. They're not together anymore, so she's not a part of that. Get it together, Keisha. Don't flake out now. I love him. He is going to be mine!"

Her thoughts raced in a whirlwind of confusion and fear. She was terrified that Brayden was slipping away from her. This would be the first time she faced the reality of an outsider affecting their situation.

Like everyone else who knew Brayden, Keisha, even in the short time she'd known him, understood he was a faithful guy—one woman at a time.

Keisha thought about how difficult it was for many women to find a man who treated them like queens, who came home every night, didn't stay out late unless it was for legitimate business, and took care of the significant bills. He's excellent with the kids and ensures the car is always in working condition.

This kind of man takes the trash out, carves out time for date nights, and surprises you with small tokens of love—flowers at your job or a sweet text to remind you that you're on his mind.

He's not afraid to express his feelings, even when upset, because there's always love behind his words. He's unapologetically affectionate, and his lovemaking is unforgettable. This type of man is complex to let go of, even when he slips up, even if he makes a mistake and cheats. Still, many women would do almost anything to keep him.

And Keisha wasn't about to let him slip away. She was working to get to know Brayden in all those ways.

He walked out of the bathroom, a towel wrapped around his waist, right below his rock-hard six-pack. He'd already put lotion on and entered the walk-in closet to get dressed. Keisha sat up in bed, pulling the covers to her waist, her bare breasts exposed. She didn't know how to break the silence, and her thoughts began to spiral again.

Why am I so nervous? He cheated on me! He should be the one nervous, trying to smooth things over. What is he thinking? Is he going back to her? Does he not want me anymore? He pleaded with me last night to forgive him, but now he's distant.

Her negative thoughts overwhelmed her as if the roles were reversed, like she was the one who had cheated.

Keisha knew she had to act fast. Brayden would be leaving soon to show a house.

When he came out of the closet, he wore dark dress pants and a collared shirt that had not yet been buttoned.

He walked over to the lounge chair near the king-sized bed.

"Brayden?" Keisha whispered, her voice soft yet catching him off guard. He hadn't noticed she'd been watching him since he came out of the shower. His mind had been elsewhere.

"Oh, good morning, sleepyhead. You scared me, girl. Didn't realize you were awake."

Keisha didn't waste time. "What's going on, Brayden? You've been ignoring me since last night, and you haven't touched me at all. I don't understand why you're so distant. It feels like I'm the one who cheated on you."

A tear slipped down her cheek as she tried to reach him, hoping to understand his silence. He felt a pang of guilt, hating that he had put her in this position.

After putting on his shoes, Brayden sat beside her on the bed and embraced her tightly. He felt he'd stepped into a situation he never wanted to face and couldn't shake it.

"Keisha, please stop crying," Brayden murmured. "I never said I was leaving. I'm right here."

He gently cupped her face in his hands, meeting her gaze.

"I know I hurt you, and I'm sorry. But I'm not going anywhere, and I want to fix this—if you'll let me."

Keisha's tears slowed, but she looked at him with intensity as he continued to speak.

"I didn't touch you last night because I thought it was the right thing to do. I didn't think you'd want that after what I did."

Keisha wiped her eyes, her voice firm but vulnerable. "Brayden, please, don't be ridiculous. I love you."

Those three words caught him off guard, but he stayed focused on her, his gaze never leaving hers. She noticed the subtle tension in his eyes but didn't back down.

"When we said we'd work it out last night, I meant it. I want to put the past behind us and work through this with you. I'm here, bae," she expressed shamelessly.

Again, Keisha pleaded her case as though she were the one who had cheated. She wasn't about to lose any ground to Brooklyn or anyone else, for that matter. Her eyes were set on the bigger prize, and Brayden was certainly that prize. She still hoped that he would make them official.

But Brayden wasn't being fully honest with Keisha. He hadn't touched her last night because his mind was with Brooklyn, like it was this morning.

Brooklyn still held his heart; he couldn't shake his love for her.

"We're okay," Brayden reassured Keisha, his voice soft. "If you want to talk about this later, we can. Is that alright with you?" He gently kissed her on the cheek before getting up to finish dressing.

"Bae, we don't need to talk about this anymore," she said, grabbing his hand as he stood. She didn't want to dwell on the negativity. She knew it could strain their relationship, pushing it to a point where they might not be able to recover from. She couldn't risk that. What scared her the most was Brayden being too honest about his feelings for Brooklyn. She wasn't ready to face that truth, no matter how much she already knew it.

Keisha gave Brayden a flirtatious look, her intentions clear in her eyes. "You don't have to rush off so soon, do you?" she asked softly, her hands slowly unbuttoning his pants.

Brayden's eyes widened, his hand gently grasping her wrist. "What are you doing? This can wait–"

Her sudden closeness and the boldness of her actions surprised him, leaving him momentarily speechless.

She moved quickly, taking the initiative in a way that made Brayden's breath catch in his throat, the warmth of her mouth surrounding his manhood. He could only watch as she continued, his body reacting instinctively to the sensation, his thoughts clouded with the overwhelming pleasure. His hand reached her head, holding it gently as she moved.

"Keisha, wait," he whispered, still trying to hold onto control. But she didn't stop. Instead, she pressed forward, balanced on her knees, determined to keep him engaged—her eyes locked on his for a second as if she wanted to ensure he felt every instance.

After a few more minutes, Brayden pulled back just in time to release, the intensity of the moment catching him off guard. He inhaled deeply and softly exhaled as he lowered his head, shaking it with a smile. The aftershocks of what had just happened pulsed through him, and he found himself at a loss for words for a brief second.

"You wild for that," he said with a scoff, the weight of their situation hanging in the air.

Keisha smiled at him, a sense of pride in her eyes. She softly brushed her hand over his chest, relieved she had gotten the desired reaction.

Afterward, she hoped that her actions would prevent Brayden from going to work and completing the mission she'd set for the morning. However, to her surprise, he didn't stay. Instead, he winked at her playfully and went to the bathroom to freshen up.

"You better be glad I'm already running late, girl," he teased with a smile. "You're working the late shift at the bank today, right?"

"Yeah. Remember, I work from noon to five today and 9 a.m. to 1 p.m. on Saturday," she responded, keeping her calm while watching him prepare.

Brayden emerged from the bathroom, fully dressed and exuding confidence and style. Before heading out the door, he grabbed his suit jacket and briefcase.

He approached the bed where Keisha lay, watching him intently, and leaned in to kiss her gently on the cheek.

He placed his spare key on the nightstand. "You'll make it back here before I do this evening. Let yourself in, and don't lose my key. Just leave it on the kitchen counter when you come in," he instructed.

Grinning widely, Keisha eagerly replied, "Okay!"

Once she was sure he had left, she sprang out of bed, her excitement evident. "Yes! I got my man back! He can't help but make us official now!"

She danced around the room, overflowing with joy. With a sense of triumph, she decided to drop her car off after work and take an Uber back to Brayden's. She was preparing to stay the entire weekend.

With a few hours left before her shift, sleep was the furthest thing from her mind. Grabbing her phone, she settled into his bed. She spent the next couple of hours browsing social media, cheerfully lost in the moment.

CHAPTER 4

It's Friday!

Zora sat at work, organizing patients' account records, but a familiar sting of disappointment worried her. Malik hadn't returned the previous night, which had become the norm since their breakup. Travel, internships, and extra projects consumed his busy schedule.

She felt the weight of his absence more each day, increasingly drained of stability. It wasn't easy to confide in him about essential matters when she never knew how long he would be around. She felt a growing sense of abandonment, even though, deep down, she understood that his commitments were ultimately meant to secure a better future for their family.

The only explanation Malik had given her for his absence the night before was a brief text saying that his parents had kept Mazo overnight; he would bring her home after church services on Sunday, and he apologized for not making it back in time.

She was okay with Mazo staying, but needing to talk things through, Zora picked up her phone and began texting.

Zora 8:30 am: Malik, call me at work. My truck wouldn't start, but Cornelius gave me a jump.

Zora 9:15 am: Malik?

Zora 11:00 am: You are so dirty! You came and got what you wanted yesterday, and now the next day, you're M.I.A.? You know what? It's all good. Lose my number! Don't come by my house unannounced, and I want my key back!

Zora 12 noon: Thanks, but no thanks for your help this morning. I don't know why I put up with you!
Zora 1:20: You want to play these games...okay, let's play!
Zora 1:35: I hate you, Malik!

Urban Coffee

On the other side of town, Brooklyn woke up on the same couch she had collapsed onto the night before, her fruity drink still beside her. She reached for her phone, intending to call in sick to work and check if Brayden had contacted her. But as she scrolled through her messages, frustration, sadness, and hurt washed over her—there were no messages from Brayden.

This was rare; he usually made a point to check in on her emotional well-being.

Brooklyn speculated that Keisha might have won Brayden's sympathy with her constant complaints and tears. Her mind raced with questions about what had happened between them.

I can't keep moping around about this man. I love him, but I should focus on myself, or I'll lose it! She thought, trying to reassure herself. *I'm strong, kind, and fulfilled. I can do this!*

She walked into the kitchen, determined to distract herself from the thoughts of Brayden and Keisha. She whipped up a hearty meal of two buttermilk pancakes, two slices of bacon, scrambled eggs, and a small bowl of strawberries paired with a glass of iced coffee.

Sitting in her cozy eat-in kitchen, Brooklyn made a bacon and egg sandwich with the pancakes, slicing them in half and dipping each bite into a side of warm maple syrup. She savored her late breakfast while watching TV on the 25-inch flat-screen, a birthday gift from Brayden.

As she took a bite, memories flooded back... Her love for experimenting with breakfast sandwiches and brunch foods had often led her to spend hours in the kitchen when they were together.

Brayden had known this and thoughtfully gifted her the TV for her birthday, knowing she'd appreciate it. He hadn't stopped there, though. He had also surprised her with a generous $1,200 spa package for that day, along with three of her closest friends.

After the spa day, Brooklyn returned home that evening to the comforting scent of her favorite food and a romantically lit, spotless house. She was overwhelmed with happiness and rushed into his arms, her heart beaming. They shared a candlelit dinner, indulging in intimate conversation and enjoying each other's company throughout the night.

Brooklyn shook her head, snapping herself out of her daydream. She had reminisced long enough and decided to finish her breakfast.

Setting her empty dishes aside, she glanced at her phone one last time before heading to the shower. The sting of disappointment hit her as she found no messages from Brayden yet again. Frustrated by the whole scene, Brooklyn tossed her phone onto the couch before heading upstairs. She grabbed an outfit from the closet and collapsed onto the mattress, her stomach turning from the overwhelming emotions.

Urban Coffee

Later that evening, Zora was getting off work and still upset with Malik. He never texted her back while she was at work. Now, she was leaving the hospital, praying that her car wouldn't give her any problems. As she approached the front exit, the security guard, Mr. Hank, a much older guy, handed her a small, sealed manila envelope.

"Hey, Mr. Hank," she approached with a smile. "What's this?"

"I have no clue, Miss Young," he said with a shrug. "The overnight parking lot security handed it to me before she left this morning. She told me to give it to you after your shift."

Zora strolled, fumbling with the envelope as she tried to unseal it with her nails.

"Okay, thanks, Mr. Hank. Have a good day!" she called out as she approached the front entrance.

"You do the same, Miss Young. Be careful out there, especially on Friday evenings. It gets busy."

She glanced back at him and flashed a smile. "Yes, you're right. And call me Zora, Mr. Hank!"

He returned a smile, swiftly saluting with his right hand.

Mr. Hank has worked at the hospital for 45 years. He began working as a transporter in the maternity ward at the age of 20. Over the years, he had become a familiar and cherished presence to all who knew him at the hospital.

Zora had managed to open the envelope halfway. Still, she hadn't finished, distracted by the cheerful goodbyes and weekend farewells around her. Everyone seemed extra happy on Fridays, especially those who didn't have to work the weekend.

That was Zora's area. The administrative staff in her department never worked weekends; there was a night shift for that.

As Zora approached the parking lot, she was thinking about the weekend plans ahead. But when she reached the usual spot where her truck was parked, she instantly panicked.

"Oh my gosh! Where's my truck?" She started spinning around, hoping to catch a glimpse of it.

"Okay, wait a second. Maybe I just forgot where I parked," she muttered, scanning the large parking deck.

As she spun around to look in the opposite direction, a small package from the envelope fell to the ground. She bent down, picked it up, and opened it. Inside was a key attached to a key ring.

Without thinking, Zora hit the panic button on the key ring and jumped out of her skin as the car alarm blared. The panic button belonged to a silver Mercedes-Benz, Malik's luxury car. It was sitting right where her truck had been.

Zora scanned the parking lot again, hoping Malik would walk up at any moment, but he didn't. She approached his car slowly, eyes sweeping the area, but there was still no sign of him.

Finally, she got into the car, still shocked that it was there, yet he was nowhere to be seen. As she settled in, she noticed a note inside the envelope that read:

"Hey, baby. I'm sorry I'm not there. See you later.

Love forever, Malik."

Zora simultaneously felt both surprised and fortunate, unsure what to do with herself.

The unexpected gesture reminded her of his spontaneous and caring nature, making her reconsider the negative texts she'd sent him earlier that morning. Instantly, regret consumed her.

"Omg! When did he get my truck? How did he get it? Did he get those texts? I was so mean!" she thought, her mind racing.

After a few moments of lightly slapping her forehead in frustration, Zora sat back in the car, lost in nostalgia. She remembered the countless nights Malik had driven her in this car, their romantic date nights, Sunday outings with their daughter, and the spontaneous weekend getaways.

When the blissful thoughts faded, she slipped on her shades and spread a big smile. The recognizable scent of his cologne filled the car, evoking memories and stirring emotions within her. At that moment, she felt the familiarity of being his girl once more as she cranked the car to drive home. Also, she wondered why she hadn't recognized his car right in front of her.

Nevertheless, she was on her way, but stopped at the gas station to refuel after noticing the tank was only half-full.

She decided to top it off as a small gesture of appreciation to him for lending her the car after work—it was the very least she could do. Because, all day, she'd been worried about her truck giving her trouble once her shift ended.

****

Zora pulled into her garage, expecting to find Malik waiting for her, but there was no sign of him. After walking inside, she quickly grabbed her phone and texted him.

Zora Text: *Hey, I'm home. Thank you so much. Where are you?*

As soon as she hit send, she heard music outside. Glancing through the window, she saw Malik pulling up in her truck. Her heart skipped a beat.

She ran in a hurry to another room and kicked off her heels. Rushing back to the living room, she quickly hit the power button on the TV remote, then darted into the kitchen to grab a bottle of water from the fridge.

As she turned to head back into the living room, Malik walked in. He looked the part of a man who knew how to turn heads.

Dressed in gray acid-washed jeans and a crisp white long-sleeve t-shirt, sleeves slightly pulled up, exuding effortless charm. His all-white Adidas sneakers completed the look, while a platinum Rolex on his wrist added a touch of sophistication. His impeccably groomed beard, mustache, and sideburns seamlessly connected, perfectly trimmed against his smooth skin. He smelled as good as he looked–a true clean-cut man. He epitomized masculinity—almost too much for one woman to handle.

Zora took it all in, her heart quickening as he closed the distance between them. "Thank you for the ride home," she said softly, her voice laced with gratitude.

"You're welcome," he responded gently, his hands resting around her waist as he leaned closer to her ear. "You know I've got you, baby. You do know that, right?"

His minty breath grazed her ear, sending a shiver down her spine. Zora closed her eyes momentarily, trying to hold onto the calm she desperately clung to.

"My girls will never go without. You believe that, don't you?" he murmured, softly kissing her neck.

His words were as comforting as they were intimate.

"By God's permission, I'll always be here for you," he added softly, his words lingering as he kissed her forehead gently. He locked eyes with her, his gaze intense and sincere.

Overwhelmed by the depth of his affection, Zora felt her heart rate speed up, sensing his steady presence. With a deep breath, Zora closed the space between them, her lips meeting his in a kiss that conveyed everything she couldn't quite say aloud. The world outside seemed to diminish, leaving only the warmth and security of his arms securely around her.

Malik gently pulled away from the kiss, his gaze locking with hers again. Zora's chest rose and fell rapidly, her body responding to his touch, to the warmth of his affection. She was instantly heated and could barely control it.

"Malik, what?" she asked, her voice breathless, her words more a soft invitation than a question.

"Shh," he whispered, his arms enveloping her lovingly, never breaking eye contact. His fingers softly traced her back as he asked, "So, what's up with those heated texts?"

Zora's lips parted in surprise, but she played innocent. "Huh?" she murmured, her arms still resting around his neck.

"You hate me now?" he whispered, his lips kissing hers softly before he pulled back, locking eyes with her again.

"Um...," she stammered, feeling guilty. "I'm sorry."

Her voice caught, overwhelmed by the depth of his attention.

He pulled her closer, his eyes never leaving hers, his hand tenderly caressing her curvaceous bum. "You didn't answer my question, baby," he said softly. "Do you still hate me?"

Zora lowered her gaze, smiling shyly. His presence was grand, and his attention was as gentle as it was intense.

"No, I don't hate you," she finally whispered, lifting her head to meet his eyes. Her voice was shy and vulnerable yet filled with the truth of her feelings.

His gaze softened as he leaned in, capturing her lips in a deep, tender kiss. Everything seemed to melt away, and when he finally pulled back, he looked at her with quiet passion. He gently lifted her into his arms without saying a word, carrying her upstairs to the bedroom.

He laid her on the bed, slowly undressed her, and tossed her clothes aside. The soft thud of her garments landed beside the lush chocolate-brown armchair. Zora watched him intently, savoring his full attention.

After a moment, Malik stood, heading into the adjoining primary suite's bathroom, leaving the door slightly ajar. She remained still, curiosity bubbling up as she patiently waited for whatever he had in mind.

A minute passed before he returned, the sound of running water filling the air as he opened the door. He had removed his shirt, though the rest of his clothes remained intact. His smallest gestures had always made the most significant impact, no matter the circumstance.

With ease, he lifted Zora from the bed like she weighed nothing, kissing her lips and then her cheek before carrying her to the tub.

Gently, he placed her in the warm, sudsy water. She leaned back, offering him a warm smile and showing off her pearly whites. Malik sat on the tub's edge, stirring the bubbles with his hand.

"Are you good, baby?" he asked softly.

"I feel perfect." Zora's voice was dripping with contentment.

"Yeah, you should. Your panties were soaked," he teased, sarcasm lacing his words.

Zora friskily pushed his hand, a soft laugh escaping her. "Hush, it's your fault!"

Malik smiled.

The playful exchange paused, and then his expression softened. "I'm sorry for not responding to your texts quickly enough and for not being there for you this morning," he said sincerely, his eyes meeting hers.

Zora shook her head. "It's okay, Malik. You don't have to explain."

"I do," he insisted, his gaze steady. "I intended to get back to you as soon as I saw the first message, but it went off during the meeting."

Zora's eyes widened. "Oh my gosh! I'm so sorry," she responded, her voice filled with remorse.

Malik chuckled, playfully flicking a little water towards her face.

She shrieked softly, turning away from the splash, and he tenderly wiped her face before continuing.

"When we finally got a short break, I checked my phone and saw those hateful texts. I thought, *no way!* I just knew I'd be on the phone for hours, listening to you tear me down while I tried to explain myself," he said, his voice light but apologetic.

Zora tilted her head, pursing her lips. "Hours?"

Malik shrugged with a mischievous grin. "I was bracing for it."

Zora scoffed, shaking her head with a smile as he resumed speaking.

"So, I made the phone call to BC. He and one of our other friends, Vince, helped get your truck... That's Brayden's copy of the key to my car that he left for you."

"Oh, okay, that figures," Zora replied, nodding knowingly. "Y'all can always count on each other when it matters. You guys are like *'My Brother's Keepers*," she said, mimicking quotation marks with her fingers.

“Yes, ma’am... we grew up together. Our moms are best friends, so that’s my bro. He’s got my back; I’ve got his. You know this.”

Zora nodded, but couldn’t shake the guilt, though. She thought about the texts she’d sent and that Malik was juggling her issue while managing his responsibilities. She hung her head in shame.

Noticing her shift in mood, he tried to lighten the moment. “Hey, lift your head, baby. Why are you so mean to me?” he teased, gently lifting her chin to meet his gaze.

“I’m not mean to you. Quit saying that,” Zora replied shyly, her lips curling into a smile. She caught the wink he shot her, his dimples appearing as he smiled back.

Silence filled the air between them again. Zora reflected on her previous uncompromising stance and wondered why their dynamic had shifted so much lately.

Being the man he is, Malik prompted her to ask the question he saw lingering in her expression, so she did.

“Why are we still not together?”

His brows furrowed in disbelief. *Was she serious?*

“Oh, you don’t remember how cold you became toward me?” he replied, his voice steady but marked with sadness.

Zora glanced up at him, her hands swirling absently through the bubbles in the tub.

“But you changed the whole dynamic of us,” she said firmly. “Not just with school,” she added. “I’m proud of your commitment to that—but the extra projects. You were barely around anymore,” she admitted, her voice softening.

“Baby, we’ve talked about this.” His tone was gentle yet firm. “I can commit to this relationship if *you’d* allow me to. But I ended things because that’s what you wanted—not me. You were so resentful back then because of my traveling.”

And it had been the most challenging thing he'd ever done, feeling like he was abandoning his family. If it were up to Malik, he would have stayed in the relationship. However, a while after the breakup, he realized their relationship was set up to fail anyway. They played house as if they were already married. He was raised with values that contradicted this.

He confessed this again to Zora, silently praying that this could be their second chance to make things right, since she had brought it up. But his hope was for her to be patient this time with his travels and to witness the long-term plans, goals, and surprises he had in store for her, for his family.

Zora felt relieved to have brought it up, so she dug deeper. She was still hoping for the opposite—a significant reduction in his traveling this time.

"Malik, I want us to return to how we used to be." Her voice was soft but earnest. "Are you willing to let go of some of these extra projects, at least for now? I have surprises of my own that might make you reconsider everything," she concluded, hoping this would pique his interest. And she wasn't offering any more hints unless he was willing to adjust.

Malik sighed heavily and knelt beside the tub, their gazes meeting. His arms rested on the edge, the weight of the conversation hanging in the air.

"Listen," he began, his voice soft but intense.

"If it were that simple, I would do it in a heartbeat. But any deviations now could affect us, especially my career, and not for the better. Zora, I love you. I'm deeply in love with you. If you can bear with me a little longer, I promise it'll be worth it," he said, his eyes filled with hope.

Zora smiled at the sincerity in his voice, and at the same time, guilt settled in her chest. She had built walls for a reason, but now she wondered if those walls were doing more harm than good. She wanted to press the issue further, hoping he would relent, but as she looked into his eyes, part of her hesitated.

Knowing how hard Malik worked to make her life easier, she didn't want to appear unappreciative. So, she digressed for the time being, hoping to spend the rest of the day with him. She knew all too well that her time with him was limited.

"I love you, too," she said softly, her smile returning as she playfully splashed water in his direction. Malik jumped back, but not fast enough; his pant leg was already soaked.

"Oh, it's on now!" he exclaimed, a smile crossing his face.

He unbuckled his belt, clearly ready to join her in the tub.

But just as he removed his shoes, his cell phone rang, interrupting the moment. The sound made him freeze. He had left his phone on the bathroom sink while preparing Zora's bath.

Her smile faded as the ringing cut through the tension between them. Her heart began to pound as she watched him pause. It was as if her whole mental process flipped.

"What the...?" Malik muttered under his breath. The blaring ringtone of *"All I Do Is Think of You"* by Troop couldn't have chosen a worse moment. They exchanged a glance, and Malik instantly felt apologetic, but the anger was bubbling up inside him.

Before the ringtone played out, Malik made no move to silence it—the damage had already been done.

Overwhelmed by frustration, Zora stood up abruptly, hastily wrapping a towel around her damp body. It was as if something more profound than the ringtone had triggered her whole mood. Without a word, she walked past him, her steps heavy with discontent.

She quickly dried off and selected an outfit from her dresser—a pink tank top paired with light blue cutoff jean shorts that accentuated her curves. Slipping into her pink and black Pastry sneakers, she raked her long natural curls into a neat, messy ponytail before heading downstairs.

From the bathroom, Malik watched her dress, struck by the sweetness and innocence she exuded, even in the middle of their tension. But all he could see was the pain in her eyes as he stood there momentarily. Soon after, he released a soft sigh, put on his shirt, silenced his phone, and went after her.

Oddly enough, Zora was in the kitchen, hastily preparing a turkey and salami sandwich. She moved quickly, layering the pepper-jack cheese, lettuce, and tomato on the buttery Captain John bread. As she reached for the sandwich spread, she heard Malik coming down the stairs. She grabbed his spare car key off the counter and tossed it at him. He caught it midair as though he expected her to do precisely that.

Zora turned back around, but Malik stepped up behind her, gently gripping her arms to turn her toward him. Her eyes were red, holding back the tears she refused to let fall.

Without looking up at him, Zora softly asked, "What's her name? That's your new girl, right?"

Malik sighed deeply, hating that Zora thought he had moved on. "No, she's not my girl, Zo. Her name is Heather," he began, his voice soft but firm. "Listen...let me explain..."

"How long?" Zora interrupted, her voice strained with emotion. "Do you like her?"

"Baby, please, listen to me," He pleaded, his frustration mounting. "And no, it's not like that. We've known her since elementary school." We all grew up in the same neighborhood," he clarified, not liking the interrogating process, but he stayed calm. He didn't want to make things worse–she deserved answers.

"Zora, she's a family friend. Her work is located right by the college, and she found me one day after spotting me on campus. Can I start from the beginning?"

Malik's words flowed easily, but Zora's heart skipped a beat from what he was saying. Looking up at him, she found comfort as Malik tenderly cupped her face in his hands.

"Baby, don't overthink this. I love you," he declared with solid conviction. My explanation is all over the place, I know. It's a long story, but I'm happy to explain everything about her, the ringtone, or whatever you need."

He wanted to hold her, but Zora's resistance became obvious. She looked at him with soft, sorrowful eyes, and without a word, she turned around to finish making her sandwich. She wanted to appear unfazed because she didn't think he was being sincere, but he was.

"It's okay, Malik. I'm not naive. This must be the real issue as to why our relationship can't be mended—not school or extra projects," she said, struggling to hold back the flood of tears. "You're a great guy and father, so I get it. It's okay."

Malik looked at her with a bit of agitation, realizing that she didn't believe him and that she had flipped her mindset to their issues being about him with another girl. Lowering his head, he ran his hand down his face, trying to collect his thoughts.

"Zora, did you not hear anything I just said to you? She's..." Zora interrupted him once again.

"Malik. Don't! It's okay...really," she insisted.

She turned back to face him, embracing him lovingly, maintaining her composure, but her heart felt injured.

Feeling the tension in her arms, Malik held her tighter, but he felt a shift in her—the barrier between them quickly grew. She pulled away first, trying to keep herself together, leaning back against the counter, avoiding his gaze.

His face, which had always comforted her, now felt distant, like a stranger. The hurt in her chest grew heavier, but she wouldn't let it show. Not yet.

Malik sensed that something deeper was troubling her.

Still, the evening had been momentarily ruined, overshadowing the opportunity for another conversation. There seemed to be nothing he could do or say to salvage the moment before that untimely ringtone.

"Can we talk later?" he asked.

"I don't know," Zora responded, shrugging her shoulders. He decided to leave well enough alone. "If you have more problems with the truck, just call me. The shop said it was only your alternator...

If not, we'll make something else happen, so don't worry about that. Okay?"

Gently, he placed his hand under Zora's chin, lifting her gaze to his.

"I'm sorry," he said softly, his voice carrying genuine remorse. "I promise you, it's nothing. Please, don't make our issues about someone else."

"No, I'm okay," Zora reassured him.

After a few moments, Malik turned to leave, closing the front door softly behind him.

Zora felt her world crumble in that instant. The weight of everything she couldn't say pressed down on her, and weakness overtook her body.

She slid slowly down the counter, eventually sitting on the cold kitchen floor, her tears falling freely. A deep emptiness settled in her chest, leaving her with nothing but uncertainty.

The ringtone triggered something in her mind—she felt it but couldn't quite explain it. It stirred anger and resentment toward Malik. At that moment, she selfishly decided to withhold crucial information from him that may affect their future.

CHAPTER 5
Crazy Love

Dressed and ready, Brooklyn was prepared to step out the door to embrace the fresh air and seek a change of scenery. To distance herself from the previous night's events with Brayden and his involvement with Keisha, her comfort was a simple act of prayer. She had spent the entire day sulking, but she was also praying to God, asking for forgiveness for taking blessings for granted. She spoke to the Lord as if he were listening in the flesh. She made her cry to Him very personally.

Keys were jingling in one hand, and her purse was slung over her shoulder. Brooklyn reached for her phone. Panic took over as the text message icon appeared at the top of her screen. "No, no, no! I missed it!" she muttered as she swiped her finger across the screen, seeing Brayden's text.

"Aw, man... thirty minutes ago?! Twice?!" She groaned, regretting her decision to leave the phone downstairs. Her heartbeat sped up as she read his texts.

Brayden 5 pm: Hey, Brook, do you have time for me? I want to talk to you and see how you're doing. Please call me.

Brayden 5:15 pm: I guess you're still feeling salty. You didn't text me last night to let me know you got home; I understand. Again, I'm sorry about how things went down. I want to make sure we're good. Love, always. Take care.

His words, although sweet, felt so final. It sounded like someone was remorseful but ready to move on. *"Take care?"* Brooklyn reread the message.

She dropped her keys and purse to the floor and sank to her knees, reading the last part of Brayden's message four times before a tear escaped her eye.

Sitting cross-legged, her right elbow propped on her knee, and her hand resting against her face, she stared at the dimming screen of her phone. She was lost and unsure of how to proceed.

"Should I keep pursuing him? Does he regret last night?"

Those were the questions that crowded her mind. She shook her head, not sure of her next steps.

After regaining her composure, Brooklyn stood up, gathered her things, and left her condo.

Urban Coffee

"No thanks, Rocco! I don't need you here! You made your choice, so stay where you are. Go get that hood-whore you've been rolling around with!"

"Chill out," Rocco replied, trying to play off the hurt she'd verbally inflicted on him. Despite his attempt to act unbothered, his voice softened. "You know you miss me. I miss you. I promise it will be different this time," he added.

"Roc, no! I don't believe you. The last time was supposed to be different, too! You hurt me, and I'm not giving you the chance to do it again!"

Amina was on the phone with her ex, **Roccorio "Rocco" Richards**, a guy she'd known since middle school. Rocco had always admired her, and in 12th grade, after years of mutual crushing, their relationship finally blossomed. But things took a drastic turn after graduation. He was well-known for his athleticism, intelligence, and popularity among his peers.

He had a hot-headed streak, especially when someone disrespected him or those he cared about. Confident and handsome, he was a guy many girls admired, but he wasn't considered "relationship-worthy" at the time. Still, his love for Amina was unmatched, though their relationship had been a rocky, on-and-off affair since graduation.

While Amina had once been infatuated with him, she had grown tired of his deceptive behavior. However, she couldn't help but love his mom. Mrs. Richards had always seen Amina as the one for her son. She frequently reassured him, saying, *"Honey, once you find your purpose, some lucky girl will strike gold."*

Mrs. Richards affectionately nicknamed Rocco her "Golden Child." While his brothers thought it was because gold was one of his favorite colors, his mother knew it symbolized his true worth—his kindness, reliability, and loyalty.

She loved all her sons, but saw something special in Rocco—a unique kindness that set him apart from his siblings. From a young age, his *"golden child"* qualities were evident. Even as a toddler, he displayed these forever attributes.

Nevertheless, as the years passed, Amina began to see too many undesirable traits in him. The breaking point came when she caught Rocco in a compromising situation—having sex with another girl in the backseat of her car, right outside her workplace.

About four years prior....

Rocco didn't have his own car at the time, so Amina generously let him use hers every other day to get around.

He worked the early shift as a stockperson at a large warehouse, such as Costco, starting at 4 a.m. and taking his lunch break around 8 a.m. This schedule allowed him to pick Amina up and drop her off at her clerical job at the phone company, ensuring she arrived on time by 8:30 am. The unfortunate reality was that with the car in his possession for most of the day, since his shift ended around 1 p.m., while Amina didn't finish work until 5:30 p.m., Rocco had access to her car far too often and for far too long.

On one particular day, Rocco parked far from Amina's building, choosing a spot in the back section of the parking lot.

Before that, he had been chatting with a young woman named Jowanda, who worked in the deli on the first floor of the phone company building.

Rocco had made it a routine to grab lunch from that deli at least once a week when he dropped Amina off at work. Jowanda's flirtatious demeanor made it clear that she was interested, and after their fourth encounter, they exchanged numbers. It was the start of something new between them.

Jowanda, a street-savvy woman with long silver micro-braids and colorful nails, had a curvaceous figure and a tiny waist. She loved the club scene with her friends and wasn't shy about playing the role of the *side chick*. Drawn to men already in relationships, she found the challenge and excitement irresistible.

Despite her looks, every man she'd been involved with had cheated on her. As a result, she adopted an unconcerned attitude toward others' relationships, embodying the persona of a young woman scorned.

Jowanda smiled flirtatiously as she rang up Rocco's sandwich. "So, what are you getting into this morning?"

Rocco shot her a quick glance. "Why?"

She leaned in, her voice dropping a little. “You know what I’m talking about.” She smiled playfully, challenging him.

Rocco smirked, raising an eyebrow. “We’ve barely talked, and when we did, it was nothing worth my time.”

Jowanda laughed, tossing her braids back, clearly enjoying the tension she created. “You talk a big game at first, but I don’t see any action behind it.”

He didn’t like that, and his pride prompted him to make a decision. “Come here,” he said, motioning toward the men’s restroom. He wasn’t interested in the teasing anymore; his mind was already elsewhere.

Without hesitation, she followed him, driven by the boldness of their chitchat. He locked the door behind them.

“Pull your pants down,” he instructed, his voice lower. She paused, clearly surprised by the directness. “No kiss, no nothing?” she asked with a smirk.

Rocco’s eyes flashed with impatience. “Do you want a kiss, or do you want this joyride?”

The back-and-forth with her felt strange to him, but he was caught in the heat of the moment. After unwrapping a condom, he turned her around, bent her over, and went to work, pounding out her insides. He didn’t care for her at all.

Something deeper lingered beneath the surface, a few seconds in—something he didn’t want to admit. The pleasure he felt, the rush of adrenaline, and the excitement of the moment clouded his thoughts. He moved quickly, trying to lose himself in the action, but a part of him knew this wasn’t right.

As they continued, a quiet voice in the back of his mind whispered about the mess he was making—about Amina and the broken promises, about the lies he kept telling himself.

But the moment was too decisive, and when it ended with Jowanda on her knees, finishing him off, he felt an emptiness—probably *after-guilt* from the brief enjoyment.

When Rocco left the bathroom, he couldn't shake the feeling that he'd made a terrible mistake. But for Jowanda, this was just another win. She knew exactly how to play the game, but in doing so, she'd only left herself more rooted in a cycle she couldn't escape.

He returned, just as she had expected, within a month. This time, however, they took a risk, deciding to meet in Amina's 2002 red Nissan Maxima. Jowanda watched as Rocco pulled up and parked, just as he always did, arriving early, his car idling. At the same time, he listened to music, waiting for Amina.

Jowanda walked over to the car, eager to speak to him.

"Hey, sexy," she greeted, her voice light and playful. Rocco scoffed, his mood shifting immediately.

"What do you want, Jowanda? You better get away from my girl's car before she flips out on you," he warned, his voice flat but serious.

She rolled her eyes, undeterred. "Please, she won't do anything to me," she said with a shrug.

"Yeah, well, you won't do anything to her either," he snapped back, his tone growing more serious.

Jowanda lightened up, sensing his frustration but knowing she needed something else.

"Look, Rocco, I need you right now." Her voice lowered to a more serious tone. "I'm feeling something... you know."

Rocco stared at her momentarily, a hint of disbelief crossing his face. "What are you talking about, man? Move on with that nonsense. I'm not messing with you no more—the first time was the last time!"

But Jowanda didn't back down. "I'm serious, Rocco," she pleaded, a smile tugging at her lips as she twisted one of her braids around her finger. "We've got time. Just a few minutes before everyone starts coming out. Let's go to the back of the lot... It'll be quick."

He hesitated, trying to suppress the urge she was triggering, but the temptation was there, undeniable. Despite his better judgment, a part of him wanted to give in.

"Dang!" he muttered, dropping his head. "Fine, I'll meet you back there. But this is the last time... you hear me?" His voice was low and serious as he made the ultimatum, locking eyes with her one last time.

Jowanda smiled, her confidence unmoved.

She didn't care about his warning; she was already planning her next move. She turned and sprinted towards the back of the parking lot, the tension between them thick in the air.

After putting on a condom, Rocco quickly lowered his black joggers; his impatience with her was clear. The act was rough, and the moment's pressure swiftly built, but it didn't take long for Jowanda to react. She cried out, the sound of their interaction filling the quiet space of the back seat.

But there was no tenderness, no affection. Rocco wasn't here for romance—he didn't care about her feelings. He cared only about satisfying his desires. He didn't want to kiss her; he selfishly focused on his needs only.

And then, suddenly, everything came to a crashing halt. A loud shatter echoed through the space, followed by a burst of glass. Rocco and Jowanda's hearts felt as if they had frozen. Amina had smashed the back window of her car with a raw fury that left them both speechless.

Without hesitation, she snatched open the car door, swinging her umbrella with all the strength her anger could gather, hitting Rocco and landing a solid blow to his neck.

"Ouch, girl!" he yelled...

"Amina, wait! I'm sorry!" he begged, desperately trying to grab the umbrella from her hands.

But she wasn't listening. Her anger burned hotter than ever, and she didn't care how she looked in her cream-colored pantsuit and high heels. All Amina cared about was the betrayal in front of her.

Rocco finally managed to break free, leaping out of the car and grabbing the umbrella from her. His chest heaving with guilt and frustration, he stood there, watching Amina's rage take over.

"Rocco?! Are you serious?! You're doing this to me—at my job?!" Amina's voice fluttered between disbelief and raw emotion as her eyes filled with hurt. Her hands trembled as she struggled to process what was happening.

When she saw Jowanda attempting to escape the car, Amina wasn't having it. Rocco stood back, frozen momentarily, watching Amina drag Jowanda out of the car, pulling her braids, and landing blow after blow to her face.

Her pain and betrayal turned into a personal, physical attack on Jowanda—she was not an innocent victim; she very well knew that Rocco was Amina's boyfriend.

It wasn't long before Security and some of Amina's coworkers arrived on the scene, stepping in to break up the fight. Jowanda, humiliated and bleeding from her nose, quickly scrambled to her feet, trying to cover herself as she fled back into the building. Her body, half-exposed, only added to her embarrassment.

Amina, still trembling with anger, could barely process what had happened. She had seen them talking from the window and watched as they disappeared into the parking lot. She wanted to rush down sooner, but her meeting was extended.

By the time she reached the parking lot, it was too late. As she got closer to her car, the truth was unmistakable.

With the last of her rage still boiling, Amina climbed into her car and drove off, leaving Rocco in the parking lot. He looked at no one and just began walking home.

When he finally arrived, his clothes were thrown into garbage bags and left in front of the apartment complex.

The relationship was over.

Current day...

"I know I messed up, but I'm serious this time. Please, give me a chance to prove it to you," Rocco pleaded sincerely. "I was stupid and immature four years ago, but I've changed. Let me show you."

He poured his heart out, but Amina remained cold and firm, refusing to give in and continuing to challenge him.

"Rocco, what do you mean you were immature?" she asked, her voice steady before posing the million-dollar question. "Answer me this... when was the last time you talked to Hoe-wanda?"

An awkward silence stretched between them, and that was all Amina needed. "That's okay, Rocco, you answered it!"

"Nah, wait!" he protested.

"Nope. Forget it, Roc. You'll never change!"

The soft click of her cell phone hanging up was the last thing Rocco heard before Amina disconnected the call.

Unbothered, he started texting her.

Rocco text 6:30 pm: Mina, please. Let me talk to you in person. I want to explain everything. I'm going crazy without you.
Amina text 6:32 pm: Rocco, leave me alone! You had your chance! You're disrespectful & stupid! I thought we were happy, but I was wrong, and you messed up! I'm over it, Roc. So, please leave me alone!!!!!!
Rocco 6:35 pm: Dang, Mina! You can say what you want, but I ain't giving up on you yet. Give me a chance. I'll do whatever it takes.
Amina 6:40 pm: Rocco, don't do this to me. It's taken me a long time to get over you. If you care about me, you'll leave me alone.
Rocco 6:43 pm: You can forget that. I miss you. I still love you.
Rocco 6:44 pm: My break's over. I'll call you later. I love you.

Amina didn't respond, lost in thought as she pondered what *"break"* Rocco was talking about and whether she should see him. What if she gave him one more chance? What did she have to lose except her time and energy?

After a few minutes of contemplation, Amina returned to reality with a sigh. "Oh Lord!" she muttered. "I can't do this with him again... There's still too much pain. I won't backtrack. I won't," she admitted aloud as if trying to convince herself.

A few minutes of self-reassurance later, she gathered her things and headed out to meet her friends at Zora's house.

****

Brooklyn text 6:20 pm: Hey, we're leaving from your place tonight, right?

Zora text 6:22: Yes. I need to get out of here to unwind. Heard from Mina?
Brooklyn 6:27: Nope, I just tried calling. That little troll sent me to VM. She should be on her way, though. I'm not sure about Devin.
Zora 6:33: Okay. Devin called earlier. You know she got this young dude she's dealing with, right? Lol. See you in a minute, girl.
Brooklyn 6:34: That poor dude, Lol. But okay, see you.

Urban Coffee

After leaving Zora's house, Malik dialed Brayden's cell. "Yo, BC, where are you?"

Having sealed a $15,000 commission for their company from one sale, Brayden felt good about ending the week on a high note.

"I'm in the field. Did you get my text? I'm heading home in a minute. What's up, bro?"

Malik nodded his head. "Yes, I got the text. Money in the bank is always good. What are you doing tonight? I need to find a place to reevaluate."

Brayden chuckled. "What's going on? You and Zo good?"

"Nah, man, I don't think so. Everything was fine right after I returned her truck."

"Uh-oh. What happened?" he responded quickly.

"We were having a good moment until my phone rang."

Brayden laughed, but when Malik didn't react, he sensed the seriousness of the situation.

"Dang, my bad, bro."

Malik sighed. "She stormed out so fast, and it was downhill from there. She didn't believe a word I said afterward. Heather put that stupid ringtone on my phone!"

Brayden's face shifted with surprise. "Wait—Heather? She's back? She didn't call me."

"I didn't get a call, either." She works for a cell phone company right across from my campus."

Brayden shook his head, clearly processing. "Ah, okay."

"Yeah, I was surprised to see her, too, Malik continued. Happy, but minus the playful flirting."

"Is she still fine like she was in high school?"

Malik chuckled, caught off guard by the question.

"Remember around 11th or 12th grade? Brayden asked another question, probing. She started embracing her feminine side. Ended up looking like *'Nia Long'* from *The Best Man,* just a little taller," he added. They both chuckled at the memory.

Malik, shaking his head, was still preoccupied with Zora but continued the story about how he had found out Heather was back in town.

"So, with the little time I could spare, we started catching up on things. She asked about you, my folks, and then brought up Malena."

Brayden smiled, nodding. "Ah, Malena—the first love."

Malik chuckled, clearly uninterested in discussing Malena. "C'mon, man, don't go there."

He had moved on and didn't want to rehash those memories, although she still held a special place in his heart.

Brayden scoffed, smiling as Malik steered the conversation back to Heather.

"So, as I was saying, Heather helped me set up my new phone. Before I left, she slipped me her number on the receipt and said, *'I already have yours."*

"Wow," Brayden chuckled, shaking his head. "She knows she's just the homie, right?"

"Exactly!" Malik confirmed.

"Coming back acting all brand new on us."

Malik scoffed. "Yeah, I was like, babygirl, *we boys*."

They both laughed.

"Getting back to the story, though... when I met her at the deli the other day, we were chilling. I didn't know she set that song under her name."

"You didn't hook up with her, did you?" Brayden asked, chuckling.

Malik laughed, not expecting that question. "What is wrong with you, man? No! I don't see her like that, nor do I want to. Man, stop playing."

"I'm just messing with you." Brayden knew full well that he, Malik, and Heather had been nothing but best friends since before puberty.

"I know you're joking, but it was obvious she's trying to prove she's not the same tomboy we used to know. I could sense it in the way she spoke and in the way she was touching my arm... You know how girls do," Malik added with a chuckle.

"Indeed, I do," Brayden said with a knowing scoff. His tone changed, becoming more focused as he shifted back to the reason Malik had called.

"Look, Mal, I know you're working to get your family back on track. So, maybe we can stick with the first project, help you cross that stage for your Master's, and delay the second project. You're just as unhappy as Zora is," he concluded.

Malik inhaled deeply and sighed. He understood the suggestion but knew it wasn't practical given his commitments.

"As much as I'd love to do that, BC, I can't. We've made promises to colleagues, vendors, and merchants. In our line of work, keeping our word is crucial... If I delay the second deal, we will miss out on $250,000 for launching the business with the current setup. And I don't want to cut any more corners."

Their goal was to wrap everything up within six months. Completing this project would enable them to hire additional staff for the business launch and bring in Malik's big sister, Melanie, who had been helping behind the scenes since the beginning.

Sticking to these plans would give Malik a more predictable schedule and time at home, positioning him to secure his future, hopefully with Zora. He has a solid plan.

"We've been working towards this for a few years. We need to see it through," Malik emphasized.

Brayden nodded, fully aware that their plans, which had started after many house flips, were finally coming to fruition. "I understand, and I know it's too late for changes now... "I just don't want you to lose Zo like I lost Brooklyn, even though my absence wasn't the cause. So, I suggest we find a way to explain things to the girls without giving away too much."

Malik exhaled. "I've been trying, man. But once Zora learns about the extra intern hours and the new projects, it will be over as soon as it begins. I can't explain without lying. She wants all or nothing—and she deserves that."

Brayden shifted the phone to his other ear, considering Malik's words. "Maybe it's best to give her space until things settle down," he suggested.

"Absolutely not! I can't imagine doing that, not even for a second!" Malik, firm in his response.

Brayden scoffed, knowing the answer before he even asked. He knows how deep Malik's love goes, regardless of their breakup.

"So, I guess it's good that Heather's back," Brayden remarked. "She was always the one we could vent to."

"Definitely. But as much as we valued her, she's been gone too long. She has to earn that confidential spot again."

Brayden shook his head. "She got a headlock coming to her for not contacting me after being here for a few days."

Quickly growing nostalgic, Malik chuckled. "Zo was the one I confided in about everything. But now? She won't even let me take her out publicly since the breakup. She's not pretending we're back together—those were her exact words." He scoffed, rubbing his face in frustration.

Malik's words hung in the air for a moment, and Brayden could sense the weight of the frustration. "Well, one thing we need to address is Heather's flirting. That's just weird," he said, deliberately lightening the mood.

"Exactly! I told her not to do that again. I get it, you've changed, but still, don't do that," Malik replied, chuckling with Brayden.

With that said and not wanting to linger on that subject any longer, Malik brought up Brayden's relationship woes.

"Zora mentioned that Brooklyn's trying to make amends."

"Yeah, I think she is. Remember what I told you about last night?"

"Yeah, I remember how she '*Mayweather-ed'* your girl!" They both laughed, though Brayden wasn't referring to the fight.

"Nah, man, I'm talking about the other details," he clarified.

Malik paused. "Yeah, I gotcha, man. I like Brooklyn—she's always been cool. And if she's genuinely changing, what's the deal? You and she are still family. You still love her, and you're not afraid to admit it."

"You're right, but Keisha, man... she's doing everything to lock me in, wanting to make things official."

"Is it hard to let go of Keisha because of... she's good at that... you know..." Malik asked, and they both chuckled.

"Trust me, she still has nothing on Brooklyn," Brayden assured him.

"Alright, we can drop that. I don't want to hear about lil' sis."

Brayden laughed. "I'm just letting you know, bro."

"Yeah, so tell me more about Keisha, though, if you will."

"Man, chill with the *'if you will'* stuff!" Brayden knew Malik was about to say something crazy.

"*You right*. I'm just running my mouth at this point, he admitted, smiling. "What's up with tonight, though?" Malik asked, quickly changing the subject again.

"I don't know... maybe the new spot in Alpine City. I heard the seafood there is the bomb! It's called 'Savory' or something like that."

"Okay, cool. Wait, is it right across from our old spot?"

"Yep, 'The Hangout,' where we used to take our girls on date nights, but I'm not going there with anyone else," Brayden replied.

"I agree. Yo, BC, let me call you back; our long-lost friend is calling me."

"Okay, we'll meet at nine, and I'll scold Heather tonight."

"Cool," Malik replied before answering Heather's call.

"What's up, homie?"

"Hey, friend. What's on your agenda for the evening?" she asked, hoping it involved her.

"You." he replied cheerfully, and Heather's wide grin was noticeable through the phone.

"Okay, boo, where?" She was so excited.

"Have you been to Savory Seafood yet?"

"No way! I've heard the food is great, but it's also super expensive. It's close to the city, right?"

"Yeah. It's all good. Whatever you can't afford, I got you."

"Okay," she replied, sending virtual hearts. "You're coming to get me, right?" she asked, still grinning from ear to ear.

"Can you just meet us there around nine?"

"Ah, yeah. Sure." Her excitement diminished slightly at his response.

He wasn't letting the issue about her weird flirting slide. He valued the friendship but knew boundaries needed to be set.

"What should I wear?"

"Jeans will be fine so that you can handle the headlock Brayden's got coming for you."

Heather's eyes widened. "You didn't tell him I was back before now?" she asked, feeling a little guilty.

"Nope. It's your business. He wants to hear it from you," Malik said, keeping it light but firm.

At that, they ended the call, after confirming the meet-up for later.

Malik quickly stopped at his parents' house to see Mazo. Then, he headed to his condo to freshen up and relax a little before the evening's plans.

CHAPTER 6

Weekend Drama

Meanwhile, the girls had made it to Zora's house to chill and figure out where to go for the night. Everyone was there except Devin.

"Hey! Let's get this party started!" Brooklyn and Amina shouted as they entered the front door. Zora left it open after they texted that they were coming down her street.

"Hey, mamas!" she shouted back as she went to them for a hug. "How did y'all end up together?" Zora asked.

"Oh, I saw Miss Princess here strolling through the mall with her cute little bun and bags," Amina said sarcastically, swinging her finger up and down toward Brooklyn. They all laughed.

"And you did," Brooklyn admitted. "They had sales abundantly out that mofo! And don't even trip, Mina. Your little butt strolled right along with me! She had bags, too, Zo. Don't let her fool you."

"Uh-huh," Zora replied. "That's one thing we all have in common. We love to shop *and* eat!" They all said in unison, exchanging high-fives and laughter.

"Speaking of things in common—where's Devin?" Amina asked, plopping down on the sofa after kicking off her shoes.

Zora answered with a shrug. "She texted me about 30 minutes ago, saying she was on the way."

"Did y'all meet her young hottie yet?" Brooklyn asked.

None had met the young guy Devin had been unusually smitten with yet.

Amina noticed the time. “That’s probably why she’s late. Somewhere performing on some poor guy’s penis, wasting his time, knowing she doesn’t have a committed bone in her body.”

Brooklyn laughed, but Zora only chuckled lightly. She didn’t want it to be too apparent that she agreed, even though Amina’s statement was spot on.

“Don’t act like you don’t wanna laugh, hooker!” Brooklyn said with a scrunched face.

“Hey, y’all stop; that’s my girl you’re talking about,” Zora said, smiling.

“*We, all girls*, honey, so it’s okay!” They fired back.

Amina changed the topic from Devin as she moved toward the kitchen. “Zora and Brooklyn, make me some of that good, iced coffee you two used to make.”

“Okay, cool. I can use the boost,” Brooklyn agreed.

“No! Y’all are not about to drink all my expensive coffee.”

Amina furrowed her brows. “Malik buys you a dozen monthly, so don’t try it.”

Brooklyn laughed at her expression but agreed. “Zora, we may not get our coffee shop for another 10 years, but we have to keep practicing our flavors and little pastries.”

“Yeah, I know, Brook, but experimenting with this coffee was getting pricey. The regular stuff from the grocery store doesn’t cut it in terms of taste. And I’m not going to ask Malik to fund our coffee experiments. He already does enough.”

Brooklyn nodded. “Yeah, I feel the same way about asking Brayden. But we can’t give up on our dream. The flavors we sold to people, especially in the hood, were awesome the first year!”

Amina chuckled, recalling those days. “I remember! Brayden liked them because some had a sweet, earthy taste, and he was like, “*This is that inner-city java*!”

“Then Malik said... *that urban java!*” Brooklyn added, laughing.

Zora’s eyes widened, remembering when Malik and Brayden called out the name at the same time. “Then, they both said simultaneously, *That urban coffee!*”

The girls laughed, reminiscing about how Malik and Brayden always played off each other’s thoughts and words. Sometimes, it was as if they were twins, often knowing exactly what the other was thinking. This unique connection was one reason their business had worked so well all these years.

My favorites were the *Cinnamon Bark* and Cardamon *Maple*. They were so delicious! But y’all let these men delay your progress,” Amina sarcastically said, laughing.

Zora and Brooklyn looked at her like she was crazy for putting Malik and Brayden in a box like that.

“Honey, if anything, they encouraged us to stick with it. They liked our coffees, hot or cold,” Zora declared.

“And the pastries.” Brooklyn chimed in at the end.

“So, what’s up with Rocco, Mina?” Brooklyn quickly swapped the vibe on her, since she was trying to be funny.

Amina scrunched up her face like the question was off-limits. “Nothing at all!” she responded swiftly.

“Dang, Mina! There’s nothing wrong with you seeing him just to talk,” Zora specified. “I mean, I know what he did was *like* unforgivable, but—”

“*LIKE?*” Amina interrupted, eyes wide.

“Yes. Like!” Brooklyn jumped in. “What if God didn’t forgive us for what we do or say? We’d be doomed,” she added.

"All I'm saying, Mina, is you loved Rocco. I believe you still do, which is why you're still mad like it happened yesterday," Zora said. "Don't get me wrong, he messed up big time! But we remember that he protected you as if you were platinum. Rocco wouldn't let anybody disrespect you. And I also remember you told us you wished we could sample his lovemaking, and then in the same sentence, you said you'd kill us if we even thought about it."

"Yep!" Brooklyn agreed as she and Zora laughed and high-fived each other.

"His mom adored you and treated you like family," Brooklyn added.

"All that's good or whatnot, but you forgot that he disrespected me to the max! I was so embarrassed! My supervisor allowed me to take a week off with pay, just to lay low! She was embarrassed *for* me!"

The girls watched Amina with sympathetic eyes as she recalled the painful details of that day.

"I love Rocco, it's true, but that doesn't mean I have to be with him." Amina's voice was thick with emotion.

Tears began to spill as she thought about the good times they shared. However, they were still overshadowed by the memory of her first love's public disrespect, which had shattered her heart into a million pieces. She was sure he would never change; he would always be a player and never amount to much.

"Amina, sweetie," Brooklyn said, sitting beside her and rubbing her back to console her and lighten the mood.

"People can change. All it takes is a made-up mind; everything else falls into place...

And I just have a good feeling about Rocco this time. It's been, what, four years now?"

Amina listened closely, torn between hope and fear. Deep down, she was saying and hoping the same things, but was scared out of her mind.

"I know you've been thinking about what we're saying because you would've cussed us out by now," Brooklyn added with a grin.

"Yep, stopped us dead in our tracks," Zora laughed, trying to help lighten up the mood.

"And talking to Rocco is better than chilling with that old dude who's always calling you!" Brooklyn chimed in a little aggressively.

"Well, old dude ain't never hurt me. I don't have to give him sex, and he's not my boyfriend! Amina clarified, feeling compelled to defend her situation.

"You better be careful with that, for real," Zora warned.

Brooklyn, shaking her head, "Nah, she needs to leave Grandpa alone altogether."

After a calmer conversation and a few sips of iced coffee, the mood lightened up again. They began sharing outfit ideas for the night and fixing each other's hair while they waited for Devin.

Urban Coffee

"Pull over right here, babe," Devin instructed her young friend, Chris, as he drove her up next to Zora's house.

"Why here? It's got a *'For Sale'* sign in the yard and looks empty," Chris said, puzzled by Devin's choice of destination.

"Yeah, it's empty. My best friend's baby daddy owns it," she explained.

Still unsure, Chris drove into the open, dark garage. The house was beautiful, situated in a well-maintained neighborhood on English Drive. All the homes here were priced in the mid-$200,000s and up.

They were well-spaced apart, with generously sized yards and thick, neatly manicured hedges. The only house with a direct view from the garage belonged to the Hudsons, a married couple who were empty-nesters, on vacation for the next few weeks.

"What's up, baby? Why are we here?" Chris asked again, still unsure.

Devin whispered, her voice laced with flirtation.

"I need some of you before heading to my friend's house."

Chris looked at her sideways, his eyes squinted in confusion. It was the farthest thing from his mind.

"What? I thought we were going to see your friends." His tone was a bit puzzled.

She moved in closer. "I know, Chris," Devin said softly, her lips brushing his as she kissed him. "But when you picked me up tonight, I didn't expect you to look this fine and smell this good."

He was both turned on and frustrated. Chris was intelligent, well-mannered, and handsome. When he smiled, his hazel eyes lit up the room.

"Come on, this is getting old... I have not met your parents yet, and that's okay. But I'm not good enough to meet your friends? Your girls?"

Devin's frustration started to show. "Babe, please, why must we keep talking about this?" She asked, trying to keep things light. She didn't want to risk losing what she enjoyed most with him.

"You're not being straight with me. That's why we keep talking about it!" he fired back... "We've been together for five months, and I like you. I thought we were making progress, but you only see me as a quick fix!"

Devin scoffed, a playful smile tugging at her lips as she licked them. "Yes, sir, *daddy*. I can't help that you fit my kitty-kat like you do," she teased, running her fingers along his arm.

But Chris wasn't smiling. He rubbed his hand down his face and sighed heavily, leaving Devin confused.

She never imagined this young man would even respect her enough to want something more, let alone desire a relationship. She didn't think she'd given him any reason to believe it could be possible.

Yet, surprisingly, she felt his emotions and instinctively leaned in, placing a hand on his chin to gently guide his face toward hers. "Babe, I'm sorry. I'm not trying to be insensitive, but you just turned 22, and I'll be 27 in a couple of months. You don't see that as a problem?"

He gave her a look that suggested she should've already known the answer. "No, I don't," he replied, his voice serious.

Devin dropped her hand and looked down, a baffled expression on her face.

Sensing her confusion, Chris gently asked, "What's wrong with that?"

"No one's ever taken me this seriously," she murmured.

Chris caressed the back of her head, his fingers running through her silky, shoulder-length bob. "I sense something good in you that you don't even realize."

His words touched Devin. She looked at him and saw the sincerity in his eyes. But it still puzzled her—she'd never been in a long-term relationship. Guys had always told her she was too much like the man—controlling, hard to connect with—and she never understood why.

She usually ended things first, needing control over her own life.

"Dev?" His voice snapped her out of her thoughts. She quickly shifted back to her usual mindset. Sentimental talk wasn't her thing.

She kissed him softly. "Okay, baby, we'll figure this out...

But first, we need to focus on you busting down this kitty. After that, I promise we'll talk about you meeting my friends... deal?"

Chris put his head down and chuckled. "Girl, you be *buggin'*."

He pressed his fist to his forehead. "How are you so fine and educated but so ratchet?"

Devin giggled. "I don't know, babe... maybe you're meant to help me figure that out. But for now, it's whatever you want after you hook me up," she added with a big smile.

Chris could tell he probably wouldn't get a chance to meet her friends anytime soon. He knew that Devin was prioritizing her needs over his feelings.

She crawled to the back seat of his truck, slipping off her black thong, the scent of sun-kissed tropical flowers filling the air.

Chris couldn't help but be drawn to it—her scent always enticed him when he was between her pretty brown thighs.

"Alright then," he sighed, his voice lined with frustration. "It's whatever I want?"

He removed his t-shirt and crawled back into the seat with her, unbuckling his pants just enough.

He paused, looking at her. He gently moved her hands away as she reached for him and gestured with his finger. *"Turn over."*

Devin furrowed her brows. "What are you doing?"

"You said it's whatever I want, right?"

"Yes, but..."

"Okay then," Chris interrupted. "You want what you want, and I want what I want. I wanna talk to *miss kitty* from behind. Are you good with that? Or should I pack this up and go home?"

Devin responded to his confident and firm request, her desire for him growing more assertive.

He entered her gently, and she felt herself melt into him, her body already adjusting to the rhythm between them.

Her breath caught as Chris braced himself with one hand on the back of his passenger seat and the other strategically placed between her sweet, lush core.

Devin was overwhelmed with pleasure, being surprised at how quickly she was getting swept away, feeling a rush of heat building inside her.

Chris's voice was low and commanding. "Tell me you want this."

"I want this!" Devin breathed out.

As their connection deepened, Chris couldn't shake the thought that if this were to be the end, he would make sure it ended with his name attached to it.

Devin's reactions matched his every movement as he went deeper, the intensity building between them. She couldn't help but lose herself in the moment, feeling both dazed and exhilarated.

Feeling the intensity of their intimacy building, he proceeded deeper with each lunge. The unattainable surge of heat they both felt within, Chris warned her, his voice barely above a whisper, "I need to pull back..."

Devin trembled as she let go, her body responding uncontrollably, while Chris followed suit; his release came soon after. They were breathless—both forgot they were in someone else's garage as they tried to steady themselves.

Afterward, they lay there, winded, caught in the aftermath of carnal bliss.

Chris reached into the middle console, grabbing a few wipes—a couple for Devin, one for himself. He quickly adjusted, pulling his pants back up and leaning back, resting his head against the backseat's headrest.

Devin rolled onto her back, wiping herself and catching her breath. Her legs bent, spread slightly apart, and she faced him as she relaxed. Chris shifted his body closer between her legs, resting his head on her chest. They slowed their breathing, still riding the high of the moment.

"You worked me over and over, Chris. I'll be sore for days," Devin teased, feeling the outcome of their session.

Chris scoffed, then chuckled. "I'm sorry... well, actually, no, I'm not," he replied with a grin.

Devin playfully hit him on the head.

"Ouch," he muttered, laughing with her. "I was just upset," he added lightly. "Had to take it out on something."

"Really?" she chuckled, hitting him harder this time.

"Chill, girl! You know you liked it," he said as he caught her hand, tightening his grip as they laughed.

Devin's smile faded as her expression softened, staring at the truck ceiling. She thought about Chris's frustration when he suggested she turn over, skipping foreplay and getting straight to it. And with that, she asked the question.

"You didn't believe me about meeting my friends, huh?" Her voice was soft.

"No, not really," he replied with a smirk. "I think you were just negotiating so *miss kitty* could have her way."

They both chuckled, but the mood lifted quickly. The air grew quiet as Chris slid his hand under her shirt, gently pulling and twirling her nipple between his fingers.

"So, when?" he asked, his tone direct.

"When what?" Devin, playing dumb as if she didn't know exactly what he meant.

"Will I ever meet your friends?"

A heavy silence settled between them, and Chris grew increasingly impatient with each passing second. Finally, unable to stand the quiet any longer, he broke the stillness.

"Put your clothes on," he said calmly. "I'm taking you to your friends." He opened the back door of his truck, fixing his pants before sliding into the driver's seat.

"Don't bother. I'll walk!" Devin snapped.

Chris shook his head in reply. "Cool. Walk your kitty and your lying ego over there, then."

Devin angrily snatched her panties from the floor, stuffed them into her hand, and quickly put on her shoes. She was determined to get out of his truck.

With no shortcuts through the thick hedges, she walked down the long driveway and headed toward Zora's house. But before she could reach her destination, Chris backed out and slowly drove beside her as she made her way up the sidewalk.

"What do you want? You can go home!" she yelled.

"I will after I know you've reached your friend's house. Then, I'll gladly leave you!" His tone was cold. "I'm done with your selfish attitude!"

"Um, you forgot, I'm older than you! So, I can take care of myself!"

"You may be older, but not smarter," he shot back. "Not smart enough to know when a man cares about you."

"Shut up, Chris!" Devin yelled, tossing her thongs at him. It almost hit him in the face, but he caught them just in time, sniffed them, and then smirked.

As he enjoyed the playful, taunting moment, Chris looked up and noticed a few women standing in the doorway.

Devin followed his gaze, her expression changing as she saw her friends looking dumbfounded.

"Hi, ladies," Chris said kindly, waving. "Hey!" they all greeted in harmony.

"I'm Chris, and I'm sorry this introduction wasn't on better terms," he added apologetically.

Devin, seething, turned back to him. "Like, I know you are not speaking to my friends!"

Chris just shook his head and drove off.

Devin, embarrassed and fuming, stomped up the driveway toward her friends.

Amina's head jerked back. "Uh-uhn! What the freak?!"

Zora quickly interfered, taking Devin by the hand and guiding her into the house. Brooklyn chuckled softly at Amina's outburst.

"There's no way! This clown has never given any guy this much time and attention! What's up with that?" Amina kept going, clearly flabbergasted.

"Please, Amina, can she at least sit down first?" Zora requested politely.

"No!" Brooklyn and Amina replied in unity.

Devin glared at them, already annoyed. "What?!" she yelled, but they ignored her anger.

"Now, Devin, don't pretend that dude didn't just drive off with your *draws* in his hand!" Brooklyn said, tilting her head and folding her arms as she spoke.

Devin rolled her eyes, but the rest of them—Zora included—burst out laughing.

At first, Devin hadn't realized how much of the screaming match they'd heard, but now, she couldn't help but cringe.

She plopped down on the sofa and covered her face with her hands, unintentionally picturing his face.

From the moment they met, Chris was strongly attracted to Devin, even with her detached attitude. Though she felt the same way, drawn to him at first sight, she had only envisioned a *'friends with benefits'* connection. But unexpectedly, for the first time, she began to picture Chris's vision of a real relationship.

His assertive yet respectful way of speaking, his kindness toward others, his strong sense of faith and family—qualities she hadn't fully appreciated until now.

Ironically, these qualities pushed her away—she wasn't used to them. No man had been this consistently committed to her, making her nervous.

Tonight, though, she was more drawn to him than she cared to admit, but her narcissistic tendencies kept her from showing that side to him.

Urban Coffee

Brayden finally arrived home after his last showing of the day. A couple of hours earlier, he had called Keisha to remind her to prepare for tonight. As he walked into his well-kept home, he called out to her. "Yo, Keisha!"

Immediately, the sweet scent of her perfume filled the air, followed by an even better sight. Keisha stood in her four-inch black Louboutin heels, wearing baby-blue silk thongs.

The string of the thongs nestled between her curves, accentuating her figure. She was braless, her firm, perky breasts exposed and ready to be fondled. Her face was done up, and she was smoothing her natural curls into a neat, messy bun.

Small diamond circle earrings dangled from her ears as she wrapped a sparkly twist-tie around her bun.

"Hey, Bae!" she responded sultrily, teasing her fluffy bun.

He walked up behind her, wrapping his arms around her waist, and kissed her neck. She had dressed so alluringly, hoping for this reaction when he walked through the door. She let out a soft sigh, leaning back into him as a welcoming gesture.

"You smell good," he whispered between kisses.

Feeling their attraction, Keisha reached back, her hand caressing his firmness. She turned around to face him, their lips meeting in a heated kiss as she undid his belt and unzipped his pants.

"Hold up," Brayden interfered. "We don't have that kind of time."

She paused, looking at him with desire, wanting him badly. Walking over to the kitchen bar stool, Keisha removed her thong and bent over slightly.

"It's okay, babe, just a couple of minutes—that's all I need," she said, smiling playfully. However, she was hoping to keep him to herself tonight without going out at all.

Brayden, already feeling the pressure, walked toward her. But suddenly, the ringtone of his phone echoed across the room. "YOUR SON IS ATTEMPTING TO REACH YOU ON YOUR CELLULAR DEVICE."

The sound immediately stopped him in his tracks, breaking the moment.

Keisha glanced at the phone, feeling extremely irritated that she hadn't thought to silence it after he had walked in.

"Hold up a minute," Brayden said, welcoming the interruption.

"Hey, what's up?" he greeted the caller.

"Hey, Brayden! How are you?"

"I'm good, babygirl. What's going on?"

Keisha immediately tensed up, knowing Brayden was talking to Brooklyn. He put the phone on speaker as he headed to the bedroom, a move he made consciously after the tension between him and Keisha over his past actions with Brooklyn.

"I just got off the phone with your mom. Are you letting Nate stay with her until Sunday?"

"Oh yeah, sorry, Brook. I meant to call you when I got home, but got sidetracked," Brayden replied, tapping Keisha on the butt as she walked into the bedroom, holding her damp panties in her hand.

"Ouch, babe!" Keisha said it intentionally, loud enough for Brooklyn to hear.

"Oh, my bad. Didn't realize you had company."

Keisha boiled internally, her thoughts cutting through her frustration. "I'm his girl, hoe... not company," she said to herself.

Brayden continued the conversation, unfazed.

"Nah, you're okay, Brook. That was Keisha. But yeah, Mom and Ms. Bria wanted the kids to come to brunch on Saturday and then to church on Sunday," he informed.

"Okay, that's right. Your mom did mention that. So, with that, if I can't pick Nate up right after church, do you mind bringing him home?"

Keisha's scowl deepened as she listened.

"Of course," he replied with no hesitation.

"Great, so I'll see you later, then."

"Alright, babygirl, be good."

Brooklyn disconnected the call, but her heart ached from hearing Keisha's voice in the background.

"Alright, Keisha, it's getting late. I'll jump in the shower right quick and throw something on, then we can go." Brayden kissed her on the cheek before heading off.

"Um...okay, bae."

This had put a damper on Keisha's plans. She had remained undressed, hoping Brayden would pick up where they had left off once he finished the call.

"Ugh! I'll be glad when that tramp gets a man!" she whispered, frustration building.

If Keisha knew Brayden had no lingering feelings for Brooklyn, she wouldn't feel so insecure about the situation.

Moreover, the fact that they had recently slept together only made it worse—Keisha's feelings became more insecure.

Urban Coffee

The ladies were dressed and ready for a fun, peaceful, exciting night. However, they had no specific plans or expectations for what the evening would bring.

"Are we rolling in the Range or the Lex?" Amina asked, grabbing her gray purse; her lengthy, black 4C hair was elegantly styled in a low, side ponytail.

"We can take the Lex, honey. I need gas," Brooklyn quickly suggested. The group burst into laughter as they prepared to head out the door.

"We can get you some gas, stinka," Zora teased, not particularly eager to drive herself.

"I'm good on gas... to be real. I just don't feel like driving," Brooklyn confessed.

Zora shrugged her shoulders. "Well, neither do I."

"Throw me the keys!" Devin hollered from the driver's side of Zora's Lexus SUV. She didn't mind taking the wheel of that beautiful, shiny, classic vehicle while Zora happily rode shotgun in her own ride.

"Ah, dang!" Amina muttered as she opened the car door and slid into the backseat.

Brooklyn heard her. "What's the matter?" She asked, glancing over at Amina's cell phone as it lit up.

"Don't ask," Amina said, raising her hand as a signal to stop.

Rocco text: Amina, where you at, beautiful?
Amina text: Why, Rocco? I'm minding my business!
Rocco: Lol, why you gotta be so mean, girl? Can I see you?
Amina: Why? I'm out with my girls tonight. I don't want to see you!
Rocco: I don't believe you don't feel anything for me. I know you. When you're done, you're done—but here we are. Please don't block me! Lol.
Amina: Oh, okay, Mr. Cocky! Lol. But it remains...I don't trust you. I don't believe anything that's coming out of your mouth.

Rocco: I wish I could see that smile in person. You don't have to believe me, though—I will prove it with actions. I pray you give me the chance.
Amina: Oh, so you pray now? Lol.
Rocco: You don't?
Amina: Don't worry about me. I pray. So, you know Jesus, too? Lol. Is this the so-called change you want to talk to me about?
Rocco: Yes, and then some. Is anything wrong with that?
Amina: No, it's not, but it's hard to imagine YOU wanting to. I didn't know liars, cheaters, and heartbreakers knew who Jesus was.
Rocco: Ouch! That's who I used to be. Just let me see you, okay?
Amina: Roc, I need to think about it. Maybe call me tomorrow, and I'll see how I'm feeling.
Rocco: That's all I ask. Take care out in those streets.

She didn't respond. Instead, Amina sat in a daze, staring out the window. She was on the verge of tears, torn between how someone she cared about deeply could cause her so much pain...and the idea of possibly giving him another chance to hurt her again. Despite the confusion, her heart pulled her toward him. She couldn't deny the curiosity gnawing at her about what he's been up to.

"Girl, let that man see you," Brooklyn said, casually reading Rocco's last text. "It won't hurt to give him a chance to say what's on his mind."

"You're right, Brook. And I'm going to let him HAVE IT. I never really told him how I felt. I packed up his stuff and never looked back."

"Okay then. Perfect time for closure," Brooklyn remarked, giving Amina a sideways glance.

Amina noticed her expression. “What?”

“Nothing… just be careful what you say.”

“Nah, I got this!” Amina snapped back boldly.

Urban Coffee

The night was clear and crisp, a cool 70 degrees, as the girls coasted towards Alpine Boulevard, where most of the nightlife occurred. They first stopped at a self-serve gas station to refuel and buy junk food for the anticipated fun-filled night.

Devin got out to pump the gas. “Zora, get me a pack of Tropical Twist Trident and a Mountain Dew,” she called out right before the girls entered the store.

They navigated through the aisles, swiftly picking out their snacks while dressed in cute outfits. Across the room, a tall, dark-skinned man watched them, his gaze primarily fixed on Zora. He wore a black Nike baseball cap turned backward and stood by the lottery machine, patiently waiting to purchase tickets.

Mina!” Zora exclaimed as they made their way toward the checkout counter. “I know you’re not seriously snacking on chips before we’ve paid for them, are you?”

Amina shook her head with pursed lips. “Girl, chill! I’m going to give these people their 99 cents. I’m hungry; get out of my business!” Brooklyn laughed.

“You little Tasmanian devil.” Zora retorted while laughing at her facial expression as well.

“It’ll be $4.62,” the store clerk announced right before Brooklyn tossed her chips onto the counter to be added to Amina’s. But if looks could kill, Brooklyn would have collapsed on the gas station floor.

"Move!" she snapped, lightly pushing Amina aside. "I'll pay for everything. You can be so stingy sometimes."

Amina chuckled. Her tactic was occasionally getting them to foot the bill, pretending she didn't have the money. "Your new total is $5.79," the chubby-cheeked clerk said.

Brooklyn turned toward Zora, who was chatting with the tall man wearing the Nike cap by the lottery machine. "Do you want me to add yours?" she asked, but Zora paid her no mind.

After the clerk had bagged their items, Brooklyn and Amina exchanged a knowing smirk before returning to the truck.

Devin had parked right in front of the store after filling the tank. They hopped into the backseat, all three of them patiently observing Zora and the tall man's conversation for about two minutes.

Afterward, Zora approached the counter to pay for Devin's soda and gum. Mr. Nike cap stood behind her, leaning in as if whispering something into her ear. Zora chuckled and playfully tapped his chest in response. The girls exchanged stunned looks with each other.

"Wait a minute! She knows this dude," Brooklyn stated as she and Amina leaned in closer from the back seat. Devin sat in silence, observing every little exchange between them.

Zora waved goodbye to the guy as she left the store and returned to the truck. When she entered, their eyes pierced her, but she remained calm and did not speak until they brought it up.

"So, are you going to sit your little narrow behind in this truck and not tell us who that tall bottle of cuteness is?!" Brooklyn shot out.

The others patiently waited for her to respond. Zora slowly looked over at Devin and then at Brooklyn and Amina, who were behind her, before returning her gaze to Devin.

"Anyway, here's your gum and Mountain Dew. Can we go now?" Zora reacted unexpectedly, throwing the gum in Devin's lap and placing the soda in the middle console's cup holder.

"Wait. What?" Amina said, but Devin quickly held her hand up, shushing her.

"Don't worry about it; her tongue will fall out before the night's over," Devin stated firmly. They all started laughing, even Zora.

"Okay! Y'all are thinking too much into this. That's Damon—he was a patient at the hospital, and we recognized each other. All I asked was what happened to the bandage he had on his wrist."

They all scoffed, chuckling and thinking it was more than that. Devin slowly backed the truck out of the parking space, and at the same time, the Nike cap cutie came walking out of the store, heading toward his car. He looked over at Zora and blew her a kiss.

They all screamed and started laughing, lightly shoving Zora's shoulder.

Subsequently, Devin's laughter halted, and she quickly placed the truck in park, jumped out, and walked briskly across the gas station parking lot. She approached a black truck parked backward into the end parking space. She started yelling at the young gentleman in the driver's seat.

"Oh, okay, this is how you get down?!

You wanna be with me, but out here posted up with some random chick this quickly?!" Devin said firmly, waving her finger in the guy's face.

"Man, you better move away from my ride," the gentleman responded to Devin.

"Okay, I will." And then suddenly... *SMACK!* She landed a solid one across his face.

He turned away from the blow, then faced her again, gently rubbing his cheek as he flashed a friendly smile.

"I know you didn't!" the random girl said as she jumped out of his passenger side and headed towards Devin, ready to swing.

Brooklyn and Amina didn't miss a beat. They also jumped out and ran over to defend their friend, but not before Devin landed the first punch in the random girl's eye. *Bop!* It was quickly followed by a left shot to her jaw from Amina.

The random girl started screaming. *"I'mma* kill you!" as she continued to swing and miss because Devin was tagging her face with every punch. Brooklyn stood there just in case the girl got the better of her friend. But it never happened, so she stayed calm.

To the random girl, it felt like 10 minutes, but it was only 10 seconds. The guy in the black truck had gotten out and grabbed the girl, and Damon grabbed Amina, who was waiting to swing again. Brooklyn and Zora quickly grabbed hold of Devin.

"C'mon, Dev, get back in the car! Zora yelled, pulling Devin by the arm.

Devin looked back at the truck and shouted, "Chris, you're wrong! You'll regret this!

The guy laughed, shaking his head.

"You're the wrong one, pretty lady. You'll regret it before I do," he yelled as he drove off.

"Oh, my goodness! That was Chris?" Brooklyn asked, her face filled with surprise.

"Wow, I'm so sorry, Dev," Zora said, opening the passenger-side door for her. She knew her friend wouldn't be in the mood to drive after what just happened. "Are you okay?" Zora asked as she slid into the driver's seat.

"I'm good, let's just go."

Zora let out a solemn sigh and continued heading down Alpine Boulevard. The first few minutes passed in silence until Brooklyn finally broke the tension.

"Dev, are you sure you're okay, sweetie? We can go back home." There was a brief pause before Devin responded.

"Yeah, I'm good. Don't worry about me. I want to have fun tonight and not dwell on what happened."

Amina chimed in, lightening the mood. "What about *Miss Birdbrain* jumping out of the truck like she's about to regulate?"

"Yeah, I know, right? She was acting wild! Brooklyn responded.

All the girls blurted out their responses to Amina's question, laughing.

"I mean, I wasn't going to do anything until I saw her leap out like that," Amina added, shaking her head.

"Exactly! Y'all had it covered, too. I didn't have to budge. And I'm so glad I didn't because I'm looking too cute tonight," Brooklyn remarked, provoking another round of laughter.

Urban Coffee

Elsewhere, the guys had arrived at the restaurant near the city. Brayden stepped out of his Navigator and took Keisha's hand as she approached from the other side. Together, they walked inside to find a table for their party.

“Table for two?” the pretty Caucasian brunette asked, eyeing Brayden up and down with a cheesy smile.

“It’ll be four—preferably a booth by the window if you can,” he replied, showcasing that alluring smile and dreamy eyes.

“Sure, follow me.”

“She’s about to get her block knocked off, looking at you like that,” Keisha whispered with a slanted smile as they followed the waitress to their booth. Brayden scoffed at her comment.

“Oh, you don’t think I will?” Keisha teased, vigorously tapping his arm.

“Ay, girl... I believe you,” he said with a sarcastic grin, lightly rubbing his arm.

She wondered if he was reflecting on the fight she had lost with Brooklyn, so she attempted to burst his bubble with a snide remark.

“Just because you hold a high-ranking belt in kickboxing doesn’t mean you can beat everybody, Brayden,” Keisha interjected swiftly.

“I never once, nor will I ever, claim that I can *beat* everybody,” he responded. “There’s always someone better than you, me, or the next person.” His humility showed as he gently kissed Keisha’s forehead, effectively ending the conversation. She pursed her lips, knowing he was right.

As he slid into the booth after her, Brayden noticed Malik outside, engrossed in a phone call.

****

“Hey, babygirl... are you okay?”

“I’m fine. And you?

"I'm good now," Malik replied with relief. "I'm at the seafood joint on the Boulevard. Brayden's inside waiting for me right now. I wanted to be sure you're good and knew how to get here."

"Oh, okay. Yes, I know the spot," Heather said. "I'll be there in about 10 minutes or so."

"Okay, cool. Look for us near the side window, closest to the sign, or call me when you arrive."

"Got it! See you soon, then."

"Alright, baby." Malik ended the call.

****

Inside, one of their contractors, Vincent, walked up to Brayden's booth. "What's up, man?" he greeted Brayden with a handshake and a smile.

"What are you doing here? We are officially off the clock, Vince."

"Nah, I was waiting on my food next door and saw your truck pull in. I was about to speak to Malik, but he's out there on the phone."

Three seconds later...

"Hey! What's up, Hammer Time?" Malik grinned at the contractor as he walked over and slid into the booth.

"What's good, Bob the Builder?" Vince laughed, dapping Malik. "I don't want to intrude too much longer, but I got some good news on that long-awaited project in the city."

"Oh, word?" Brayden leaned forward, enthusiastic.

"Referring to the space where our company's initial funds are tied up, right?" Malik asked. "I knew we had the right one keeping an eye on it."

Vince gave a quick salute. "Yes, sir, boss man. I got y'all."

Brayden glanced at Malik. “You gotta hurry up, walk that stage, man, and finalize our biggest contract. We need to achieve both at the same time.”

“Well, this is my cue to leave. I’ll see you guys at the office on Monday,” Vince said, exchanging handshakes with the guys, then turned to Keisha and raised his hands in a prayer gesture.

“I apologize, miss lady.”

“You’re good... no worries.”

“Looks like you’re third-wheeling it, aren’t you, playboy?” Vincent sarcastically remarked to Malik as he backed away to leave.

“Vince, get out of here,” Malik retorted, “before I flip you over these tables.” They all laughed, the sound filling the booth.

“Alright, boss man,” the contractor smiled, throwing his hands up, surrendering.

“Are you guys ready to order?” the cute waiter, speaking in a native accent, approached just in time.

“Sure, why not?” they all agreed, ordering the lobster and shrimp special.

“Are we not waiting on your friend?” Keisha asked, glancing at both of them.

Before Malik could answer, Heather appeared, dressed in a mid-thigh, blush pink mini-dress with a lace-open back.

It was completed with taupe high heels and a clutch purse.

“You’ve got to be kidding me! She comes all beautified, and I’m just in jeans!” Keisha blurted out.

Brayden chuckled, shaking his head. “Keisha, chill. You’re still fine,” he reassured her, glancing at Malik, who was looking at Heather.

“Girl, I don’t know you like that, but that dress is cute!” Keisha commented. Heather smiled, thanking her for the compliment.

“Whoa!” Malik whispered to himself as he stood to let Heather scoot in. She sat there in all her girly splendor, looking at him in deep thought.

“Sorry I’m late, friend,” she addressed Malik.

“No, you good... *fashionably late*, huh?

Heather, shrugging her shoulders and smiling, “Well, you know what it is.”

“What’s good, homie? It’s been a long time,” Brayden greeted her.

“Hey, Brady-bear!” Heather replied, grinning widely and feeling remorseful for not contacting him sooner.

“Brady-bear? Keisha asked, raising an eyebrow as she looked at Brayden.

“Man, don’t do that, he said to Heather, chuckling at the nickname she used to call him back in the day. “I’m a grown man, and nobody’s Brady Bear.”

They laughed, drawing a few glances from nearby tables. But for the next couple of hours, they reminisced and laughed throughout their meal, thoroughly enjoying each other’s company.

Malik explained the ringtone situation to Heather, who promptly apologized. She admitted she was only trying to be funny and expressed regret for any unintended consequences that had occurred between him and Zora. Heather and Brayden also had a heart-to-heart, and she apologized for not reaching out when she returned to town.

She explained how embarrassed she had been about her entire ordeal, but promised to update them soon about what actually happened during their five-year friendship gap.

Urban Coffee

Oddly enough, the girls were having the same sort of night. They had been at their destination for a while, ordering lemon pepper and spicy honey-glazed wings with crinkle fries. For a fun dessert, they opted for chocolate chip cookies and an ice-cold ginger ale to drink.

When the girls get together, they don't order alcohol. They are naturally high off each other's unique sense of humor and diverse personalities—a group of friends who believe they need nothing to alter their brain cells to have fun.

****

Hours had passed, and the night had been eventful. Devin's night had started rough at the gas station, but she had her dad's credit card and offered to pay for everyone's meal.

The tab was roughly *$120*. Yet, she couldn't shake the feeling that she needed some space and wanted to just sleep.

"Y'all, it's after midnight, and I'm tired. Ready to go home—I've got work tomorrow," she announced.

The girls all agreed. Each left a tip, totaling $23, and waved to their waitress as they exited their booth.

"I call shotgun," Amina shouted as she strode a little faster, going down the restaurant's steps.

Devin looked at her like she was crazy. "I don't think so. I drove here, so I get first choice, Miss delusional."

"You did not drive here, but whatever, troll." Amina shot back, giggling. She let it go, not wanting to bring up the gas station incident.

"Will somebody walk next door to the *Cream Bar* with me for some Häagen-Dazs?" Brooklyn asked, looking for company.

"I'll go with you," Zora said, and Amina joined in.

"I'll wait in the truck, but y'all hurry up." Devin firmly demanded. I'm so ready to go!"

A cool Friday night breeze still filled the air. The sounds and sights of restaurants, department stores, game rooms, theaters, and a nearby carnival ride were always part of the experience on the strip of Alpine Boulevard, especially on the weekends. It was the nightlife enjoyed with real friends, family, close-knit coworkers, or a significant other.

Traffic typically bustles until around 9 p.m. By midnight, it tapers off, with people retreating inside to enjoy their chosen activities on the Boulevard. Couples walked hand in hand, parents strolled with their little ones, and uniformed security guards were sprinkled about.

The girls wandered through the parking lot toward the Cream Bar. They couldn't help but admire the city's charming, tree-lined streets. They imagined a life filled with spontaneous evening strolls, brunches at the local café, and weekend trips to farmers' markets, where fresh, organic produce would be abundant.

Zora and Brooklyn, in particular, often envisioned one day moving into one of the up-and-coming homes with their coffee shop nearby. But for now, it remained just a dream.

As the girls neared the sidewalk, Zora suddenly stopped, her gaze fixed into the distance as if she had seen a ghost. They all followed her gaze, and there, across the street, sat Malik and Brayden, nestled next to the window inside Savory Seafood, accompanied by two women.

Zora's breathing quickened, and she could feel the anger and pain rise in her chest, each breath heavy with the weight of what she was seeing. Her shoulders heaved as the emotions took over, and tears welled in her eyes, threatening to spill but not yet falling. Devin noticed the shift and quickly exited the truck, rushing to Zora's side.

"It's okay, Zora. Let's go," she said softly, her voice concerned. Amina nodded in agreement, but Zora didn't move. Brooklyn, however, was already crossing the street toward the restaurant.

Surprisingly, Brayden noticed her first. He excused himself from the table and got up. "Hold up, y'all, I'll be right back," he said calmly, addressing his party.

"Alright, BC, make it snappy. I gotta pick my daughter up in the morning. I need some sleep," Malik replied, his tone light, unaware of the tension building outside.

"Why you gotta go home so early?" Heather asked playfully, lightly pushing against Malik's shoulder.

"Daddy's tired, and I've got a lot planned with my babygirl for tomorrow," he replied, smiling.

Keisha giggled at his response, *'daddy's tired,'* unaware that Brayden had quietly left to go outside. They assumed he was excusing himself to the restroom.

Brooklyn arrived at Savory Seafood's parking lot just as Brayden stepped out of the door. She smiled warmly, then gave him a big hug. Brayden gladly returned the embrace.

"How are you?" he asked kindly, holding her left hand when they pulled away from the hug.

Brooklyn smiled. "Not as good as Keisha, out here having fun with you,"

Brayden fixed his gaze on hers, and Brooklyn felt a slight blush, not able to maintain her composure.

"What? Why are you staring at me like that?" she asked shyly, feeling self-conscious.

"Is it a problem... me looking at you?" he softly questioned.

She tried her best not to smile wider. "Of course not."

Brayden lightly scoffed, his gaze never leaving hers. There was a brief, intimate pause between them.

His smile slowly extended, and she bashfully chuckled, lowering her head. It felt good to reunite in such a natural way. They hadn't discussed the night before, but nothing more needed to be said. This quiet, cozy moment spoke volumes. They were content with that.

But their brief moment was quickly consumed by the flames of emotional fury. Brayden watched as Zora crossed the street, her face grimacing in a frantic, upset expression. The memory of him telling Malik that he didn't have a good feeling about tonight flashed rapidly in his mind.

Devin and Amina greeted Brayden with quick, friendly hugs before he walked straight to Zora. Placing his hands on her shoulders, he looked her in the eyes.

"Hold on, don't overthink this, Zo. It's nothing... trust me," Brayden softly pleaded.

"Sure." Zora snapped, her voice mixed with frustration. "You'd say that. He's your best friend."

"I would never lie to you. You know me," he countered, his tone sincere.

Zora glanced at the restaurant window, where Malik remained seated, laughing with Keisha and Heather. The sight of it struck her with an unfathomable pain she'd never felt before. Tears began to fall, their presence now unavoidable. A storm of hurt, anger, and confusion began swirling inside her, like a thunderstorm slowly forming. Malik must've sensed something because his laughter abruptly stopped, and his brows furrowed.

"What? What happened... You okay?" Heather asked, noticing his sudden shift.

Malik glanced out the window and saw Brayden and the girls. "*What the...?*" he muttered before standing up from the table.

"Malik, you good?" Keisha asked as he started to walk away. He briefly glanced back and threw up his hand, a silent gesture that he was fine. He stopped at the counter to give his server $400 to pay the bill. "Keep the change," he said before exiting the restaurant. The server was elated as he ran up their ticket and found his tip was $84.

Malik reached the parking lot just as Zora started walking toward him, her heart heavy with anger.

"Baby, what's wrong?" he asked, reaching out to hold her. He saw the grief etched on her face—something he had never seen before—and his protective instincts flared. He was ready to rock someone's world over it. He didn't know that his world was about to be rocked.

"Don't touch me!" Zora snapped, jerking away from him.

"What's wrong, baby? What did I do?" Malik's voice carried genuine concern as he tried to reach her.

She fired off questions, her heart racing with the hope that it wasn't what it seemed. But deep down, she felt it was exactly what it looked like to her.

When Zora was upset, she talked with her hands. They moved as fast as her thoughts, urgently punctuating each question and statement.

"What is this, Malik? Are you for real right now?" she asked, pointing toward the restaurant window. "Huh? So, I was right earlier? What are you doing here?!"

"Zora, stop. Let's go somewhere and talk," Malik gently requested, trying to steady the storm between them.

"I can't believe I trusted you!" she shouted. "All this talk about wanting our family back, about making us your priority, and now this?! You told me earlier it wasn't what I thought it was, but look where we are now! Is this her?! The ringtone?!"

Malik had no words. He didn't take his eyes off her, letting her vent while maintaining his calm.

"So, this is what you call a priority? You're out here with randoms? You're seriously on a date?!" Zora's voice cracked, tears falling despite her best effort to appear cold. "I'm done! I'm so done with you!"

"Zora, stop. Hold on," he said, furrowing his brows as he stepped closer, looking into her eyes. His heart felt like it was being ripped out of his chest.

By this time, Keisha and Heather had come outside.

Malik stared at Zora as if he were seeing a different person. This was unlike him—handling personal matters in public was never his style.

"You're overreacting. Let's go talk," he said softly, his voice filled with pain. "Please."

"How am I overreacting when you're the one out here... ON A DATE?!" Zora screamed, her voice laced with betrayal and heartbreak.

Heather watched with concern. "Malik, are you okay?" she interrupted.

"Uhn-uhn! You don't speak to him!" Amina snapped aggressively as she and Devin began walking toward Heather.

"Say something else!" Zora added, turning to face Heather. Both Heather and Keisha's eyes widened in surprise, unsure of what the girls were about to do next.

"Whoa, hold up, ladies... chill," Brayden intervened, stepping between them with Brooklyn beside him.

"Y'all, please stop, for real," Brooklyn calmly requested, looking at her friends with a gentle but firm expression.

Brayden then approached Heather. "It'd be best if you didn't insert yourself," he said softly.

Heather nodded, regret filling her expression as she acknowledged her mistake.

Meanwhile, Malik was growing increasingly frustrated with the unnecessary drama and Zora's behavior. He lightly grabbed her arm and pulled her a few steps from the group.

"Your problem is with me, so address me. She has nothing to do with this," he added, gesturing to Heather.

Malik moved closer to Zora, looking her in the eyes, trying to be as honest and sincere as possible. He needed her to hear him and understand.

"Not that I need to explain myself, especially with you acting like this, but Heather's an old family friend," he began. "This is what I was trying to explain to you earlier. I'm not on a date. She means nothing to me in that way—only that she knows how I feel about you."

Heather felt embarrassed at Malik's honesty, wishing she could shrink away from the moment.

"Omg!" Keisha muttered, glancing at Heather's uncomfortable expression.

"I don't know why you're acting like this," Malik continued, his voice softer now...

"I love you, but you keep pushing us apart. I need to understand what's going on because this isn't you." His gaze softened as he tilted his head slightly.

But Zora's stare was icy and unyielding. She didn't respond—his words seemed to fall on deaf ears.

Malik didn't give up just yet, his voice low and pleading, "Can we please talk somewhere... just the two of us?"

But Zora's gaze didn't fade. The presence of Heather, standing there in the background, was too much for Zora to ignore.

"Malik, forget about me and just take care of your daughter," she finally said, her voice trembling with emotion. "I can't do this anymore with you."

Malik took a step back, his brows furrowing in disbelief. He couldn't believe what he was hearing. His mind was flooded with all the beautiful memories they'd shared, but just as quickly as they came, those memories began to fade.

Brayden swiftly acted, hoping to reduce the mounting tension before things escalated further. He became the peacemaker, pulling $50 from his wallet.

"Heather, take this for gas and make sure Keisha gets home," his voice steady but firm.

Keisha's expression immediately soured. She shook her head, eyes wide with disbelief, not agreeing with Brayden's request. He caught the look, aware of her frustration.

"Keisha, go home. I'll talk to you later," he insisted, his tone steadfast.

She stared at him for a few seconds, clearly struggling with the urge to argue. But knowing better than to make a scene, she stepped up to him, trying to kiss him. He stopped her, holding his hand up, politely but firmly urging her to leave.

Keisha paused, attempting to play it down. "Brayden, did you forget? I left *my* key on your table before we left the house tonight," she said purposely, making sure Brooklyn could hear her words.

"No. Go to *your* house, and I'll call you tomorrow."

"Oop!" Amina muttered aloud before realizing.

Keisha caught the sound and glanced toward Amina, but Amina met her gaze without flinching.

Before anything else could escalate, Heather quickly grabbed Keisha's hand, preventing any more tension from building.

"C'mon, girl, let's go. He's your man; you'll see him tomorrow," she said deliberately as she passed by the girls, heading toward her car.

Brooklyn giggled lightly, shaking her head.

Amidst all this, Malik, his emotions swirling, stepped forward to get confirmation one last time.

"So, this is it?" he asked, his eyes locked on Zora's, his voice weighed down with hurt and uncertainty as he stepped closer. "You want me to forget about you? Forget us?"

Deep down, Zora wanted to go to him, forget everything she had said, and embrace him. However, to avoid further humiliation after her outbursts, she held her ground, keeping a straight face as she locked eyes with him.

"Take care of your daughter... and forget about us, Malik," she repeated, her voice trembling. A slight stutter betrayed her decision. He lowered his head, a heavy sigh escaping him, his pain visible.

At that moment, a gut-wrenching ball of emotion formed in Zora's chest. She felt as though she were drowning, struggling to breathe, and no one—least of all the man who had always been able to save her—could pull her out of the mess she had just created. She was ripping his world apart, and it shattered her just as much. It was as though she didn't recognize her own words—her actions.

The girls, including Brayden, were left speechless, the heaviness of the moment pressing down on them. But what came next was the ultimate shockwave.

"Because I love you so much, I will honor your request. And don't worry, I'll *always* take care of our daughter." Malik's voice was steady but marked with pain.

Zora began to tremble from within, feeling like pieces of herself were slowly breaking apart.

Malik turned to walk away, tossing his keys to Brayden without a word, heading toward his vehicle. He climbed into the passenger seat, drained—Zora had taken every ounce of emotional energy he had left tonight.

Knowing precisely what Malik needed without him saying a word, Brayden handed his own keys to Brooklyn. "Here, could you take my car home, please? I'll pick it up tomorrow."

"Of course," she responded with a nod, her voice soft and understanding.

"Thank you, baby." Gratitude and sorrow intertwine in his tone.

Brayden climbed into Malik's car and backed out of the parking lot. The drive back down Alpine Boulevard was long, quiet, and full of unspoken weight—about a 30-minute drive back home, but it felt much longer for Malik.

Zora watched as Malik rode past her, not once glancing her way. Her anxiety escalated, and she began crying as though the world was falling apart. The girls rushed to help her across the street and back to the truck.

"Zo, sweetie, are you okay?" Brooklyn asked, noticing her pale complexion.

Suddenly, Zora gagged and sprinted to a nearby bush, her body convulsing as she vomited up the wave of nauseating emotions.

Devin hurried over, gently holding her hair back, staying by her side until everything calmed.

They heard a car honk its horn, and Heather and Keisha were driving past. Keisha laughed and waved her hand as they went by.

She and Heather had been sitting in the car, away from everyone else, watching everything unfold. They had seen Malik and Brayden drive off, noticed Zora vomiting, and realized this was the perfect moment to pass by.

Keisha was determined not to leave until the coast was clear, but she hadn't expected Brayden to leave his car behind with Brooklyn. It stirred up her insecurities, taking them to an entirely new level.

After ten minutes of consoling Zora and waiting for her to regain some composure, Brooklyn went inside The Hangout to grab a ginger ale to settle Zora's stomach.

After a while, they all headed back down Alpine Boulevard, the night that had started with fun and laughter fading into a sea of heartbreak.

Urban Coffee

Instead of going home, Malik asked Brayden to drop him off at his parents' house. He needed to be near his daughter, his family.

"I'll get the car sorted tomorrow," Malik said.

"Alright, man, get some rest," Brayden replied, his voice a little heavy with concern. "Don't make any sudden moves. Everything's still fresh."

Malik chuckled lightly. "Yeah, I hear you."

"Tell Mama Bria and Pops I'll see them tomorrow." Brayden dapped Malik before heading home, worn out from the night.

Malik's parents lived in a charming five-bedroom brick home with a manicured lawn, a three-tiered marble water fountain strategically placed out front, and a custom ocean-blue pool in the back. Some of the additions were designed by Malik himself, showcasing his architectural skills.

He slipped in through the side door around 1:30 AM.

His mom was tidying the pantry, and soft voices echoed from the cozy office beside the kitchen.

"Son, you scared me," Mama Bria whispered, turning to Malik as he walked up behind her and kissed her cheek.

"Sorry, ma. What are you still doing up... and where's my babygirl?" Malik scanned the open-concept area with a slight unease.

"You just missed her. Mazo went to sleep about 30 minutes ago. Your dad's in his office, watching TV and waiting for me. He's probably asleep by now, though, since we just got back from our road trip..."

Mama Bria continued to organize her pantry. "We met some family members we didn't even know we had. It was a wonderful time. Even the oldest member, Ms. Evadine, a lovely 107-year-old lady. A few of them will be here tomorrow for the brunch."

Malik's mom paused, unsure of what she was feeling, then turned to face him. "But the real question, son, is what are you doing here? And be straight with me—I can feel it, and I see it all over your face."

Malik sat on the kitchen bar stool, gathering his thoughts as his mother closed the pantry door. Silence hung between them, the tension heavy. Finally, she walked closer, concern clear on her face. Malik leaned against the kitchen island, propping his elbow and resting his chin on his fist. Sensing his emotional weight, his mother immediately rushed to his side.

"Son, what is it? What's going on?" She nestled him in her arms as he began describing every detail of the night and more.

Ms. Bria felt deep empathy for him, knowing her son loved hard and was always honest. She responded with love, wisdom, and unyielding support.

"Malik, you're an alpha male gifted at expressing your heart and soul. That trait makes you highly desirable and suited for successful relationships, both personal and professional...

You're just like your dad," she added with a smile. "So, don't feel defeated, son—you'll get through this."

She lifted his chin to meet her gaze. "If anyone can't see your value, it's their loss. I love Zora, and I've always loved her for you. I have no doubt you'll make the right decision moving forward. Just take your time and pray for guidance."

Malik listened intently to his mom's wise words, grateful for her understanding and reassurance. After thanking her and giving her a warm hug, he said goodnight. Before heading to bed, he briefly stopped by the office to speak with his dad, then made his way to Mazo's room.

When he peeked through the door, she turned over and noticed him. "Hi, Daddy." Her soft-spoken voice was barely audible as her eyes fluttered open.

"Hey, baby. I love you. Go back to sleep," he replied, lying down beside her.

"Okay, Daddy, goodnight." Malik felt tired and dejected, but finally at peace.

CHAPTER 7
Almost 2 am

Brayden was only a couple of minutes away from home. Keisha had called his phone for the tenth time.

He reluctantly answered, “Yeah, what’s up?”

“Oh, now you decide to pick up. I’ve called you twenty times!”

“Twenty? Yo, Keisha, this is not the time. I’m tired and sleepy. If all you have for me is attitude, we can talk tomorrow.”

“Well, fortunately, it is tomorrow. Where are you now?” she asked boldly.

“I’m headed home. Is everything okay?”

“Yes, everything is fine. I called to see how things were with you on your drive home, Brayden.”

“Well, you should know since you left after we did.”

Keisha’s eyes widened in surprise. She hadn’t realized he had spotted Heather’s car behind them as they drove down the Boulevard. He also knew they hadn’t left the parking lot of Savory Seafood when he first asked her to leave.

“So, where is your car since you’re driving Malik’s?”

“Keisha, don’t ask me a question you already know the answer to.”

She was upset, but she did not want to spoil the surprise she had planned for him.

After a few minutes, Brayden pulled up to his house, and to his disbelief, Keisha stood on his porch. He parked the car and didn’t get out for at least a minute.

His stomach knotted. He exhaled abruptly, head dropping, trying to swallow the frustration building up inside.

Keisha started walking towards his car, but he got out before she arrived.

"What are you doing here? I told you to go home, and we'll talk later." She tried her best to find the right words to change his mind.

"I just wanted to be here for you after everything that happened." Her voice pleading.

"I appreciate that. I do. But I don't want company tonight. So, please, go home, and I'll call you later."

To his benefit, though, Heather was still there, parked across the street from his home.

Keisha had asked her to stick around just in case.

"Okay, Brayden, I'll go home, and we'll talk tomorrow," she hesitantly complied, appearing sad and defeated.

Brayden took her by the hand and walked her to the car. Heather was shaking her head. *"Poor thing,"* she said to herself, chuckling, right before Brayden opened the car door and kissed Keisha on the cheek.

"Alright, Heather, text me when you drop her off and when you get home, too".

"I will do that, friend."

Keisha got into the car, her posture stiff and her face a mixture of anger and frustration. Brayden carefully closed the car door and sprinted back across the street as the girls drove off.

Urban Coffee

"Hey, hand me my purse back there. I'm ready to go home," Devin requested, glancing at Brooklyn and Amina as she parked the truck in Zora's driveway.

"Here you go. And c'mon, if you still want me to take you home," Brooklyn replied, handing Devin her purse.

Zora blurted out as she got out of the front passenger seat. “Oh, no... this can’t be happening!”

“What’s wrong? Girl, you good?” Amina asked, concern in her voice as they all watched, waiting for Zora to respond.

“Yes, I’m fine... I just... my cycle started,” Zora explained, her voice shaky, tears quickly rolling down her face. “I’m a whole mess tonight, y’all!”

Amina took the house keys from her hand and unlocked the front door while the others followed Zora inside.

Brooklyn felt so bad for her. “Honey, it’s okay. Just get some rest, and let tonight be what it is. God willing, tomorrow will be a new day to fix whatever’s necessary.”

Devin nodded in agreement as she went to hug Zora and wish her well. However, Amina stood there, shaking her head in annoyance.

“What, Mina? I see you shaking that big head,” Zora said, her expression hard and angry.

“I hope you do because you need to help me understand something.” Amina’s tone was blunt and assertive.

“Mina, not now, please!” Devin begged, sensing she was about to go off in her typical no-filter way.

“No, no, no!” Amina’s voice rose as she kept going. “Let me get this off my chest, and then I’ll be on my way...

I don’t get what your goal was tonight, Zora. Who in their right mind tells a man, who’s doing so well for himself and loves you, to forget about her... and in front of a whole woman who probably wants him?!

This man is an architect! Been in school for almost six years, building a future for his daughter and your stubborn self!”

Brooklyn quickly turned her head, wide-eyed, her cheeks puffed out as she silently agreed with Amina’s rant.

"And then this man, with the courage that most men only wish they had, told you in front of that lady that she meant nothing to him! And you told him twice... to forget about you!

What were you trying to prove?" Amina asked, her brows furrowed in disbelief, her expression clearly showing her confusion.

"I didn't try to prove anything!" Zora shouted angrily.

"Okay, Mina, that's enough," Devin said, reaching out to touch Amina's shoulder, hoping she'd cut Zora some slack. But Amina quickly pulled her shoulder away and pointed at Zora, continuing.

"Nah... what you thought, after embarrassing yourself, was that Malik would go hard for you in front of that lady, and you could prove something to her. But it backfired!...

What you should've been doing was apologizing to that man when you had the chance, and he would be here tonight instead of us!...

You are dealing with a real man!" she continued. "And he may be getting tired of you acting all unsupportive... Malik's out there working hard, being away from his family, being as legit as a negro can be! And you out here playing games—Grow up!"

Zora angrily dashed toward Amina and shoved her, but Amina matched her energy just as forcefully.

"Dang! Y'all, stop!" Devin yelled as she and Brooklyn rushed to pull them apart.

"Get out of my house!" Zora screamed.

Amina remained unfazed, yelling right back as the other girls tried to shove her out the front door. "Yeah, I know... the truth hurts!"

Zora slammed the door behind them, breathing heavily. For a moment, the silence in the house was loud, the weight of the argument lingering in the air.

Outside, Brooklyn glanced back at the closed door, her concern etched across her face.

"Mina, you may have gone too far. She's hurting."

"No, I didn't go far enough. All y'all hoes are clueless!" Amina was still fuming as she walked toward her car, pointing at Brooklyn and Devin.

"Uhn-uhn! Don't address me. I've realized the *errors of my ways* and owned up to them," Brooklyn replied, climbing into her car and sticking her tongue out at Amina as she started the engine.

"And you, Devin. Mr. Young Hottie wants something serious, but you're too busy stealing clothes from your job, treating life like you've got several more to live... Then you got the nerve to act like a fool when you saw him with another girl.

Make up your mind!" Amina concluded, slamming her car door shut.

Brooklyn glanced at Devin, then burst out laughing. Surprisingly, Devin did too, realizing that Amina was speaking some truth.

A few moments later, Brooklyn gathered her composure and slowly pulled out of the driveway. She shouted out the window to Amina, "Bye, crazy girl. It's late. Let me get Devin home, and you get home safe. Text us!

Amina waved back, smiling and shaking her head. She followed them briefly out of the driveway before turning in the opposite direction toward her own home.

Zora contacted her mom after slamming the front door behind her friends and running a hot bath. Ms. Shanel and Zora talked about the incident for an hour. Zora fully grasped the depth of her hurt, concern, and heartbreak, which sent her stress levels skyrocketing. The weight of it all became so overwhelming that her mom felt compelled to make an emergency visit, a gesture Zora kept hidden from everyone else.

Urban Coffee

The following day, at 8 a.m., Zora was awakened by the hum of a high-tech commercial stand-on mower, the buzzing of a low-emission lawn edger, and the faint sound of two guys laughing in her front yard.

She rushed to her bedroom window and saw an older man, along with what seemed to be the young guy who used to cut the neighborhood's yards. Zora leaned against the window, and an unexpected sadness flashed over her. Malik's voice echoed in her head from Thursday's visit:

"It's all good. I'll get my OG by early Saturday morning to hook you up."

Last night, Zora dreamt of the beautiful moments she and Malik once shared, when they were happier than ever. But this morning, the reality hit. The events on the Boulevard last night weren't a dream—they were real, a painful nightmare in real life. And Zora was far from happy.

She pulled herself away from the window, pushing aside her unrealistic thoughts of happiness with Malik. For the first time, she questioned her stance on their relationship. The agonizing thought of losing him for good became overwhelming.

"What have I done? I've been so stubborn, so impatient... for what?!" Zora thought to herself as she sank onto her bed.

Her stomach churned, and the stress still weighed heavily on her. Tears began to rise again, but before they could fall, the ringing of her cell phone pulled her from the emotional whirlwind.

"Hello?"

"Hey, girl. How are you?" Brooklyn's voice came through, filled with unease over the aftermath.

"I'm okay. I'm just cramping badly right now."

"Did you talk to your mom last night?"

"I did... and mom is not happy with my decision. She suggested that I fix it—and fast."

Brooklyn chuckled, knowing how much Ms. Shanel adores Malik.

Zora sighed, still feeling the weight of her mom's words, and as she did, she got dressed and made her way downstairs, still on the phone with Brooklyn.

Before heading to the kitchen to fix herself something to eat, Zora opened the front door to speak to the gentlemen caring for her yard.

"Good morning, Ms. Zora, the young guy greeted when he saw her.

Zora, appreciating his presence, smiled. "Hi, Thomas. We haven't seen you in a while."

"Yes, ma'am. I injured my arm playing football, so my doctor had me resting for the past six to eight weeks."

"Oh, okay. I'm glad to see you're doing well."

"Yes, ma'am, thank you... This is Jimmy John, my uncle," young Thomas said, pointing to the older gentleman with him.

"Good morning, ma'am," Mr. Jimmy greeted with a deep voice, respectfully removing his hat.

"So, I guess you're the OG Malik was talking about?" Zora asked, a smile spreading across her face.

Jimmy John chuckled and nodded. "Yes, ma'am, that would be me. Your husband called to have us hook you up, and those were his exact words," he added with a light laugh.

Zora's eyes widened, and she let out an awkward, hopeful sigh, lightly chuckling at the kind gentleman's statement. That *"husband"* word had her spellbound for a split second.

"Well, I appreciate you accepting the job," she said.

"Yes, ma'am, but this isn't my first rodeo with Mr. Malik. I've done a few houses for him and his colleague. After I'm done here, I'll head over to touch up the one next door," Jimmy John explained.

"Oh, okay. So, what's with all the plants on the sidewalk?" Zora asked, admiring the beautiful pots of flowers.

"Mr. Malik wanted us to plant some of your favorites on each side of your front steps," young Thomas explained.

The older gentleman smiled. "Yes, ma'am, he certainly did. He mentioned you liked colorful hydrangeas, so we've got purple, pink, and white ones. We're also adding a few yellow chrysanthemums and fresh ferns to finish it off. It's going to look beautiful!"

Zora scoffed softly, smiling. "Thank you both so much. I'm looking forward to seeing it. Let me know if I can do anything for you."

"Oh, don't worry, ma'am. Mr. Malik asked me to call him when we were almost done so he could settle up with us. It was nice meeting you, though," Jimmy John said.

“Likewise,” Zora retorted, waving as she closed the door. She then turned her attention back to her phone call. “Are you still there, Brook?”

“Yes, I am, and I heard the whole exchange. Are you okay? I know that hit home a little bit.”

Zora stood leaning on the front door with her forehead resting against it. “To be honest, I don’t know how to feel, Brook, except for these cramps and my anxiety after that conversation with them.”

“Well, if you’re not sitting down, go sit and gather yourself. And put something on your stomach.”

Zora took a few deep breaths, calming herself a little.

“Can you stay on the phone while I fix a quick breakfast? My mom will be here soon with Tylenol for the pain.”

“Of course, I’ll stay. We should talk about how you and Amina will squash things, too.”

Zora rolled her eyes. She wasn’t ready to talk about that—at least not this morning.

Urban Coffee

“C’mon, baby. Let daddy wash your face so we can put some clothes on you,” Malik called to his daughter, who was lying on the floor in her pink pajama pants and shirt, watching one of her favorite cartoons on her iPad.

“Okay, Daddy. Where *we* going?” she asked, climbing onto the bed and jumping into his arms.

“Whoa! babygirl, that was a quick jump. You gotta warn Daddy first,” Malik chuckled.

Mazo laughed but apologized sweetly. “Sorry, Daddy.”

“It’s okay, baby. Let’s get you situated.”

He lifted and carried her to the bathroom, setting her down on the sink as his dad called out from downstairs.

"Malik, can I speak to you when you're done with the little princess?"

"Okay, Pop. Give me a minute."

Malik tried putting toothpaste on her little toothbrush, but Mazo grabbed it and helped Malik squeeze it.

"I can brush my teeth, Daddy. I can do it by myself."

"Okay, baby, but daddy wants to assist you a little so we don't make a mess."

"Let me hold it, Daddy," she insisted.

He gave in, and she began brushing her teeth in the mirror. Malik watched with a smile, verbally guiding her in a kind tone so she'd feel proud for doing it on her own.

After they were done, he picked out a cute outfit for her, and they headed downstairs for breakfast.

Malik's mom greeted them as he sat Mazo at the kitchen island. "Good morning, grandma's baby and mama's brokenhearted grown man."

"C'mon, Ma. Did you have to put 'brokenhearted' on it?" Malik chuckled, kissing her on the cheek.

"Well, your heart was broken last night, right?"

"Yes, indeed."

Mom giggled and lightly grabbed his face. "Aw. You'll be okay, son."

"Where's Dad?" Malik asked, grabbing a piece of buttered toast from the stove and returning to sit beside Mazo.

"He was just in here," Mom replied, busy making some scrambled cheese eggs for Malik. Although he initially had no intention of eating, she persuaded him to add a bit of protein to the toast.

"Malik, come ride with me!"

"Oh, there he is. Okay, Dad. I'll be right behind you."

Mr. Nelson was heading to the store for the afternoon gathering, so Mom placed Malik's eggs in a paper bowl. He grabbed some orange juice from the fridge, kissed Mazo on the cheek, and headed to the car.

Mazo's little voice yelled, "Daddy, can I go *wit'* you?"

"Can you stay with me a little while longer, baby? Daddy will be right back." Grandma Bria quickly intervened.

"Okay, Grandma."

****

On the way to the grocery store, Malik and his dad shared a casual conversation and a few laughs.

"Dad, it's 9 a.m. Why are we going to the store?"

"So, you forgot about the brunch your mom is having?"

Malik's head slumped in distress. "I do not want to be around other people today."

"I know, son, but it will mean a lot to your mom if you stay for at least an hour. I understand you're a busy man, and for good reasons, but please consider it," his dad pleaded, glancing back and forth between the road and his son.

Malik grabbed the grocery list from the cupholder and scanned the items his mom had put together:

Pasture-raised eggs - 2 dozen

Organic blueberries

Organic oranges - 2 bags

Turkey meatballs

Chicken drumettes

Sweet potato fries – family-size bags

He mentally prepared himself to help his dad quickly and get home. Choosing to shop for the meats, knowing they'd take the most time, Malik's goal was to get in and out fast.

They collected everything within fifteen minutes and met back at the front registers.

"That'll be $98.44," the slim male cashier with the curly afro said.

"I got it, Dad." Malik pulled out his debit card, handed it to the young man, and then helped the other employee bag. Dad grabbed a couple of bags, and Malik took the other two. They were back in the car in no time.

Silence filled the air for the first two minutes of the ride home. Mr. Nelson observed his son, who was sulking in grief. Malik's elbow was propped on the car door, staring out the window.

"Are you done moping?"

Malik, with furrowed brows, snapped to attention. "Sir?"

"Are you done torturing yourself, replaying what you might perceive as missteps?"

What do you expect, Dad? It's clear I've done something wrong, and it bothers me. I'm losing the person I thought was meant to be part of my future," Malik articulated, reclining in his seat as his mind replayed flashes of last night's events...

The things she said were hurtful, and no matter what I said, she wouldn't let me fix it...

I've been working so hard, but I must have made a huge mistake somewhere." Malik sighed, a deep breath of hopelessness escaping. "I'm mentally exhausted, Pop."

Mr. Nelson lightly scoffed with a hint of a smile, listening intently to his son. He was proud of Malik—proud of his courage and his vulnerability.

They finally reached the house and pulled into the driveway. Dad lightly touched Malik on the arm before he got out to grab the grocery bags.

"Listen to me carefully, son. If you know you've done everything possible to protect, provide for, and love your family, never doubt it."

"Admittedly, we tend to put the horse before the cart, making things harder when life hits us. It causes us to harbor misplaced emotions."

"What do you mean by 'misplaced emotions?"

"Well, son, you're hurting because she's hurting. But I can guarantee that if she were your wife first, your journey would've

been met with much more patience and support...

And that's not to say you should've gotten married before now—because clearly, you guys weren't ready. So, I can assure you that something much deeper is going on here."

Mr. Nelson opened the door and glanced back at Malik before getting out. "You are a grown man... a smart man, so I won't tell you what to do in your situation. But sometimes, an individual has to sit with their words for a while to gain perspective."

Malik nodded, agreeing but pondering the phrase *"sit with their words."* Still, the conversation with his dad had lightened his mood. He decided to make the rest of the day festive by spending time with his family. He helped his dad gather the bags and headed into the house.

When Mazo heard the front door open, she dashed over to hug her granddad, only managing to wrap her arms around his legs as she noticed he was carrying grocery bags. But with all her strength, she leaped up to embrace Malik after he walked in.

"Daddy...you're back!"

Malik placed the two bags on the floor and kissed her little cheeks. She hugged him tightly, smiling from ear to ear.

****

It was nearing 10 a.m., and Mom had prepped much of the brunch food. The cleaners were busy tidying up the place, and Rosa, the pastry chef and longtime friend of the Nelsons, was baking apple crisps and mini lemon cupcakes.

Ms. Bria handed her a container of organic blueberries for the mini muffins, which would top off the desserts. Meanwhile, Mr. Nelson washed his hands and added eggs to the boiling water on the stove, which his wife had prepared for the deviled eggs. Shortly after, she kindly guided him out of the kitchen.

"Thank you, honey, for the grocery run and the eggs, but Rosa and I got the rest. You're always cooking, so have today off."

"Okay, baby, I'll leave you to it." They shared a quick kiss, and Mr. Nelson headed to his office. Soon after, Malik peeked in to thank his dad for their earlier conversation.

"You're going to be okay, son. Focus on your trip to Paris. You've got bigger fish to fry," his dad said with a smile.

"I am. Everything's set for Paris. All I need to do now is finish packing, and I'll do that tomorrow after I drop Mazo off with Zora. This is why I need another assistant, Dad."

"Yeah. Finding someone you trust, like your big sister, would be nice. But I have no doubt you will."

Malik scoffed and smiled at his optimistic father. He closed the office door behind him and headed upstairs, dialing Brayden's number as he walked.

"Daddy, where you going?"

"Upstairs to call Uncle BC. You coming?" Without hesitation, Mazo took off running behind him.

"What's up, bro?" Malik greeted Brayden, settling with Mazo on the giant bean bag in his old bedroom.

"Everything's everything. You ready for your ride?"

"I guess, man. I'm still with my parents. I'll be here for a while today. You are staying for brunch, too, right?"

"Free food? Of course."

Malik chuckled at his quick response before continuing.

"The real reason I called, though, was to discuss the possibility of allocating funds from the company budget to hire another assistant—specifically, an around-the-clock PA if needed."

That suggestion was music to Brayden's ears, as he'd been thinking the same thing recently. "I don't know how you knew, bro, but I could use the extra help when I'm in the field."

Malik nodded his head. They were on board with the idea of bringing on another assistant for their soon-to-launch realty company, agreeing to discuss the matter in more detail later.

"Let me go ahead and call Brooklyn so she can meet me at your parents' house with my truck. I'll see y'all soon."

"Alright, man... later." Malik ended the call.

Urban Coffee

Since early this morning, Zora and Brooklyn have been on the phone for over two hours, even bringing Amina on a three-way call. They had a heart-to-heart, and all was well.

"Y'all, let me talk to you later. Brayden is calling me on the other line. I know it's about his truck."

"Okay, girl. Tell him we said hi."

"Alright, Zo. I will... bye, guys." Brooklyn switched over to answer Brayden's call, exchanging warm greetings.

Brayden spoke to her about the brunch and asked her to drop his truck off at the Nelsons.

"Okay. I'll be there around 1:30. I'll see my baby boy for a minute, too. I'll get Amina to follow me to bring me back home."

Brayden raised an eyebrow. "Why do that? I'm perfectly capable of dropping you off at home."

"No, I didn't mean it like that. I'm going to the store later this evening, so I'll need my car," Brooklyn explained.

"You did me a favor, so let me return it. I'll take you to the store and drop you off at home. Is that okay?"

Without hesitation, Brooklyn agreed, smiling.

"That settles it, then. I'll see you at the brunch, babygirl."

After ending the call, Brooklyn contacted Zora again to update her on the plan for returning Brayden's car.

She also hoped to persuade Zora to attend the brunch, thinking it might be a good opportunity for her and Malik to talk.

CHAPTER 8
The Brunch

It was 1:00 p.m., and the Nelson family brunch had officially begun. The setup was beautifully decorated, with a theme of whites and creams, accented by pops of yellow and marigold, creating a welcoming, vibrant atmosphere.

The sun cleansed the air in radiant warmth, a crisp 72-degree day complemented by gentle winds and low humidity. The menu offered a selection of the finest organic fruits, veggies, meats, and cheeses, all set against the stunning backdrop of the ocean-blue pool in the backyard.

Brayden's mom, Ms. Joy, and little Nate arrived a bit earlier than everyone else, eager to help with the last-minute details—details that can often turn into a headache. Miss Kizzy, Heather's mom, was also in attendance, as was Brayden's dad, Mr. Coleman, and a few other family members and friends. The house offered ample parking along the side, allowing guests to enter the brunch through the side gate, which set the tone for a relaxed yet festive gathering.

"Oh, my goodness, Bria, this is beautiful back here!" Miss Kizzy exclaimed, her eyes scanning the backyard with awe. Simultaneously, Bria and Joy turned around, surprised and delighted, as they greeted Miss Kizzy at the gate.

"Hey, girl!" they exclaimed, enveloping her in a group hug. Their laughter filled the air. Ms. Joy, eager to catch up, pulled back slightly and smiled at Miss Kizzy.

"You and your daughter left us for about five or six years. What's been going on with you two?"

Miss Kizzy hesitated, her eyes momentarily clouded with a mix of emotions. She was reluctant to share, unsure of how the words would land.

"You're right, Joy, and it's been a lot to handle... but to sum it up, Heather started getting disrespectful, the cops were called, and we were kicked out of the neighborhood I'd lived in my whole life."

The words hung in the air, and everyone was astonished. The awkwardness Miss Kizzy had hoped to avoid now filled the space between them. Still, she knew the truth could reach the surface, no matter how hard she tried to bury it.

Malik was going through the patio doorway to greet everyone, but he halted upon hearing Miss Kizzy's words. Brayden, entering through the side gate, overheard it too, and his footsteps came to a halt. He opted to turn around, heading back toward the front instead, and texted Malik to join him in the front yard.

As Malik stepped out of the front door, Brayden's eyes widened in surprise. Malik chuckled at his expression, but he understood exactly why.

"Man, the homie didn't say any of this last night at the restaurant. She talked about everyone and everything but herself."

Malik nodded, his expression serious. "She sure didn't... but we're getting to the bottom of it today."

Just then, Brooklyn pulled up in Brayden's truck, parking near the end of the driveway. Her curly tresses were pulled back in a ponytail, and she was dressed in a long, burnt-orange maxi dress with a subtle side split.

She completed her look by wearing cream-colored Bosco sneaker loafers and minimal jewelry—just a Rolex watch on her left arm. Brooklyn radiated beauty and effortless style, and Brayden couldn't help but admire her glow and warm smile as she approached.

She greeted Malik with a hug first and then moved on to Brayden.

"So, you give this clown a hug first?" he teased, pulling her into a tight embrace.

She looked up at him with a shy smile as they pulled away. "I saved the best for last."

Malik, watching them, placed a hand over his mouth and chuckled. "Ahh, okay now!"

They all chuckled until the moment was interrupted by a call from Keisha. Brayden reluctantly answered it.

"Where you at?" Keisha asked.

Brayden furrowed his brows, prompting her to backtrack a bit. "Should there be another way to address someone when they answer your call?"

Keisha giggled before responding. "I'm sorry... hey, bae, how are you?"

At that point, Brooklyn decided to excuse herself and head into the house. She had no interest in that conversation.

"I'll talk to y'all later. I'm going in to speak to everybody and kiss my baby boy." She headed inside.

Malik followed suit. "I'm going, too, man... give you space to chat."

"Okay, I'll be right behind y'all," Brayden responded, then returned his attention to his phone call.

"Was that Malik?"

"Yeah, what's up, Keisha?"

"Who was the female voice I heard before that?"

"That was Brooklyn. She's here to return my truck. I'm at Malik's parents' house for a brunch gathering."

Instantly, Keisha became heated, feeling powerless and afraid. She'd never been this insecure before meeting Brooklyn.

However, Brooklyn's personality left Keisha feeling more insecure than Brayden's actual act of sleeping with her. Strangely, she subconsciously aspired to be more like Brooklyn, which only frustrated her more.

"Bae, I would've helped get your ride back after work."

"I know; I appreciate it. Can I call you back later, though? I haven't been here long, so I need to speak to everybody."

Keisha entertained an apparent thought, wondering why Brayden hadn't invited her to the brunch.

"So, I don't get an invite to the party?"

He let out a subtle sigh. "It's not my party... Malik's mom had a specific list of people. But I'll see what I can do and call you back."

Keisha wasn't satisfied with that answer. Unbeknownst to Brayden, she had plans to show up regardless. "Okay, bae, I'll see you soon," she replied.

Brayden ended the call, entered the house, and headed to the backyard patio to greet and hug everybody.

****

After two hours, everyone was still enjoying the brunch festivities. They swapped jokes and laughter, sharing amusing and not-so-amusing memories. The children played cheerfully in the yard under the watchful eyes of the adults. The trays of fruit, meats, and cheeses were nearly empty, and the dessert bar was currently being relished.

Malik's phone rang, and he excused himself from the lively chatter to find a quieter spot. "Jimmy J, what's up?"

Thomas and Jimmy John had finished working on both yards, and the job was nearly complete. They called, as Malik had requested, to update him on their progress and to let him know that they were ready to settle up.

"Hey, Mr. Malik! Thomas is blowing the excess to tidy up the place, so we should be done in about 10 minutes."

"Okay, cool... I'll be there shortly."

After ending the call, Malik returned to the brunch, briefly informing his dad that he had business to attend to but would be right back.

"Mazo? C'mon, baby, ride with daddy."

Without wavering, Mazo dashed to her dad, her small hand eagerly finding his as he led her to his truck.

At the same time, Brooklyn could be heard chuckling, trying to convince little Nate, who had dashed off right after, to follow Mazo.

"Nate, where are you going? Mommy's playing with the jumbo blocks with you! How are you *gonna* leave me like that?"

Malik paused, giving Brooklyn a knowing look. "It's okay for him to come with me."

Brooklyn giggled, still trying to keep Nate close.

"No, go ahead, man. Handle your business. I got him." Brayden intervened, scooping Nate into the air. His little voice gave an adorable scream while he laughed.

Just as Brayden was settling Nate, his phone rang. It was Keisha again, her voice filled with frustration. She had not heard back from him in two hours.

Brayden sighed, feeling a little guilty before he even answered.

"Keisha, I am so sorry... I honestly forgot after speaking and catching up with everybody."

At first, she was silent, carefully choosing her words.

She knew the wrong phrasing could derail her plan to show up, but she also needed Brayden to feel guilty for his actions.

"Brayden?" Her voice hesitated slightly. "You know all of this started Thursday when you cheated on me."

She went straight for the emotional guilt trip, knowing it would tug at his heartstrings.

Her desperation was evident as she leaned into it, hoping it would make him want to spend more time with her.

"I mean, you haven't been affectionate with me since then. Now, it feels like you don't even want me around anymore. I can think of several times you've excluded me. I haven't even officially met your parents."

Brayden's stomach tightened as he listened, his guilt rising. He could feel the weight of her words, but as she spoke, he felt something else—constrained. They weren't even an official couple, yet she was trying to push them into that role.

At that moment, Brayden realized that making things official had never crossed his mind. During their *on-and-off* six-month interactions, it was never a priority. He felt torn between his remorse and the pressure Keisha placed on him.

"Keisha, you're right, and we should talk about this."

She furrowed her brows, her confusion plain. After making him feel guilty, Keisha had expected that Brayden would quickly invite her over to resolve things.

"I can come where you are, Brayden, so we can talk."

"No, we should talk alone, with no interruptions...

I can see you later tonight or tomorrow if that's okay."

Keisha's heart sank as anger, rejection, and fear engulfed her. She felt like Brayden was slipping away, and the thought of losing him was almost too much to bear. Her emotions swirled like a storm, and she could no longer hold them in.

"Okay, Brayden. Whatever!" she said forcefully.

He took the phone away from his ear, releasing a subtle sigh before continuing the call.

"Keisha? Hello, Keisha?" She had ended the call.

As he lowered the phone, the weight of the conversation hung over him like a cloud. He'd made a hasty decision six months ago, which now felt like one of his biggest mistakes.

The reality of it all hit him harder than he expected—Keisha's desperation and his uncertainty.

Nevertheless, it was clear now, more than ever, that he'd let things spiral without truly understanding how it would end.

Urban Coffee

Malik arrived at English Drive to settle the payment with Jimmy John and young Thomas for their landscaping services. He parked between Zora's residence and his other property, got out of the car, and went to his daughter's side to help her out.

Realizing they were in front of Mommy's house, Mazo looked up at him with a worried expression.

"Daddy, I'm going home?" she asked in her soft voice.

"No, baby, not yet... It'll be tomorrow," he reassured her.

"Okay, Daddy." Mazo grabbed his hand and strolled around the properties with her dad, carefree and joyful.

Inside the house, Zora heard the chatter from her bedroom window. Her heart raced as she spotted Malik's car and saw him outside with Mazo. She rushed to the bathroom to ensure her hair was neat, then hurried to her dresser.

In her rush, she removed the blouse she had stained earlier while eating a jelly biscuit, swapped it for a cute pink tank top, and dashed back to the window. But when she looked outside, there was no sign of Malik. Realizing he might be inspecting the guys' work next door, she hurried downstairs to get a clearer view of them through the kitchen window.

Breathing anxiously, she discreetly peeked through the curtains, her eyes locking on Malik. Her breathing paused as she took in the sight of him. He looked incredibly handsome, especially when he was in business mode. He looked effortlessly good-looking, dressed casually in wide-flare, mid-tinted blue jeans, a crisp white T-shirt, and light blue and white Air Jordan Low sneakers. His wrist was adorned with a stainless-steel Cartier watch.

After Malik inspected the guys' work on the neighboring property, they returned to the front and gathered on the sidewalk near his car.

The air was filled with light chatter and laughter as Malik signed the check made out to both Jimmy John and Thomas. He added a generous cash tip of $200 for accepting the gig on such short notice.

As the guys shook hands, Malik expressed his satisfaction with the yard services again. He is known to be a perfectionist, especially when it comes to maintaining curb appeal and ensuring the quality of their properties, so he made sure they knew he was pleased with the outcome.

Inside, Zora noticed the men shaking hands and immediately began scanning the room, ensuring the house was tidy and smelling fresh. Her heart ached with anticipation. She desperately hoped Malik would walk through the door, ready to patch up their relationship.

She felt she was finally ready to open up to him and articulate the deep-seated reasons behind her growing resentment.

Despite her frustration, the thought of losing him was the farthest thing from her mind. She was ready to swallow her pride and take back all the hurtful things she had said to him the night before.

With a sense of urgency, she paced back and forth in the kitchen, her anticipation growing each second. She was waiting for the sound of the doorbell or the key turning in the lock.

Minutes passed, but no knock came. Confusion crept in. *Why hadn't he come inside?* Tiptoeing to the window, she carefully cracked the curtains just enough to peek outside. She froze as she saw the back of Malik's car pulling away. Tears formed in her eyes, and her breathing quickened, anxiety rising within her.

Amina's words echoed relentlessly in her mind: *"What you should've been doing was apologizing when you had the chance. You are dealing with a real man, and he may be getting tired of you acting unsupportive. Grow up!"*

Overcome by emotion, Zora collapsed onto the sofa, her hands covering her face as tears flooded her. She was overwhelmed, unsure of what to do next.

At the same time, Malik found himself at the end of the street, his car idling as he debated putting it in reverse. The weight of Zora's rejection and words, however, echoed in his mind: *"Take care of your daughter and forget about me."*

The pause lasted longer than usual, even in Mazo's young mind. Tucked securely in her car seat, Mazo looked out the side window before turning her attention to her dad through the rearview mirror.

"Daddy, are you okay? I don't see cars. You can go now."

Her soft, calm voice broke through the heaviness in the air. Malik glanced at her through the mirror, a faint smile on his face.

"Okay, thank you, baby... Daddy is going."

Urban Coffee

Malik arrived back at his parents' house just as Heather pulled up. After parking his truck, he carefully helped Mazo out of her car seat, and she immediately dashed toward the backyard, where the brunch festivities were still in full swing.

Heather exited her car with a big smile, walking toward Malik. They exchanged a familiar dap—the handshake they'd developed growing up in the same neighborhood.

Brayden saw that Mazo had returned, so he assumed Malik must be back as well. Mazo didn't waste a moment letting Uncle Brayden know her dad was in the front yard. When he made his way to the front, he greeted Heather with the same mutual dap, followed by a hug, and informed her that her mom was at the brunch.

"You've got some explaining to do, ma'am," Brayden said, his tone slightly teasing.

"What are you talking about? What do I need to explain?" Heather asked, a wave of unease rising in her...

"I just got here; let me speak to everyone first. I'm sure my mom is back there running her mouth as usual."

With that, Brayden and Malik exchanged a look, brows furrowed, before following Heather to the backyard.

"Hey, everybody!" Heather called out as she entered. The group greeted her with warm smiles and hugs, but Miss Kizzy remained seated in the corner. She barely shifted in her chair, her expression icy. Even Brooklyn couldn't miss the tension.

Heather settled in, trying her best not to let her mom's cold demeanor affect her, at least, not on the surface.

But just as quickly, the uneasy calm shattered.

"So, did you tell your guy best friends how you were *laying up* in my house with that nasty girl you called your girlfriend and got us kicked out?"

Sensing the brewing tension, Rosa quickly ushered the kids—Mazo, Nate, and Diego —into the house.

A heavy silence descended, the air dense with tension. Everyone froze, eyes wide—everyone except Malik's and Brayden's. Neither one appreciated how Miss Kizzy phrased that question.

They saw Heather's expression and felt the urge to protect her. However, Heather's restraint finally snapped in response to her mother's embarrassment. She revealed long-held secrets, exposing the painful truth of her past for everyone to hear. No longer concerned with protecting her mother, Heather spoke from a place of raw frustration.

"Um... did you inform them that your first boyfriend used to discipline me by slapping me while I was in middle school, and you did nothing about it?!

And that he also taught me how to kiss when I was eleven years old?... or what about the time I started high school, and you caught the second one in my bedroom pulling up my pajama shirt at midnight, and you blamed me?!"

As Heather's last words echoed through the backyard, Mr. Nelson and Brayden's dad, Mr. Coleman, exchanged uncomfortable glances before excusing themselves. Shaking their heads in disbelief, they made their way inside the house. Mr. Nelson, in particular, quickly realized he didn't need to witness any of the painful truths unraveling before him.

"Heather, stop right now!" Brayden's voice rose, his patience running thin. Heather glanced at him, taking a deep breath to calm herself—she'd always respected their protective brother-sister relationship for years.

Malik, sensing the escalating tension, stepped in, grabbing her gently by the arm to guide her away from the scene.

At the same time, the moms took charge of Miss Kizzy and tried to escort her in the opposite direction toward her car. But Miss Kizzy wasn't done yet.

"Where were you when I was getting my behind beat?!

I tried to protect you, but you're the one who left for all those years!" Miss Kizzy's voice rang across the yard, raw and hurtful.

Heather, unable to hold her tongue, snapped back, her emotions surfacing. "I wonder why, ma! You never protected me after my daddy died!"

Before the words could linger, Malik moved swiftly, grabbing Heather's arms and turning her to face him. His voice dropped to a low, controlled tone. "That's enough."

When Heather met his gaze, she saw the seriousness in his eyes, a quiet but powerful demand for her to stop. She took a deep breath, feeling the heaviness of his words.

Glancing over at Brayden, she saw his expression mirrored Malik's—silent but firm. Slowly, her chaos settled into an uneasy silence. She lowered her head, resting it in Malik's chest, and cried.

****

Some time had passed, and the remaining extended family and friends had finally left. Ms. Bria, Ms. Joy, Melanie, Brooklyn, and Rosa took charge of cleaning up and packing away the remnants of the brunch.

Despite the lingering disbelief from earlier events, the day had been filled with joy and laughter.

After the cleanup, Brooklyn joined Brayden, Malik, and Heather in the jacuzzi area at the far end of the house. The jacuzzi was under a galvanized steel double-roof gazebo painted rich chocolate brown, adorned with a seven-piece chocolate brown outdoor sofa set, burnt orange pillows, and a cozy fire pit.

The sky had darkened to a dusky gray, and the trees rustled with the evolving breeze. A faint scent of rain hung in the air, signaling the possibility of a light shower. It had gotten a little bit cooler.

Brayden received a text from his mom, letting him know she, his dad, and Nate were about to leave. He stood up, took Brooklyn's hand, and led her inside.

"My mom just texted—Nate's about to leave," he said, pulling her gently along.

She quickly got up, and as soon as they entered the house, her eyes met little Nate's. Without missing a beat, he ran to her and jumped into her arms, enveloping her in a tight hug.

Afterward, she handed him to Brayden, who smiled and hugged his son tightly in a big bear hug.

Ms. Joy and Bria exchanged warm hugs while their husbands shook hands.

"Honey, we'll talk tomorrow when we're both a little clearer," Joy said softly to Bria. "What happened earlier was too much to process in one sitting."

"I know... my heart goes out to both of them...

We can call Kizzy tomorrow and visit her soon in person to see how we can help," Bria concluded, her voice filled with concern.

Brayden took his mom by the hand and led her toward the car while his dad and Brooklyn followed, with little Nate trailing behind them. Brayden kissed his mom on the cheek before opening the passenger door for her.

"Bye, Dad... see you tomorrow," Nate called out to Brayden as Brooklyn fastened his car seat.

"See you tomorrow, baby boy... I love you!" Brayden replied with a warm smile.

"Okay, love you, too, Dad."

The Colemans backed out of the driveway, heading home, as the Nelsons stood at the front door, waving goodbye.

After closing the door, Mr. Nelson turned to his wife as he approached the side door leading to the jacuzzi area.

"Baby, I'm going to speak to Heather for a quick second."

"Okay, sweetie... I'll put Mazo in the tub and pack her clothes. I know Malik's taking her home with him tonight."

Mr. Nelson proceeded out the side door, still processing the disturbing information he had heard earlier.

Heather's eyes filled with sorrow when Mr. Nelson opened the side door. She recognized him and quickly apologized.

"I'm sorry, Judge Nelson... It wasn't my intention to act like that in your home."

Mr. Nelson approached her, offering a comforting hug.

"First of all, you don't have to address me like I'm a stranger. I've known you and your family since you were around eight, probably before that."

Heather chuckled softly. "Yes, sir."

He smiled gently and continued. "Secondly, I need you and your mom to seek help for what's going on. Honor your relationship with your mother because we only get one."

Heather nodded, the weight of his words sinking in.

"Thirdly, I'm sorry you didn't find comfort in telling us the horrors you went through growing up, not even your best friends here," he gestured to Malik and Brayden. "You three were like peas in a pod, always getting into trouble in the neighborhood..."

He paused, his face softening with a smile. "I can see you now, with your baggy clothes and that attitude, fighting anyone who dared to cross those two."

This prompted a round of laughter, and even Brooklyn smiled, realizing how much Heather was a part of their family.

"Get help soon. Within 30 days, or I'll make it a mandate by the courts," Mr. Nelson added, his smile disappearing into a serious expression. "My wife and Joy will speak with your mom about the same thing, okay?"

Heather nodded, nearly in tears, as the warmth of their love and concern enveloped her. Mr. Nelson embraced her again, then hugged Malik, shook Brayden's hand, followed by a hug, and finally embraced Brooklyn before heading inside for the night.

Brooklyn, still processing the moment, spoke up softly.

"It's hard to believe you were a tomboy... although this is only my second time meeting you."

Her comment surprised Heather, but it also made her smile. "Well, I still have days where I just want to dress like a boy, but I try not to...

I was dressing like that mainly to hide myself... I think," Heather explained, revealing more hurtful things about her past.

Feeling it was time to open up, Heather finally shared why she left for those years. It was a vulnerable moment for her, but she found the courage to let her best friends in on the part of her past she had kept hidden. Surprisingly, she felt comfortable enough to let Brooklyn hear it, too—something she never thought she'd do.

From middle school to high school, Heather detailed how she was mistreated and physically abused by her mother's boyfriends, a total of six incidents. Shockingly, though, she'd never been penetrated by these guys until one night.

On the night of her graduation, the third boyfriend tried to do just that. He was a large, burly man with long, nappy dreadlocks and an overpowering smell of beer and weed.

Heather's mom, an LPN, had an overnight shift scheduled, but by some miracle, she was sent home early due to her overtime hours. Miss Kizzy walked in and saw him pinning Heather face-down in the bed, trying to penetrate her from behind.

Heather couldn't move and could barely breathe due to his overbearing strength.

At the sight of it, Miss Kizzy flew into a rage, using her car keys like a weapon. She struck him repeatedly in the lower back, the keys digging into his flesh with such force that they damaged several spinal nerves.

"My backside bled heavily from him trying to force himself," Heather continued, looking down at the floor. "And from that day until I moved to Florida, I didn't want a man to even bat his eye at me."

Tears began to stream slowly down her face, each one carrying the burden of years of pain and unspoken words.

Malik and Brayden didn't look away; they stood there, quietly offering her the space to express everything that had been building inside her. Brooklyn sighed quietly, her heart heavy with empathy for Heather's suffering.

After a few moments of silence, Brooklyn finally asked the question, her voice soft. "What happened to him?"

Heather sighed, wiping tears from her face. "To this day, he walks slightly bent over with a limp at 49 years old..."

He never called the cops or told anyone about what happened. My mama hurt him good, but it was too late for her to protect me."

She paused before continuing with her story. "Do y'all remember calling me the day after graduation, trying to hang out?" Malik and Brayden nodded...

"Well, I met Megan, a radiologist, in the hospital after my injuries. She had just graduated from community college and connected with me—she understood what I was going through. She became the person I spent the most time with. When she received a better job offer in Florida, she asked if I wanted to go with her. Given everything I'd been through, I said yes—I needed to get away."

Heather paused again, her voice growing heavy as she found the words. "She paid for our flight, and before we left, I went home to pack... and that's when my mama caught me making out with her at the house. You can imagine what happened after that with the cops and all...

"Long story short, I went to Florida with Megan. We stayed together for almost a year...

However, I eventually realized I was still miserable. I felt like I was missing out on something real, something meaningful," Heather admitted. She didn't regret her decision to move, but the *weight* of it, the reason behind it, lingered.

After her breakup with Meagan, Heather secured a job at a cell phone company in Florida and saved enough money to move out independently. She settled in another part of the state and established herself over the next five years.

Within that time, she had a brief on-and-off relationship with a kind young gentleman that lasted two years. After that, she remained single until she decided to move back home. Her job in Florida allowed her to transfer, making the move easier.

Malik and Brayden listened attentively, though both wished the story had ended after hearing about the high school graduation night. But, for Heather, sharing her story was a necessary part of the healing process.

Aware of the weight of her words, the guys stepped aside momentarily and devised a plan to help their friend rebuild her personal and professional life. And consequently, Malik and Brayden approached Heather with a proposition:

Would she consider becoming their assistant on a probationary basis?

Heather stared at both of them, a smile spreading across her face, radiating pure joy. Without hesitation, she eagerly agreed. She would balance both jobs—working part-time at the cell phone company and dedicating her remaining time to Malik and Brayden's needs.

"I won't let you down, I promise! And I need to tell you something else," Heather continued. "Leaving you guys like I did after graduation hurt me more than I could imagine. You were my best friends, and I've always felt safe around you, but I was too embarrassed to tell you what was happening all those years."

Heather paused, her voice softening as she remembered an essential part of her journey. "You know who helped me a lot through all of this? Malena. We spoke often."

"Word?" Brayden responded, his appreciation obvious. "You guys stayed in touch all this time?"

"Yeah," Heather replied. "Until I moved and lost her number when I changed phones. And Malik, she asked about you every time we spoke. Malena still loves you."

Heather's voice trembled as she spoke, and tears welled up in her eyes. "I was so grateful for her."

Malik smiled, recalling just how kind-hearted, selfless, and supportive Malena had always been to him, his family, and his friends.

Heather paused again, gathering her words and wanting to clarify one last thing. "Malik, I'm sorry for how I acted when I returned—the flirting...

I thought that if I could get my best friends to see me as a changed person, as this beautiful woman instead of the tomboy I used to be... then... I don't know. I don't know what I was thinking! I just wanted to feel like I was worth more than I had felt about myself before I left—before I left my hometown and the people I love."

She hung her head, offering a faint smile, though it was hard to disguise the shame. Sensing the remorse in her voice, Brayden stood up and enveloped her in a tight hug. She returned the embrace, already feeling forgiven. As they pulled away from the hug, Brayden looked at her with renewed hope.

"Don't focus too much on that. Remember, we know you and saw straight through the act."

Malik scoffed, smiling. "So, whether in all your feminine glory or rocking the tomboy look, you're still beautiful—inside and out. Okay?" Heather nodded, feeling so relieved.

Brayden's eyes softened. "And from here on out, every legitimate life goal you've ever prayed for is within your reach. As your best friends and family, we're here to support you. Just make the effort, alright?"

"Yes, Brayden. Malik. Thank you, guys!"

Heather's face lit up. She and Brayden shared one more hug before she wrapped her arms around Malik. It was as if someone had pushed the reset button on their friendship.

Brayden turned his attention to Brooklyn, who sat nearby. Her emotions were apparent as she took in everything that had transpired.

"C'mon, Brook, let's hit the stores, then I'll take you home." He offered his hand to help her up from the comfy patio chair. "And I'm sorry—I know you're tired after all this drama today."

Brooklyn took his hand, and they walked toward his truck. As they went, she reassured him that no apology was necessary. She had learned a lot, was intrigued by everything that had happened, and appreciated the opportunity to get to know Heather a little better.

Brayden opened the car door for Brooklyn, but before he could close it, Keisha came speeding down the street, her tires screeching as she came to a halt. The front passenger tire burst loudly as she parked dangerously onto the sidewalk's edge. She was so focused on Brayden and Brooklyn that she didn't care about the tire; she was determined to get answers.

Seeing the situation, Brayden turned to Brooklyn and told her to stay in the truck. He shut the door behind her and met Keisha halfway before she reached his vehicle. Her voice was already rising in anger.

"Brayden, I know you didn't ditch me to be with your baby mama!" she snapped, glaring at Brayden while aggressively pointing her finger at Brooklyn. "I'm your girlfriend now, not her!"

Brooklyn could only shake her head.

A sense of discomfort flooded her. The confrontation triggered a brief flashback to her insecure and immature behavior after her breakup with Brayden.

"Keisha, we're not in a relationship. Go home! And look at your tire!" Brayden shot back, his anger growing as he eyed the flat tire. He reached for his phone to call his and Malik's friend with the tow truck company.

In a rush, Malik dashed from the gazebo area to the front door, concerned about the loud noise. He quickly reassured his father, confirming that the situation was under control.

The noise had scared Mazo, who had jumped into her granddad's arms, burying her face in his neck and hugging him tightly.

"It's okay, sweetie. Your dad is taking care of it," he said softly, offering her comfort as he closed the front door.

"Okay, Papa," Mazo responded, reassured by her grandfather's calming words.

Brayden strolled down the sidewalk, expecting Keisha to follow, and she did. He needed some distance to manage the escalating situation in front of the Nelson's house.

"Keisha, I'm not talking to you if you're *gonna* be out here yelling—not tonight, tomorrow, or ever."

The intense look in his eyes hit her hard. She saw the disconnect in him—a look she'd never seen before—and it filled her with fear. Perhaps for the first time, she realized she was on the verge of losing him for good.

Keisha stood silently, pacing back and forth. Her arms stayed folded for the next few minutes while Brayden was busy on his phone, texting Brooklyn a stream of apologies. He finally got a response from her:

"Trust me... no worries."

Moments later, the tow truck driver, Chingy, arrived and swiftly changed Keisha's tire. Brayden handed him $200 in cash, and they shook hands. Chingy waved at Malik before driving off.

Keisha stood there, still furious, her arms folded, glaring at Brayden. "So, you're not talking to me? Are you still going somewhere with her?" she asked him, gesturing toward Brooklyn.

Brayden shook his head, clearly over it.

"I'm taking her to the store and then home... but I'm still not talking to you right now, Keisha. Go home, and I'll see you later," he said gently, trying to maintain his calm as he turned to walk to his truck.

Keisha, seething with rage, stormed off to her car. She slammed the door so hard it shattered the window. The sharp sound of breaking glass made her flinch in the opposite direction, closing her eyes tightly, hoping to protect her face.

Without a moment's hesitation, Brayden rushed toward her. "Keisha, are you okay?" he asked, panic flooding his voice.

She shot him a deathly glare, her anger still burning, before revving her engine and speeding off. Her tires screeched as she tore away, leaving the scent of burning rubber hanging in the air. Her sudden reaction caught Brayden off guard, and he had to jump back to avoid being hit by her car.

Malik rushed to the edge of the yard after she sped off, leaving tire marks on the street.

"You good, bro?"

"It's all good, man. I'm *gonna* apologize to your parents right quick," Brayden replied, heading into the house.

Malik checked on Brooklyn to see if she was okay. Despite the chaos that had just unfolded, she was unbothered and calm.

He returned to the gazebo, where Heather was still seated, in shock. She had texted Keisha the address earlier, right before she arrived at the brunch, not knowing this would happen. She deeply regretted it and was extremely scared to admit it now. But she knows she has to tell her friends eventually. Right now, she was tired, drained, and ready to call it a day.

"Okay, Malik, give me a hug. This was too much. I'm ready to go home."

Malik shook his head, agreeing. "Alright, homie. We'll probably sync up before I head out to Paris. If not, Mel will fill you in on everything."

He grabbed her hand and gently pulled her up from the chair. They shared their familiar handshake, followed by a warm, friendly hug.

But then, out of nowhere, Malik overheard something that left him frozen. He turned around, a whirlwind of joy, confusion, and anger mixing in his chest.

"So, is this why you didn't say anything earlier when you came by the house... waiting to get back to this?" Zora said softly, pointing at Heather. She had spotted Heather's car and parked in front of the neighbor's house so as not to be seen right away.

Still in the truck, Brooklyn was engrossed in a phone conversation with Amina, unaware of Zora's arrival.

"Zora, what are you doing here?" Malik asked, approaching her and placing his hand on her shoulder. He instinctively tried to walk her away from Heather, but Zora pulled away from his touch, leaving him irritated.

Just then, Brayden emerged from the house and walked toward the truck. When he saw Zora, his face instantly shifted to concern.

"What do you mean, what am I doing here, Malik?! she snapped. "I have a child here, and I came to pick her up! Your hands seem pretty much full."

As Zora tried to walk past him, Malik kindly placed his hand in front of her.

"Zora, you're not taking her tonight. I'll bring her to you tomorrow after church—that's what we agreed," Malik's voice was calm but firm. "And your issue isn't about our daughter being here. Can you talk to me, please? Tell me what's going on with you."

Suddenly, Zora's frustration boiled over.

"You want the truth, Malik? I don't like her!" she snapped again, pointing at Heather as she walked toward her.

Heather's eyes widened in surprise, stepping back slightly at the sudden outburst. Malik quickly grabbed Zora by the waist, pulling her back to prevent her from going further.

Brayden opened his door to make Brooklyn aware. She heard Zora's voice rising and turned around to see the argument unfold.

"Mina, let me call you back. Zora's over here acting crazy," Brooklyn said and quickly hung up. She got out of the truck, hoping to defuse the situation, but not before Zora kept firing.

"It's funny how you have time for her when I'm the one who needed you! She's not your friend, Malik!

She's an opportunist! She just showed up out of nowhere!"

Malik stared at her, a mixture of confusion and annoyance on his face. "What do you mean you needed me?"

Out of everything Zora said—that one statement stuck with him. "Zora, what do you mean—*you needed me?*"

His voice carried a mix of desperation and concern. More than anything, he wanted her to open up to him. He could feel that she was holding something inside, something deeper than what she was letting on.

"I'm always here for you. You know that. I don't understand where all this is coming from."

Malik's words faltered as a long pause followed. He grew tired of being blamed for his work ethic and desire to provide. The weight was starting to wear on him, and at that moment, he realized the conversation needed to stop...at least for now.

He couldn't keep going with Heather still standing there, especially when Zora kept making her the issue.

"Heather... could you give us some space?" Malik asked, his tone firmer now. But Zora, still upset, quickly interjected.

"No, she can stay," she said nonchalantly.

Brooklyn shot Zora a look, an unmistakable side-eye that signaled her disbelief. Zora caught the glance but ignored it, casually folding her arms. She wasn't about to let Brooklyn's stance distract her. She turned her attention back to Malik, her position cold. But he was definitely over it.

"It frustrates me, Zora, that you keep making me out to be the villain." His voice was calm but firm. "But it's okay. I allowed it. I didn't want to lose you... But this stops now."

His words were measured, but the seriousness in his tone was unmistakable. He didn't raise his voice, but he meant what he said. Zora felt it; her short, rapid breathing showed it as she lowered her head.

"Stop making Heather the issue between us," he continued. "If she has disrespected you, speak up. If not, don't tell me who I can be friends with. You don't understand what's happening and haven't given me a chance to explain anything. Why is that?"

Zora kept her head lowered, arms still folded. She couldn't look at him, struggling from the inside out.

Malik looked away briefly, then refocused his attention on her, gently cupping her face with his hand. His touch was soft yet firm as he guided her gaze back to his.

"I leave for Paris in less than 24 hours. All I want is to fix whatever's happening between us. Don't shut me out."

Zora briefly lifted her gaze to his, her face betraying the turmoil she was trying to suppress. She wanted him to understand the pain she was still carrying, the ache she could never seem to put into words. Instead of confronting her pain, Zora remained outwardly stubborn, her appearance unbothered as all eyes were on her. Internally, though, she was crumbling without his support.

"Malik, like I said before—do I need to repeat it? Worry about your daughter and move on."

Brooklyn, desperate to stop Zora, firmly grabbed her arm, trying to guide her toward her car. "Zo, what are you doing? Stop!"

Zora froze for a moment, Brooklyn's words fighting to break through.

The weight of Zora's actions hung heavily on her. Each word pushed Malik further away. She had tested his love and patience too many times, and now, she knew deep down she was bound to face the consequences alone.

At Zora's last words, Malik's mind drifted back to his dad's advice, which hit him hard: *"Sometimes, an individual has to exist in their words before gaining perspective."*

With a deep breath, Malik turned and walked inside his parents' house to gather Mazo. He needed to leave and head home to his condo.

Heather, eyes wide, waved goodbye to Brayden as she headed to her car, her mind filled with worry for Malik and herself as she drove off.

Brooklyn stood outside Zora's car, trying to understand her friend's behavior over the past few days.

"Zora, something's bothering you. You're pushing the man you love, the father of your child, to move on. I don't get it... I'll tell Brayden he can leave, and I'll come with you, okay?"

Zora shook her head, exhausted both physically and emotionally.

She knew she was the cause of the strain and didn't have the energy to explain it all. "No, Brooklyn... Thank you, but I need to be alone."

Brooklyn stood there for a moment, feeling helpless. She didn't know what else to do for her friend at that moment.

As Zora drove away, Brooklyn pulled out her phone and called Devin. She quickly explained the situation and asked her to contact Zora later to check on her. Devin promised to call as soon as she clocked out for the day.

With that conversation behind her, Brooklyn felt a tad bit of relief. She could focus on something as simple as grocery shopping, which was a minor but needed distraction.

"Are you okay? We can take a long drive somewhere first to decompress if you want." Brayden's words were warm. He'd always been this way when it came to her mental well-being.

"No, I'm okay. Thanks for asking."

He nodded, and as she and Brayden made their way to the store, she took a deep breath, feeling a weight lift off her shoulders—if only for a moment.

CHAPTER 9

Casual Chaos

Amina reflected on Brooklyn's advice earlier in their phone conversation. And after considering it, she gave Rocco a chance and allowed him to pick her up from her apartment.

As 6:30 p.m. approached, a knock on her door unexpectedly engulfed her, causing her to feel nervous and anxious.

"Who is it?" she asked, standing a few feet away from the door, hesitating before gathering the courage to open it.

"It's your husband."

Amina couldn't help but smile, a small giggle escaping her as she pressed her lips together. She opened the door to find Rocco standing there, looking different—in a good way.

He had always been handsome, but tonight, he seemed more mature. He wore straight, wide-leg cargo pants in a deep bronze color and a cream designer t-shirt. A pair of cream and white Air Force One Low sneakers, complemented by a black check, completed the look.

His sleek designer watch, paired with a black leather band, accentuated his grown-up appearance, and his fresh, low haircut with natural waves completed the polished, mature vibe.

"Hey, Roccorio," Amina greeted softly, her smile beaming as she looked at him. Rocco returned the greeting, spreading his arms wide.

"Hey, Amina. Can I get a hug if it's okay with you?" he asked sincerely.

Amina gladly stepped forward, wrapping her arms around him. His cologne was pleasant, and she lingered a little longer in the embrace, subtly inhaling his scent before pulling away.

After they separated, Rocco closed the door behind him and walked over to the sofa, where he sat.

"Can we talk for a second before we leave?" he asked, his voice steady but filled with intent, looking at her, hoping she would agree.

As Amina approached the sofa, he gently grabbed her hand, guiding her to sit closer. He wanted to ensure he had her full attention before speaking his mind.

"I think things need to be said on my end before I can leave here in good faith," he began, gesturing to his chest. There's no straightforward way until I clear up the past...

Rocco sighed softly before continuing. "I know I embarrassed you, humiliated you, and hurt you badly a while ago... and I never got the chance to apologize appropriately for my foolishness, for the dumb choices I made back then..."

His eyes locked with hers, feeling compelled to release the burden he had carried for a long time...

"I am so sorry for betraying you like I did those years ago. That's been one of my biggest regrets in life—hurting you... losing you. And I don't know how I'm even blessed to be in your presence now, except by the grace of God. And I don't take that lightly. So, thank you... Thank you, Amina, for giving me this chance."

A long pause stretched between them, and he watched as her eyes softened, yet there was still a trace of doubt in her expression. She opened her mouth to speak, but he gently intervened. "I love you. It's been almost four years, and I've never stopped loving you."

Amina, pleasantly overwhelmed, smiled as she listened to Rocco's heartfelt apology. She felt that this was all she needed to hear to move on, whether they would get back together or not.

"Roc," she said softly, gently touching his face. "I forgive you. I was upset when you started calling me again, and I tried to play hard because I had never heard you say those words. But I forgive you now. Thank you for finally saying them. Honestly, I forgave you a long time ago," she added, her smile warm.

Rocco scoffed, a playful smirk crossing his face. "Oh, so you forgave me back then, huh? After you came over to use my body three months after we broke up, only to turn right back around and be mad at me again?"

Amina scrunched up her face, a big smile spreading across it. "I was just feeling a little hot and bothered—blame it on the flesh." They both laughed.

A warm hug followed, sealing the long-overdue apology session they both needed. Although Amina still felt a bit skeptical about him, his apology for cheating on her years ago somehow made her feel more at ease. And let's be honest, the fact that he looks as good as he does didn't hurt either.

"So, are we ready to go... You hungry?" Rocco asked, standing and gesturing towards the door.

Amina quickly stood up, grabbing her purse and umbrella. She let Rocco exit first, then locked her apartment door, and they headed out for the evening.

Urban Coffee

Across town, Brayden and Brooklyn arrived at the massive Whole Foods store to gather the items from the list she had prepared earlier. With the rain picking up, Brayden dropped her off near the entrance. He found a parking spot nearby before grabbing an umbrella and joining her.

"Alright, babygirl, where should we start?" he asked casually, his hand resting on her back as they leisurely scanned the grocery list.

"Since we're near the veggies, I'll grab the asparagus, cherry tomatoes, a bag of kale, and some sweet potatoes. You can get the watermelon and a bag of oranges, lemons, and limes.

That should cover this side," Brooklyn instructed, placing her phone in the shopping cart.

"Okay, Miss Bossy," Brayden teased.

She paused, glancing at him with a smile. "No, I'm sorry... I didn't mean to sound bossy."

Brayden chuckled and wrapped his arm around the top of her shoulders, pulling her in for a quick hug and a kiss on the forehead.

"I'm just joking, baby."

Brooklyn playfully tapped him on his chest as he turned to grab the items. "You play too much," she teased.

He looked back at her, giving a quick wink and a smile, sending a flutter of butterflies through her stomach.

After navigating the organic meats aisle, Brooklyn finished her shopping by picking up a bag of almond flour and restocking some seasonings she was low on. Brayden, meanwhile, selected a variety of delicious organic snacks that little Nate would love, too.

During their time at Whole Foods, Keisha had called Brayden several times.

He answered two calls, telling her he'd call back after finishing up with Brooklyn. He never hesitated to give Brooklyn his full attention.

"We got everything, babygirl?"

He asked as he saw Brooklyn coming up an aisle as he was about to pass. She gave the *I'm ready nod and smile*, and they headed to the front registers.

The cashier, clearly taken with Brayden, had an obvious, instant crush on him. She couldn't hide it well but tried to play it cool as she checked him out, perhaps hoping for a chance to make her move.

"Are y'all married? You look so cute together," the cashier said with a smile.

Brooklyn smiled back, tempted to respond with a playful lie. She wanted to keep it light and funny.

"Oh, no, this is my brother."

Brayden quickly scoffed, looking away with a chuckle, thoroughly enjoying Brooklyn's playful response.

"Oh, okay... You are so fine! We've been scoping you since you walked in. Can I please get your number?"

The cute cashier was shooting her shot with a hopeful smile. But Brooklyn's expression quickly shifted, regretting the joke. She stayed quiet. It was a blunt reminder that she and Brayden weren't together, even though this trip through Whole Foods had felt so familiar and natural.

Noticing the change in Brooklyn's demeanor, Brayden smiled and responded sincerely to the cashier.

"I appreciate you, but I'm in love with this beautiful young lady right here—who's not my sister," he said, nodding toward Brooklyn with a grin.

"Oh! I'm so sorry! I thought she was serious about the *brother* thing. Your total is $318.92," the cashier stuttered, clearly embarrassed.

Brayden pulled out his debit card, handed it to her, and began gathering the groceries. Once the transaction was complete, Brooklyn took the receipt and card. A smile played on her lips as she blushed from his response to the cashier, grappling with a mix of emotions.

She followed Brayden out of the store, feeling surprisingly lighthearted despite everything.

Fortunately, the rain had slowed considerably, leaving just a drizzle here and there. Brayden unloaded the groceries into the back of his truck, and Brooklyn returned the cart to the designated station. As she walked back toward him, he opened the passenger side door for her. Their eyes met, and for a moment, time seemed to stand still between them. Without a word, he leaned in and gently kissed her. She gladly reciprocated, feeling a warm sensation spread through her body, making her feel both safe and cherished.

After a few lingering seconds, Brayden reluctantly pulled away, closed the door behind her, and got into his truck. He proceeded to pull out of the parking space, the hum of the engine filling the brief silence that had followed.

"Are you okay?" he asked, noticing her silence as he drove through the busy Whole Foods parking lot, searching for the best exit.

Brooklyn smiled, nodding her head. "Yeah, I'm okay. Thank you so much for coming with me. I used to love grocery shopping with you."

He smiled, gently caressing her hand. "Me, too."

Brayden navigated through the parking lot, and a brief, peaceful silence dwelt between them. It didn't last long, though. As they headed down the street toward the interstate, they spotted Amina and Rocco at the Self-Serve gas station.

Without Brooklyn needing to ask, Brayden pulled into the station so she could speak to her friend.

Amina and Rocco stood outside his car, talking while he filled the tank. When Amina saw Brooklyn approaching, she rushed to greet her with a hug. Next, she hugged Brayden.

Brooklyn turned to Rocco, smiling as she hugged him. "Hey, Rocco... long time no-see."

He smiled, pointing at Amina as if blaming her for making him wait so long to see everybody in person.

Brayden approached Rocco, and they exchanged a firm handshake.

"What's up, boss man?" Rocco said with a quick salute after shaking Brayden's hand.

"Don't be greeting my friends like that!" Amina playfully scolded, laughing as she wrapped her arm around Brooklyn's.

Brayden smiled and shook his head, looking at Rocco.

The men continued talking momentarily while the girls, stepping a few feet away, shared their little huddle.

"So, I see things are going well with you two."

Amina grinned. "Yes, it is... and all I want to do is jump his bones." Brooklyn started laughing, caught off guard by Amina's blunt remark.

"Rocco's been attentive and respectful since we met earlier," Amina continued. "He says he has much to share but didn't want to spill everything in one day... He's talking about how he wants us to reconnect and get to know each other again."

Brooklyn smiled, genuinely happy for her friend. "Sounds like he's on the right track. And look at you—rocking that cute short denim jumper dress with those crispy white Air Force Ones and your hair in a bun. You go, girl!"

Amina struck a pose, flaunting her outfit, and they both laughed. Rocco glanced over, shaking his head.

"Alright, baby, you ready?" he called out, holding the door open for her.

Brooklyn whispered in her ear as they hugged.

"Keep your dress on, sweetie."

Amina giggled, "I'll try." She made her way over to Rocco.

Urban Coffee

When Brayden and Brooklyn arrived at her house, she removed her shoes and began putting away the groceries while Brayden brought in the last two bags.

"I thought you only grabbed one watermelon for us," Brooklyn said, struggling to lift one onto the bottom pantry shelf. "And they're huge!"

Brayden quickly rushed over to help. "Excuse me, please, before you hurt yourself," he said with a smile.

"No, I grabbed two for you guys. I like cutting mine into cubes and keeping some in the fridge for snacking and juicing. I vacuum seal the other one and freeze it into individual servings to make smoothies."

Brooklyn leaned on her peninsula, arms folded. "Good idea! You should do the same for Nate and me."

Brayden smiled, stepping closer. He placed both hands on the peninsula, trapping her between his arms. His gaze turned serious. "No problem," he murmured, then gently kissed her.

Brooklyn inhaled, feeling the heat of his kiss intensify. The softness of his lips against hers sent shivers down her spine. She wrapped her arms around his neck, and their kiss deepened. He pulled her closer, and they lost themselves in each other's embrace. Nothing else mattered—just their undeniable connection.

As they continued to savor each other's lips, losing themselves in each other, it felt as if time had stopped, but in an instant, a phone call from Keisha shattered the moment.

Their lips eventually parted from the kiss. Brayden pressed the silent button on his phone, then gently rested his forehead against Brooklyn's as their breathing gradually slowed, leaving both feeling a sense of physical craving.

"Whoa, I need a shower," she whispered, smiling. Brayden chuckled softly, moving closer to her ear, his tongue brushing lightly against it.

Brooklyn took a deep breath as he gently pulled her earlobe between his lips, speaking affectionately.

"You think you're the only one needing a shower?" he muttered softly, pulling away slightly, his eyes locking with hers.

Brooklyn smiled, her heart fluttering as she looked up at him, wishing the moment could last forever.

He gently hugged her tightly, and she returned the embrace, draping her arms firmly around his neck.

But as the lightheartedness passed, Brayden saw a flicker of sadness in her eyes. He could sense the moment's weight, and his smile faded slightly.

"I can't do this anymore," he said, his voice more serious now. Brooklyn's brows furrowed in confusion.

"No, baby, not you," he quickly clarified, chuckling softly at her surprised expression. She smiled, but the concern didn't leave her eyes. He gently lifted her chin, locking her gaze with his.

"Hey, I think I should head out," he said softly, his voice filled with reluctance. "Neither of us wants me to walk out that door, and if I stay any longer, I won't.

But I need to talk to Keisha, and afterward, I need some time to myself, you know?"

Brooklyn sighed, but nodded in understanding. She, too, was on a journey of self-improvement. Neither had taken the time to process their breakup and grieve what was lost.

Brayden gently kissed her lips, his eyes lingering on her momentarily. Then, with a quiet sigh, he went to grab one of the watermelons from the pantry.

"I'll cut and package this up for you guys tonight," he said, offering a small smile before heading toward the door. He paused just before leaving, looking back at her one last time before softly closing the door behind him.

Urban Coffee

Devin had gotten off work for the day and was heading to her car. She decided to call Zora to check on her, knowing she was struggling emotionally. Fortunately, though, Ms. Shanel had arrived, so she answered Zora's phone to update Devin.

"Alright, Mama Shanel, thanks for the update.

Please let Zora know I checked in on her, and I'll give her a call tomorrow." Before ending the call, Devin decided to chat with Zora's mom for a few more minutes, grateful she was there.

It was one less thing for her to worry about—especially when something else was weighing on her mind that had bothered her since the gas station fight.

She was determined to resolve it after ending the call with Ms. Shanel.

"Hey, Siri, call Chris."

"Calling Chris...Young Hottie...mobile."

The first two attempts went straight to voicemail after just one ring. Frustrated, Devin decided to text instead.

Devin text: *"Chris, you pissing me off! Answer your phone!"*

It wasn't until her third attempt that the call finally went through.

"Why are you calling me? And how you pissed off at a person you care nothing about?" Chris answered, annoyed.

Devin snapped, her anger bubbling to the surface. "I know you're not getting an attitude with me after what you did!"

Chris took the phone from his ear, confused, before placing it back. "Woman, what are you talking about? And I know this ain't you coming down my street," he exclaimed, spotting Devin's royal blue Honda Accord.

He ended the call and shook his head as Devin swiftly parked behind his truck in front of his house. She jumped out of the car and headed straight toward him, pointing her finger.

"You claim you want a real relationship with me, but not even a few hours later, you're out in public with some random female?!"

Chris's eyes furrowed in confusion, but it lasted only a moment before he smiled, unfazed. He stepped closer, attempting to wrap his arms around her.

"So, you are feeling me, huh?"

Devin quickly pushed his hands away. "Chris, stop playing with me! That's exactly why we can't be together!"

His head tilted slightly, his eyebrows furrowing in disbelief.

"Wait, I'm the reason we can't be together?" He placed a hand on his chest, shaking his head. "No, it's your twisted way of thinking—you not recognizing the worth of a man like me."

Devin raised her hand abruptly, signaling for him to stop talking.

"There's nothing decent about you. You can't even apologize for what you did! You embarrassed me in front of my friends!"

Chris shook his head, chuckling at her nonsense.

"Tell me exactly what I did wrong, and then be prepared to apologize to me."

Devin stood there, her frustration building. Without thinking, she stepped toward him, lightly swinging her hand to slap him across the face. But before her hand could connect, Chris swiftly moved back, intercepting her mid-swing.

"Man, don't put your hands on him."

Devin froze at the command. She whipped around, her eyes widening in shock. It looked like she'd just seen a ghost.

Chris's identical twin brother, Nicholas, had exited the garage's side door.

Devin glanced back at Chris, and reality hit her all at once. "OMG!" she exclaimed, her laughter bubbling up despite herself. She instantly felt embarrassed about her earlier actions with both Chris and his brother.

Still chuckling, she walked toward Chris, hugging him tightly around his waist and burying her face in his chest.

"Uh-huh...we're waiting," Chris said sarcastically, expecting her to apologize to both of them.

She pulled away slightly, holding Chris's face gently in her hands. "I am so sorry, Chris," she said sincerely.

He smiled, his eyes softening at her awkward expression, before introducing her to his brother.

"Baby, this is Nick," he said, gesturing toward his brother.

He gave Devin a firm handshake, his smile warm.

Still a little rattled, Devin explained what had happened the night before. It was clear that Nicholas hadn't filled Chris in on any details.

"I knew you were the one my brother always talked about, especially after you cold-slapped my girl and me," Nick said nonchalantly, shaking his head and chuckling.

They all laughed, but Devin's expression turned more serious as she apologized to him. She even urged him to apologize to his girlfriend on her behalf. She was still trying to make sense of what was happening.

"You guys look so identical... It's honestly scary!" Devin said, glancing back and forth between the two of them.

"Yeah, you have to know us to tell us apart," Nicholas smiled, dapping his brother. He hopped into his truck, ready to leave, but not without giving Devin some advice.

"Hey, my brother's the good one, so don't snooze on him too long," Nick winked at her as he started the engine.

Chris pressed his lips together in amusement. "She's living that casual chaos, man. She doesn't care about nothing."

Devin lightly pushed him in the chest, eyes widening. "What do you mean by that?" she asked, her mouth slightly open, unsure whether to be offended or just curious.

"It means you navigate life with reckless energy, not prioritizing what matters, not even yourself. Those are the kind of girls my brother has time for," Chris explained, his tone firm.

His brother nodded, a smirk tugging at the corners of his mouth, clearly agreeing with Chris.

"Yep, that's all I have time for right now, and messing with me leads to confusion, heartbreak, and all kinds of chaos," Nick added, shifting his gear in reverse.

Devin let out a baffled chuckle, shocked that Nick was calmly agreeing with his brother, as if this was how things went. She shook her head, watching him back out.

"Don't forget to tell your girlfriend about my apology," she called out after him.

"She's not my girl, sweetheart," Nick replied with a grin. Devin glanced at him sideways and then looked at Chris, who shrugged and confirmed,

"She's not his girl, baby."

Her eyes widened in confusion. Last night, the girl at the gas station seemed so serious about fighting for Nick, and now this. Devin felt uncertain but decided to let it go for now.

"Turn off the lights in my place!" Nicholas yelled out the window as he drove away. Chris threw his hands up in disbelief. "Bro, seriously?"

After watching his brother drive off, he turned to Devin with a smile. "Coming with me to secure his place?"

She chuckled, piecing it all together. It was clear she had the *good twin.*

They entered the garage, where Chris fumbled with his spare keys to unlock the side door. After a brief struggle, he opened it and led Devin downstairs to the basement.

To her surprise, Nick's apartment was a certified magnet for women. As Chris started to turn off the lights, she stopped him with a gentle touch, her eyes scanning the space. He noticed her surprise and chuckled, realizing she was impressed by his brother's well-maintained living space.

The apartment was tastefully decorated, featuring an open-concept living room and a large TV screen mounted on the wall. The flow into the kitchen area, immersed in natural light streaming through the windows, was eye-catching. Even the appliances were upscale, stainless steel—something that stood out in contrast to the typical bachelor's pad.

"Wow! This is a full two-bedroom apartment down here, and it's so spacious!" she exclaimed, still examining the area.

Following Devin's view of the apartment, Chris switched off the lights, including the large TV and PlayStation 5 console. "C'mon, baby, let's go," he said, taking Devin's hand and leading her back upstairs, securely locking his brother's door behind them.

Devin's demeanor shifted as they walked back through the driveway, and a look of curiosity appeared in her eyes. She stopped, causing Chris to pause.

"Where are you going?" she asked, raising an eyebrow.

"I'm walking you to your car."

Her eyes narrowed as she rested her hands on her hips. "I know *you* lying! I can't see your place?"

Chris chuckled, knowing that question was coming. "Alright, alright, let's go."

Devin followed closely behind, smiling widely, intrigued by what he'd show her next.

Once again, she was in awe as Chris opened the front door to reveal the home. It was a charming three-bedroom, two-bathroom house with a perfect blend of rustic and modern touches that created a cozy, intimate atmosphere.

Wooden beams stretched across the ceiling, and rich wood flooring added warmth. The living room featured a large sectional sofa, a stylish round coffee table in the center, and a beautiful area rug, making it the ideal spot to relax and unwind.

As Devin explored the bedrooms, she admired how beautifully designed and serene each was, including the cabin-inspired bathroom in the primary suite, which had a stone backsplash and a lavish jetted tub. Chris's third bedroom was converted into a gaming office, outfitted with a sleek, modern L-shaped desk, two large monitors, a fancy keyboard, and more.

Devin returned down the hallway and passed by the second bathroom, which, with its double sinks and spacious, wall-to-wall shower, embraced the cabin theme and completed the home's warm and inviting atmosphere.

After finishing the tour, Chris led Devin back to the living room. He pulled out his cell phone, connected it to the surround sound system, and played soft R&B music.

Gently, he twirled her around before pulling her close, swaying to the smooth rhythm. He looked at her with a smile, shaking his head.

"You don't care about anything, do you?" he asked, a playful but serious hint in his voice.

Devin furrowed her brows. "What do you mean?"

He smiled, twirling her around slowly. "You haven't asked once how, at 22, we can afford to live like this."

Though the question had crossed her mind, she didn't want to pry or seem entitled. "Yes, I thought about it, but I didn't know how to ask," she admitted with a shrug.

He scoffed, still smiling, but his expression quickly turned serious. He took a deep breath and let out a heavy sigh.

“This is the house we grew up in until we were 15. Then, my parents were killed in a head-on collision by a drunk driver. They died instantly.”

Devin’s eyes widened in shock, and a sympathetic expression crossed her face as she processed his words.

“With the help of our parents’ life insurance, and once we were old enough,” Chris continued, “my brother and I decided to come back here, to the place we were happiest with them, and fix it up,” he added quietly...

“We still need to do something with the front and back yard, but it’s decent for now, so it wasn’t a priority. The $200,000 left over—we split it down the middle, bought our cars, and deposited the rest into our accounts.”

Devin wrapped her arms around his neck—the most nurturing he had ever felt from her. “I’m so sorry,” she whispered, gently caressing him as she held him close.

Chris welcomed the gesture, tightening his arms around her.

After a long, comforting embrace, the heaviness lifted between them. They soon sat on the couch, Chris leaning back with his body slightly turned toward Devin, feeling the calmness settle in.

She stretched out her legs, resting them across his lap, and he gently caressed them as they shared light conversation, laughter, and playful flirting. The easy chitchat continued for about ten minutes until Devin’s hormones, clearly stirred by his touch and attention, began to surface.

“May I take a shower?” she asked softly, standing up in front of him.

“Sure, you can.”

Chris rose to his feet and planted a gentle kiss on her lips before going to grab one of his T-shirts and a pair of shorts for her.

Devin swiftly shed her maxi dress and panties, leaving them behind as she walked toward the primary bathroom with only her purse. Chris laid the clothes on the bed, along with lotion and deodorant.

"Do you want something to eat? A sandwich, maybe?" he asked before stepping out.

"No, thank you," she called out from the bathroom, calm but appreciative. "I'm good. But you can eat."

Chris left the room, giving Devin space to freshen up. She took her time in the shower, cleansing and refreshing before drying off, applying deodorant, and the fragrant lotion.

Slipping into Chris's T-shirt, which fell nearly to her knees, she walked back into the living room. Chris sat at the butcher block peninsula, waiting for his noodles to settle before adding hot sauce and extra seasoning.

She pulled out a barstool and hopped onto the peninsula, keeping her T-shirt underneath her. Crossing her legs, she positioned herself next to him.

Chris glanced over, a playful grin spreading across his face as he saw her in his shirt. "So fresh and so clean, clean," he teased as he went to retrieve his noodles.

Devin chuckled, shaking her head. When he returned, she gently stopped him before he sat down, removing the noodles from his hands and setting them aside, far enough to avoid any spills. Then, she reached out and pulled him closer.

"When I said you can eat, I meant *me*," she whispered with a mischievous smile, lifting the hem of his shirt.

Her playful gesture was met with an intensity in his eyes, revealing that he wanted a deeper connection than a carnal one.

"Every time we've met up for months, it's been all about the physical," Chris said, gently pulling on her shirt... "Sometimes, I just want to chill with you," he continued—go out to eat, maybe shop, anything besides just... sex...

I want to know what's in here," he said, gesturing gently to her head. "What makes you happy, sad, or angry? What's your favorite color? Do you like to travel? Do you believe in God? There's *got* to be more to you than just your body," he added, raising his brows, as if pleading for answers...

You really almost lost it earlier when you thought I was seeing someone else," Chris said, frustration building in his voice. "What's with all these assorted emotions you keep tossing at me? I can't tell what's real."

Devin sat still, her eyes flickering with mixed feelings, but she decided to only answer the part about him seeing someone else. "You're right," she admitted. "I would've lost it if I thought you were putting someone else in my place. You wouldn't want someone else satisfying me, so stop *trippin'*," she added, smiling to keep the mood light.

Chris, however, didn't share her amusement. His face remained serious as he absorbed her words. And Devin, realizing his expression didn't change, let out a frustrated sigh and answered a few of his questions:

"Yes, I believe in God. Yes, I like traveling, and my favorite color is blue. Happy?"

Chris shook his head with a small, tired smile; frustration was overwhelming. He stood there momentarily, lowered his head before lifting it back up to look in her eyes.

He began lifting her shirt off slowly.

As he leaned in, he kissed her softly, his lips lingering on hers as he held her close. The kiss was slow, tender, and filled with the kind of unspoken understanding they had been dancing around. Devin held onto him tightly, drawing him closer.

He slowly pulled away from the kiss and lifted her legs, placing them on his shoulders as he went down between them to feast in her sweetness. He skillfully teased, lightly grazing over her rosebud with his tongue—Devin, moving her hips to its rhythm, widening her legs.

She inhaled deeply from the pleasure, her legs spreading to their limit as they began to quiver. She looked up towards the ceiling, her eyes tightly closed, waiting for a massive release that was soon to come. At that moment, Chris abruptly stopped and stepped back from her, wiping his mouth.

"Go waste somebody else's time. Leave my house!" he said softly but firmly, pointing toward the front door.

Devin froze, shock flooding her system. She felt an intense surge of defeat and disbelief, her body trembling as she tried to hold the throbbing feeling together.

"Chris, you can't be serious right now!

Please, don't do this!" she pleaded, her voice breaking with insistence.

"It's already done. Get your stuff and leave," he replied, still calm but firm as he walked off.

Devin's anger flared. She pushed herself off the countertop and quickly put her shirt back on. As she stormed into the primary bedroom, she couldn't stop herself from ripping into him verbally. But Chris remained silent, focusing on the TV as he flipped through the channels.

She grabbed her purse and pulled her hair back into a quick ponytail, trying to calm herself. "So, you're just going to let me leave like this?" she declared.

He didn't respond, but his silence spoke volumes. Devin didn't believe he would ever do this to her.

"Chris, you're just like all the rest of them, saying you want something real but then treating me like this?!"

He shot her a sideways glance, clearly unfazed by her words, and turned his attention back to the TV.

Devin's frustration boiled over. She scanned the room, looking for something to make him react.

Her eyes landed on his noodles, and she shoved them off the counter, sending them crashing to the floor, and stormed toward the door.

He barely glanced at her as he uttered, "Maybe I should've passed you off to my brother after I got what I wanted the first time."

Devin stopped in her tracks, her hand still on the doorknob as her eyes blazed with hurt and rage. The pain was real, mixing with a shooting anger that made her chest tighten. She slammed the door shut behind her with a force that matched the storm brewing between them, her heart pounding in her chest as she stomped the walkway to her car.

Chris sat there momentarily, rubbing his hand over his face and feeling deeply exasperated. As the sound of her leaving echoed in the silence, he stood up and saw the noodles scattered on the floor. He sighed heavily, muttering to himself... *"Psycho!"*

For a brief moment, guilt crept over him. He did like her, but he couldn't deny the gravity of the situation. He cleaned the mess silently, mopping the floor and spraying the countertop with fresh-scented bleach to wipe it down.

The motion felt almost automatic, a way to stay calm and ground himself after the madness. Once the mess was cleaned, he showered, brushed his teeth, and put on a fresh white T-shirt and shorts. His mind was still buzzing from the confrontation, so he made another quick serving of noodles and settled in front of the TV.

****

In the meantime, Devin hurried home to alleviate the throbbing sensation. As if things weren't already complicated, a police officer pulled her over for speeding. The next twenty minutes felt like an eternity as she received her citation.

Finally home, she hurried to her adult toy box and found her favorite one. Lying on her back across her bed, she was desperate to get whatever relief she could muster—but the release was weak. She turned to her side, curling up like a baby as tears streamed down her face, overwhelming emotions she couldn't sort out.

CHAPTER 10

Do the Work

After an enjoyable evening, Amina and Rocco exited *Savory Seafood* and strolled toward their car. His arm draped comfortably around her shoulders, and she responded by wrapping hers around his waist. They moved in perfect sync, like a happy couple.

Surprisingly, Amina found herself having an amazing time with Rocco. There was something genuinely different about him now, but still, past experiences prevented her from fully embracing it. Tonight, though, she wanted to savor the moment, imagining that things had always been this way and he had always been faithful.

"Whoa!" Amina exclaimed, squeezing Rocco tighter as she was startled by the sudden darkness in the parking lot. He chuckled and wrapped both arms around her securely.

"It's just a light post, baby. It blew out," he reassured her.

She giggled, glancing up at the lamppost beside Rocco's truck. "Oh, okay. I didn't know what that was!"

Shaking his head with a smile, Rocco opened the car door for her. Once she got in, he walked around to his side and started the truck, preparing to back out.

But before he could shift gears, Amina surprised him by turning off the engine and moving closer to him. She straddled his lap with a teasing yet serious look in her eyes.

"What are you doing? We're still in the parking lot," he said, glancing around to ensure no one else was nearby.

She smirked, her fingers lightly brushing his chest. "Relax, there's no one around, and the windows are tinted," she teased, settling in, her presence making his heart race.

Rocco smiled, shaking his head in amusement as their gaze met. They began kissing intensely, their tongues reacquainting with each other. His fingertips slowly traced her thighs; their panting getting heavier, their embrace tighter.

Amina's fingers were just about to unzip his pants when Rocco gently grabbed her hands, stopping her. Her expression shifted between irritation and confusion, briefly pausing for an explanation.

"What, Rocco?" she whispered.

"I don't want this night to end like this... not in a parking lot," he said softly, looking into her eyes honestly. "This wasn't my intention."

Amina pulled away, moving back into her seat and adjusting her dress. Her emotions conflicted, and she couldn't entirely hide the anger that began to build inside her.

"So, now you have a problem with doing this in a parking lot?" she retorted, her voice sharp. She turned her gaze away from him, staring out the window as a cold distance settled between them.

"Amina, don't do that." His voice was filled with tenderness. "I care about you too much to let it happen like this, especially after all the time we've been apart. I've changed, and I want to show you respect. I want something more than this."

Her chest tightened, a deep sigh escaping as she tried to process his words. She didn't know if she was ready to accept this *"new version"* of him or if it was even what she truly wanted at all.

The familiar tension between them had shifted, leaving her with more questions than answers.

"So, what are your intentions, Roc?" Amina's voice was softer now, but still carrying the weight of her confusion. "We had dinner, you shared your plans to pursue a construction degree, and talked about your mentor who's been helping you. Don't get me wrong, all of that sounds good. But this new version of you... I don't... I don't know if..."

Rocco shifted in his seat, leaning back against the headrest, his eyes fixed on her.

"Say it," he urged, his voice calm but insistent. "Go ahead. Let me hear it."

Amina let out a heavy sigh, her words coming out slowly as she wrestled with her feelings. "I'm struggling to recognize who you've become, Roc. That's the truth."

Rocco scoffed lightly, shaking his head, his expression unreadable. "Let me help you out. It's because you don't trust me, right?" He looked at her directly, his voice low but filled with a hint of sadness...

"You're still haunted by the pain and humiliation I caused you four years ago. I don't blame you. You have every right to feel that way."

He paused, letting the silence sit between them before continuing... "And it's okay to tell me that. I deserve it."

Amina rested her elbows on her lap, hands covering her face. When she finally looked at him, her gaze met his with vulnerability and raw emotion.

"No, Roc... It's not just about trust. It's about fear. I'm terrified. I don't even know how to start trusting someone again without the constant fear of history repeating itself."

Rocco sighed deeply, the weight of her words sinking in. The truck fell silent as they stared ahead, lost in their thoughts.

After a moment, he reached out, gently taking her hand in his, their fingers interlacing. He didn't turn to face her but asked the question lingering in his mind.

"Do you still love me?"

Amina glanced at him, her brows furrowed in thought. She took a deep breath before responding softly.

"You know me, Roccorio," she said, her voice quiet but firm. "I may put up a tough front, trying to shield my heart, but you know I wouldn't be here if I didn't still love you."

Rocco nodded, a sense of relief sweeping over him.

"Okay. Okay," he replied gently, taking a moment to collect his thoughts before continuing.

"If you're willing to give us a chance, I promise you—God willing—that you won't regret it. I will earn your trust again and make sure you're happy—that we're happy. Can we do that? Are you willing to give us a real chance, no matter what?"

Amina lowered her head for a moment, gathering her thoughts, then met his gaze with a soft smile, her voice echoing his words.

"Okay. Okay. I'll give it a real chance. No matter what."

He leaned in toward her, and they kissed, sealing their commitment. However, Rocco needed to clear up some things before leaving the parking lot.

"By the way, lil' mama, I recently earned my associate's degree in Construction & Contractors Management and was blessed with not one, but two mentors who've helped me out.

See, you don't be listening to me," he teased, playfully pointing at her as if she should feel guilty.

Amina burst into laughter, apologizing for not catching those crucial details.

"I'm proud of you, Rocco," she said sincerely. "Tonight was a much-needed wake-up call, and I'm glad we had this heart-to-heart."

Rocco chuckled as he started the truck. "C'mon, let's head to the Ice Cream Retreat. I can tell you more about the last four years, and I wanna hear all about what you've been up to, too—your goals, dreams—everything!"

Amina's excitement was obvious, and a blush crept across her cheeks. "Oh, I'd love that. And I especially love the Ice Cream Retreat!" she said, smiling brightly. "It's so cozy in there with the dim lighting, lush couches, and the soft music playing. It's the perfect spot to unwind."

Rocco started to reverse out of his parking spot, but his cell phone rang. His younger brother, Cray, called with news that made Rocco's heart drop. Their mom had been rushed to the hospital in an ambulance.

Amina's eyes widened in concern as Cray's voice came through the truck's radio system.

"What happened? Who's with her?" Rocco asked, his voice tight with anxiety.

"I don't know... and it'll be you once you get there!" Cray snapped angrily.

Rocco slammed his finger on the end call button, cutting off the conversation, and without hesitation, he sped off toward the hospital. *"So stupid!"* Rocco muttered under his breath, his hands gripping the steering wheel tightly. Amina shook her head, disgusted by his brother's attitude.

Rocco's foot pressed harder on the gas, pushing the truck to 80 mph on the highway as he raced to the hospital, his mind spinning with worry.

****

After swiftly exiting the truck, they walked briskly, hand in hand, into the hospital. Inside, Rocco inquired about his mom, and the front desk clerk directed him to her room.

Amina did a double-take as they made their way toward the elevator. She spotted Keisha sitting in the waiting area, engrossed in her phone and unaware of Amina's presence. Keisha's leg shook nervously, but Amina ignored her for now—Rocco's mom was the priority.

Once they arrived on the third floor, they made their way to his mom's room, where two nurses were attending to her.

"How is she? Can you please give me an update on my mom?" Rocco asked urgently, approaching one of the nurses he seemed to know.

Ms. Richards was resting, appearing weak as she breathed with the assistance of a respirator. She was saying very little, her eyes barely opening.

Seeing the concern on Rocco's face, the young nurse addressed him calmly.

"She's doing okay for now. Your mom is in and out of consciousness, but she's good. It will take a little more time for the medication to take full effect, but Dr. Douglas has been notified," the nurse added, smiling. "He's ordered tests and should be here soon to discuss the results."

Rocco sighed deeply, shaking his head in frustration. "Thank you," he replied to the nurse. And I'm sorry, I forgot your name."

"You're welcome," the young nurse said kindly. It's London. And I didn't forget yours, Mr. Roccorio," she smiled...

But your mother is comfortable now. We'll return to discuss the results as soon as Dr. Douglas arrives."

Once the nurses left the room, Amina glanced at Rocco, a bit puzzled by the exchange. He noticed her expression.

"Oh, baby, that's the nurse who works at my mom's doctor's office," he explained, his worry for his mom still evident. "I'm sorry I didn't introduce you, but I completely forgot her name."

It's okay, baby, no biggie," she replied reassuringly.

She decided it was nothing to worry about since he had forgotten the nurse's name. However, Amina couldn't help but notice the nurse's beautiful, dark skin and pretty smile. Still, she chose not to let it bother her.

Gently, she took Rocco's hand and guided him to the small turquoise leather couch tucked in the corner of the room, where they sat to wait for the test results. Amina softly caressed his back as he sat, his gaze fixed on his mom, who was connected to the machines. Tears welled in his eyes as he watched her struggle to breathe. The room's silence was only broken by the hissing and beeping of the medical equipment.

They sat in quiet solidarity, their hearts heavy, their eyes never leaving Ms. Richards.

About fifteen minutes later, the door opened, and Dr. Douglas entered, holding the test results. Rocco immediately stood, recognizing his mom's doctor. The two men shook hands warmly, and Dr. Douglas smiled at Amina, extending his hand before turning to read the test results aloud.

"There's no need to worry too much right now," the doctor reassured Rocco, noticing the deep concern on his face... "Just try to relax. Your mom is currently experiencing mild respiratory issues, likely aggravated by her asthma, lack of sleep, and possibly her environment," Dr. Douglas explained...

"We've administered zolpidem to help her sleep tonight, which is imperative for her condition...

While I can't speak to her situation at home, I recommend a humidifier to improve air quality and help manage stress, as stress can worsen respiratory problems."

Dr. Douglas gave Rocco a reassuring look. "You can speak with her before the medication takes effect, but she'll need rest soon.

We'll monitor her throughout the night, and if anything changes, I'll contact you."

"Thank you, doc," Rocco said, shaking the doctor's hand.

Meanwhile, Amina was standing by Ms. Richards' bedside, quietly waiting as the doctor and Rocco spoke.

Ms. Richards woke up again, her eyes brightening as she saw Amina with Rocco. She smiled, comforted by their presence.

"I always knew he was my Golden Boy," she said softly. "I had faith my son would get himself together and get his wife."

Amina's eyes widened in surprise, and they both shared soft laughter. She couldn't help but blush, pleased by his mom's kind words.

Approaching the opposite side of the bed, Rocco leaned down to kiss his mom on the cheek and gently caressed her salt-and-pepper hair. She smiled at him, reassured that he would always be there for her.

"It's alright, sweetie," she said, her voice softer now. "You know my asthma can flare up sometimes. I'll be discharged in one or two days. You should head home and rest."

Rocco adjusted her covers, tucking them around her as the room was cold. "Do you need anything, Ma? What can I do for you?"

“Just bring me a couple of comfortable dresses and my purse tomorrow,” she replied, wrapping him in a warm hug before they left. As the medication took effect, her eyes grew heavier. Rocco, noticing, reassured his mom before he left that he would bring her what she needed. He leaned down to kiss her forehead before stepping back.

“Goodnight,” Amina whispered, glancing back before closing the door.

“Goodnight, sweet baby,” Ms. Richards said, her voice soft. “Stay close to him... Remember, things aren’t always as they seem at first. Just stick by him, okay?”

Amina furrowed her brows slightly at the statement but nodded with a smile before shutting the door slowly.

They approached the elevator, heading to the first floor to exit the hospital. As they passed the Pharmacy counter, Amina noticed Keisha again, though she couldn’t see what she was buying.

Keisha glanced over and waved at Rocco, but Amina didn’t dwell on it—her focus was on spending the rest of the evening with him.

Back at the truck, Rocco let out a deep sigh as Amina fastened her seatbelt. He glanced at her, his expression a mix of frustration and sincerity.

“I’m sorry we had to cut our night short. I had so much to tell you.”

Amina turned toward him, offering a reassuring smile. “You don’t need to apologize, babe. None of this is your fault.

I’m grateful you’re the kind of man who arranges to care for his mom, and I’m happy I could be here to support you,” she encouraged him.

Rocco scoffed softly, a smile tugging at his lips, before leaning in to place a tender kiss on hers.

"Okay, my queen supporter," he said with a playful grin. "How about we swing by my mom's place, help me pack a small bag, grab her purse, and then I'll take you home?"

Amina giggled, nodding. "I said I support you, so I'll be more than happy to help.

Let's go," she replied as he started the truck and headed toward his mom's house.

During the drive, they discussed their plan for the remaining weekend: He would pack his mom's things tonight. The following day, he would pick Amina up to visit his mom at the hospital before they head to church services.

A light drizzle began as Rocco and Amina approached his mom's house. He parked his truck in the front, making it easier for them to run in, pack the items, and then take Amina home for the night.

Before they got out, they sat there momentarily, watching the tiny droplets hit the windshield. The streetlight ahead flickered, threatening to go out. Despite the distant sound of gunshots and the shabby appearance of the neighborhood's homes, they found comfort in each other's presence.

With Rocco by her side, Amina felt unafraid and unbothered by her surroundings. At this moment, a rush of overwhelming emotion surged through their bodies simultaneously—the same love they had felt for each other years ago, but this time, it felt stronger.

Neither of them wanted the night to be over so soon.

Rocco adjusted his seat slightly and gestured for her to sit on his lap. Without hesitation, Amina complied, stretching her legs over the cupholder console in the middle of the truck.

Their eyes met affectionately as she wrapped her arms around his neck, settling in with him. Their lips met in a passionate kiss, the warmth of their tongues softly joining. Their heartbeats and breath quickened with the desire to reconnect.

After a minute, they parted from the kiss, and Rocco gently caressed her face, his gaze filled with deep openness. "I love you," he whispered affectionately.

"I love you more," she playfully replied.

"Impossible," Rocco responded with certainty, giving her another quick kiss before suggesting they get started before the rain worsened.

As he approached her side, Amina was already stepping out of the truck when a familiar voice called out.

"Hey, Rocco, you need to come get..."

Amina turned toward the sound, spotting the young woman just as she was about to speak.

Without hesitation, she moved toward the dimly lit porch, interrupting the woman's request.

"Roc, what is this?!" Amina shouted, moving back towards him and pushing him in the chest.

Jowanda's eyes widened, and she quickly fled back into the house when she recognized Amina. The rain began to pour harder as Rocco tried to calm Amina down by holding her arms. She yanked them away, visibly upset.

"Mina, just wait a minute, please!"

Tears streamed down her face as she stormed down the pavement, the shock of the situation overwhelming her. It felt like a nightmare unfolding in real time.

Rocco rushed after her, trying to stop her from walking further, especially at this late hour in the rain.

"Amina, will you listen to me, please?" he pleaded, but she didn't stop. "At least get back in the truck so I can take you home." He hoped to explain what had just happened during the drive.

"No!" she screamed, suddenly turning around to slap him across the face. She then began to fight him.

And Rocco did his best to dodge her swings, backing away as she lashed out.

As the rain lightened, neighbors' porch lights flicked on, and doors creaked open as a few onlookers peered out to witness the commotion.

Rocco wrestled with Amina, trying to gently grab hold of her without causing further harm. She kicked and screamed in his arms, but he managed to lift her and guide her back to the truck, carefully placing her in the passenger seat.

Despite his efforts, she continued kicking him, her cry of pain echoing in the air as her tears flowed freely. Rocco kept his hands in front of him, shielding himself from her force.

Amina suddenly stopped kicking, her breath coming in heavy gasps. She turned her face forward, attempting to regain control, but her body trembled with the weight of her emotions.

She rocked back and forth, her hands covering her face, before finally looking at him with cold, bitter eyes.

"You got Jowanda at your house?! I hate you! Don't ever touch me again! I'll never trust you! You are a liar!"

Rocco's heart shattered at her words.

"Baby, please, stop! She's not here for me... Just listen!" he begged, desperation in his voice.

"Get away from me, Roccorio!" Amina screamed.

"I'll get myself home!" With a forceful motion, she slammed his truck door shut, leaving him helpless. She pulled out her cell phone and dialed quickly.

Rocco stepped onto the front porch to escape the rain. He sat on an old wooden crate, his gaze fixed on her, waiting until her ride came. The pain of her words still stung as he tried to steady his emotions.

"Brook, could you please come pick me up?" Amina's frantic voice broke through the phone. She was full-on crying.

"I'm alright, but I can't talk right now. Just come get me, please!"

Brooklyn didn't hesitate. She knew something was terribly wrong, so she didn't ask any more questions.

"Okay, sweetie. I'm on my way. Stay on the phone with me until I get there," she reassured Amina, her voice steady.

Twenty minutes later, Brooklyn arrived, parking behind Rocco's truck. Amina stepped out, her eyes red from crying.

She glanced at Rocco on the porch before sliding into Brooklyn's car. Without a word, they drove off, leaving Rocco behind in the rain-soaked night.

He inhaled deeply, then exhaled slowly, a single tear escaping down his cheek as he listened to the sound of Brooklyn's car fading into the distance.

After sitting still for a few more minutes, Rocco finally gathered himself. He stood up, walked inside, and began packing his mom's belongings. He grabbed her purse and carried everything out to his truck. As he walked back through the house, he kicked aside dirty clothes, beer cans, and scattered dishes. The place was a mess—crowded and filthy.

Rocco went to the family room, which was cluttered with junk. His little brother was slouched on the couch, smoking weed and watching television, Cray's rap music blasting in the background as he got high.

Jowanda was lying across the loveseat, her two-year-old son sleeping beside her, covered only in a diaper.

The ceiling fan spun on high, the air thick and sluggish. Rocco couldn't help but feel disgusted by the scene.

"You need to step up and be a better mother to your son," Rocco said sharply, gesturing toward his nephew. "And put a shirt on him!"

Jowanda smacked her lips in irritation and reached for a shirt from the soiled nightstand, dressing her son.

"Man, you better mind your business... talking to my wife like that!" Rocco's little brother, Cray, interjected, standing with a beer in his hand.

Without hesitation, Rocco knocked the beer out of Cray's hand, watching as it splattered across the wall. He shoved Cray back onto the couch, the frustration from his earlier confrontation with Amina still fresh.

You got one more time to talk to me like that. You'll be picking yourself up off the floor next time," Rocco warned, glaring at his brother with a scowl.

Turning his attention back to Jowanda, Rocco's expression softened, but his disappointment was evident.

"You should want more for yourself and your son by now. You've been with my brother for four years and married for two, yet this is all he has to show you as a family...

You okay with that?" he asked, his words carrying weight before he turned and walked toward the back door.

Jowanda hung her head in shame, gently rocking her son.

"Man, go on with that noise. This is *my* family!" Cray mumbled dismissively, his voice slurring from the alcohol, just as Rocco closed the back door behind him.

Rocco went to the guest house at the back of the property. It had once been a rundown shed far from the main house, but Rocco had renovated it over time, turning it into a small, comfortable living space. His current goal is to keep working hard so that he and his mom can one day leave the chaos of the main house behind and move to a better place.

Urban Coffee

Meanwhile, Keisha remained parked in the hospital lot, the rain pouring relentlessly. After gathering her courage, she dialed Heather's number, asking if she could visit, though she wasn't entirely sure if she wanted to go.

Once she got directions, she arrived 15 minutes later at Heather and Miss Kizzy's two-bedroom duplex. Then it hit her: Heather lived just five blocks from her apartment.

Nevertheless, after parking, Keisha called again to let Heather know she had arrived.

"Okay, girl... I'm coming out now," Heather confirmed as she answered the call. She grabbed the nearest jacket, throwing it over her short, pixie hairstyle.

But when Heather reached for the car door, she found it locked. Keisha quickly unlocked it, letting her inside.

"Girl! I already didn't want to come out in this weather, and you got the door locked?" she said, reasonably annoyed. Heather removed her jacket and glanced at Keisha.

She noticed a subtle hesitation in her response, an uncomfortable mood hanging in the air. Heather's worry began to grow.

Upon closer inspection, Heather noticed Keisha's red eyes and her leg shaking as if she were on edge.

"Are you okay? What happened?" Heather asked, furrowing her brows with genuine concern.

"He just broke up with me," Keisha muttered, her expression quickly shifting to anger. "He had the nerve to come to my house—after he cheated on me and broke up with me!" she exclaimed, punching her clenched fist into her hand at each statement.

Heather remained silent. As Brayden was one of her best friends, she wasn't sure how Keisha expected her to react. She didn't want to make things worse, so she decided to fake the support for the moment.

"Tell me what happened, girl," she prompted softly.

Keisha wiped her eyes with both hands, took a deep breath, and recounted the scene that had unfolded earlier.

"So, Brayden calls me and says he's just leaving Brooklyn's house and heading my way..." She paused, her anger still simmering. Heather stayed quiet and waited for her to continue.

"Despite my anger when he mentioned leaving her house, I felt the need to get myself together before he showed up," Keisha continued. "I rushed to shower, put on lotion, and brushed my hair... Just as I finished, the doorbell rang."

Keisha chuckled, clapping her hands and shaking her head at the memory. "Girl, I answered the door butt-naked." She was clearly amused by the shock she'd caused him by doing that.

Heather held back a laugh, her eyes twinkling at the situation's absurdity. But she kept her expression neutral, not wanting to make Keisha uncomfortable.

"Girl, it's not funny," Keisha said with a chuckle, noticing Heather trying to hold back her laughter.

"Nah, nah... I'm not laughing. Go on with your story," Heather replied politely, though she couldn't hide her grin.

“Anyway, to cut it short... Brayden and I are no longer together. He feels he needs to be alone because he never fully healed from his breakup with Brooklyn. Then he started apologizing for involving me in something still broken,” she explained further, her voice trembling with emotion.

Heather felt torn, unsure of what to say. Brayden and Malik were her best friends, and she was still trying to rebuild her relationship with them after being away for so long.

“Keisha, maybe this is a blessing in disguise. At least he’s being upfront with you...

Many guys would have just sent a text or ghosted you. Honestly, it was clear he wasn’t ready to commit to something new so soon after Brooklyn,” Heather added, trying to keep her tone calm.

“What do you mean it was clear? You told me you’ve been gone for a few years, so what do you know?!” Keisha snapped, her eyebrows raised, but there was a glimmer of interest.

“Yes, I was gone for those years, and we texted for a while until I stopped. But I’ve known them since I was seven. I left when I was 19. That’s twelve years of friendship. Seventeen if you count the break when there was eventually no contact.

Our parents knew each other even longer,” Heather explained, a slight pride in her voice as she spoke, and her eyes sharpening with a hint of sarcasm.

“Whatever,” Keisha responded dismissively, brushing off Heather’s explanation as she searched for more clarity.

“So, what makes you say it was clear?” she asked.

Heather hesitated for a moment before continuing. “Okay, I’m going to ask you some personal questions. Are you okay with that?”

Keisha gave her a look—one that said, *Spit it out! I'm a grown woman. Ask whatever you want.*

"Alright," Heather began carefully, "How many times have you two been intimate?"

"Twice. So what?" Keisha replied, her voice a mixture of smugness and embarrassment.

"And how long have you been seeing each other?"

"We've been kicking it for about six months. What's your point?"

"Has he performed oral on you?" Heather's eyebrows raised, almost as if she already knew the answer.

"No," Keisha reacted defensively. "But that's not a big deal. As long as he's satisfied with what I offer, I'm good."

At that, Heather's stomach turned. Keisha's confident response felt like a red flag, confirming she was only a temporary placeholder in Brayden's life, never meant to be a permanent fixture.

"What about gifts, trips, or introducing you as his girlfriend to anybody?" Heather had fired off the last of her questions, folding her arms, knowing the truth.

Instantly, Keisha screamed for her to stop, the realization emerging on her all at once—her relationship with Brayden had always been a facade. Despite her hope for something real, she understood now that Brayden had been using her to numb the pain of his breakup with someone he truly loved.

Deep down, Keisha knew the truth all along but was willing to tolerate it. She was committed to waiting for Brayden to eventually reciprocate her feelings, no matter how long it took.

"None of this matters to me!" Keisha shouted, her voice trembling with emotion as she neared tears. "I love Brayden! And I'm not giving up on him!"

Heather's eyes widened in shock, unsure of how to respond. She watched helplessly as Keisha rummaged through a white plastic bag and pulled out a small box. She gasped when she realized what it was. "Girl, you pregnant?" Heather asked in disbelief, her voice barely above a whisper.

Keisha smiled faintly, then asked, "Can I use your bathroom?"

They hurried into the house from the rain.

Keisha headed straight for the bathroom.

After a short while, Heather could hear her sniffling and faint sobs through the door over the next fifteen minutes.

"Keisha, are you okay?" Heather softly called, knocking gently on the bathroom door.

There was a brief pause before Keisha opened the door. Her eyes were bloodshot from crying, and her posture seemed defeated. Heather waited, expecting her to say something about the test results, but instead, Keisha stood there, folding her arms, her gaze locked on the floor.

Suddenly, Keisha's body seemed to give way, and she collapsed to her knees, sobbing uncontrollably. Heather immediately knelt beside her, wrapping her arms around Keisha in a comforting embrace.

"It's going to be alright," Heather whispered, her voice gentle but firm as she tried to offer some reassurance amid Keisha's grief.

After a long moment, Keisha slowly wiped the tears from her face, gathering herself enough to stand up. She still held the pregnancy test box tightly in her hand.

Without saying a word, she walked to the door.

"Thank you for letting me use your bathroom," she said quietly, her voice barely above a whisper. "I'm going home to get some rest. Goodnight."

She turned and walked out the door, quickly making her way to her car, leaving Heather in the doorway, her heart heavy with concern.

"So, is she pregnant or not?" Heather thought to herself, shaking her head. *"She couldn't be bursting into tears like that."* Confusion and worry swirled in her mind as she locked the front door and headed to her bedroom for the night. She decided she would call Brayden in the morning to fill him in and to come clean about giving Keisha the address to Malik's parents' house—she just needed to process what had happened first.

Urban Coffee

"Good morning, babygirl," Malik gently woke Mazo at 9 a.m., his voice soft as he disturbed her for church services.

He'd been up since six, busy finalizing his upcoming business commitments to Paris for Monday morning.

He was sipping his coffee when Mazo finally moved, and he quickly began preparing one of her favorite breakfast meals: oatmeal with sausage, freshly squeezed orange juice, and mango chunks.

Mazo stretched, letting out a sleepy yawn as she went to the restroom to brush her teeth and wash her face—part of their usual morning routine when she was with Dad.

She entered the kitchen, and Malik helped her climb onto the barstool at the butcher block island. "Good morning, Daddy," Mazo said, sipping her juice before diving into her oatmeal.

"Good morning, baby," he responded, sitting beside her. "Eat all your oatmeal so we can get dressed, okay?"

Mazo nodded eagerly and continued eating. They chatted and enjoyed their quiet morning together before getting dressed and leaving the condo.

Urban Coffee

It was a beautiful Sunday morning, with birds chirping and the sun shining brightly, casting just the right amount of warmth on the skin. Church services were set to begin at 11 a.m., and the parking lot was quickly filling up with cars. Churchgoers exchanged warm smiles and firm handshakes, eager to greet one another.

Mazo's excited shout broke through the morning calm as she spotted her grandparents walking across the parking lot. "Grandma and Papa here!" she pointed out, her voice filled with joy as Malik parked the car.

Brayden parked next to Malik's and stepped out, with little Nate eagerly jumping from his grandparents' car to rush over and grab his father's hand. Together, the family walked toward the church entrance.

Inside, the service began with the deacon standing before the congregation. *"First, we want to give honor to the Almighty God, the creator of all things, for bringing us here today. A day to be glad and grateful for the fellowship we share. A day He has blessed us with His grace and mercy, granting us life, health, and strength. Let us all give God the glory!"* He clapped his hands, joining in the praise that filled the room.

"Before we get to the main part of the service today, hearing the Word of God from our teacher and guide, Pastor Cobb, let us first be blessed by a selection from our choir," the deacon announced.

Amina arrived with Brooklyn just before the choir started singing *"Second Chance"* by Hezekiah Walker.

After the problematic experience at Rocco's house, Amina knew it was critical to be with a friend, but even more so, to find peace in the church.

"Lord, I need to feel the touch of your hands.
Your will for my life I want to understand.
Lord, forgive me like only you can.
For you're the God of a second chance."

As the choir's voices filled the space, Amina felt the lyrics resonate deeply with her. The song moved her, and tears began to fall as she reflected on her past and future.

Sensing her friend's emotional vulnerability, Brooklyn embraced her tightly, tears flowing freely.

Shortly after, Amina's eyes widened as she spotted Rocco walking down the aisle toward the front. Not far behind him was his little brother, Cray, reaching for Jowanda's hand as she carried their son on her hip. Amina sat up straight, her gaze flicking briefly to Brooklyn before returning to Rocco, who sat on one side of the aisle next to Brayden and Malik. Cray settled with his family on the opposite side. Both Amina and Brooklyn exchanged puzzled looks at what they were witnessing.

Amina lowered her head, feeling like a heavy weight had developed in her chest. A mix of relief and guilt churned in her stomach. She buried her face in her hands, tears flowing generously. The overwhelming emotions caught her off guard, but she felt the release was necessary—too much was swirling inside her, and she had to let it out.

The choir concluded their uplifting spiritual song, prompting the congregation to rise to their feet and applaud in praise and glory to God.

After the usual service proceedings—testimonies, the church offering, and announcements—the highlight of the service was Pastor Cobb's delivery of the Word of God.

His heartfelt teachings resonated deeply with the congregation for the next hour and a half, confirming their faith through the scriptures.

As the service neared its conclusion, Pastor Cobb shared his final words before the benediction.

"Okay, dear hearts, in closing, remember that our true purpose in this life is to serve and worship God. Make up your mind today about whom you will serve—God or Satan. When choosing the Creator, strive to cultivate a sincere and personal relationship with Him. What does that mean, church?" Pastor Cobb asked, his voice steady as he watched the congregation hang on to every word. *"It means to begin working on 'self.' Start changing those habits and behaviors that are not aligned with God's will...*

All it takes is a made-up mind, and once your mind is set, it will resonate in your heart. Then, humble yourself and pray—seek God and turn from your wicked ways."

Many stood up, clapping and shouting, "Amen!"

"It won't happen overnight, dear hearts," the pastor continued, *"and God doesn't expect it to.*

Take your time. Focus on one unrighteous habit at a time and move on to the next," Pastor Cobb said.

"Tomorrow is not promised to any of us. So, repent of your sins daily—pray and ask God for guidance."

Pastor Cobb concluded with a brief, prayerful benediction and directed everyone to fellowship as he dismissed them from the service, marking the end of a blessed day.

After the benediction, some attendees headed outside, either chatting amongst themselves or leaving in their cars, while the majority remained inside to shake hands with the pastor before departing. Malik and Brayden were among the first to do so. Afterward, they joined others outside, waiting for additional family members and friends to exit.

Brooklyn and Amina finally exited the church and stood on the porch. In the parking lot, they spotted Malik, Brayden, Rocco, and a few other guys gathered together, chatting.

Shortly after, Jowanda hurried out of the building with her son on her hip. She passed by Amina, making it clear she wasn't interested in interacting, likely due to their history and the dramatic episode of the previous night.

Her son wiggled free from her hold, running toward his Uncle Rocco, who scooped him up, spinning him around in the air. "Wooo!" the little voice yelled, making the men laugh.

"C'mon, *lil'* boy, let's get you buckled in so we can go," Jowanda called out, smiling as she watched them. Her hand rested on her hip as she observed their playful interaction.

Rocco gently set the boy down and told him to go back to his mama, which he did obediently.

Suddenly, Cray appeared beside Amina. "Hey, Sis."

Amina jumped, startled by the unexpected voice.

"Cray, you scared me! Hey!" she exclaimed, giving him a one-armed side hug.

Brooklyn smiled and waved, recognizing Cray but not being as familiar with him as she was with Rocco.

"Cray, what's up with you and Jowanda?" Amina asked, wasting no time.

Seeing them together at the church this morning had already shocked her, and now, witnessing Rocco playing with the little boy only added to her confusion. Her mind raced as she tried to make sense of it all.

"Yeah, that's my wife and our son, Uno," he replied casually.

"Wife?!" Brooklyn and Amina exclaimed simultaneously, their eyes wide with surprise. Cray chuckled, leaning back slightly at their reaction.

With a smile, Brooklyn excused herself, leaving Amina with Cray as she went to join Brayden, Malik, and Rocco, greeting them warmly with hugs.

"How long have y'all been together?" Amina asked, still processing the information.

"Your boyfriend didn't tell you?" Cray said with a grin. "We were kicking it strong for about a year before marriage...

Uno came along almost a year after that—now he's two, so it's been about four years or so." He glanced briefly over at Amina, watching her digest the news.

She gulped, trying to wrap her head around it all. Learning this information weighed heavily on her. She realized Rocco was innocent all along, but she hadn't given him the chance to explain it last night. She glanced at the parking lot and noticed Rocco watching her and Cray talking. She quickly tried to look away, regretting the moment their eyes met. His expression was unreadable, which worried her. She felt uncertain about how to start over with him or how to offer an apology.

As Jowanda maneuvered the car out of the parking space, Cray took it as his cue to wrap up the conversation.

"Alright, sis, I gotta bounce... Need a quick smoke," Cray said, giving Amina a brief side-arm hug, which she reciprocated.

"Already talking about smoking right after church. Shame on you."

Cray scoffed and threw up the peace sign. "Pray for me, man; I need it, seriously," he said before getting into the car.

"Alright, bro, y'all be good! Cray shouted to Rocco and the group, extending his hand out the window as they drove off. Rocco and the others waved goodbye.

Amina made her way over to the group, greeting everyone with a hug, except Rocco. He kept his hands firmly in his pockets, hoping she'd pick up on his signal to stay away. And she did. It felt like a punch to the chest. No matter the circumstances, she never imagined he would react like that.

After Brayden and Malik's parents hugged their sons and grandkids, they soon went home.

"Bye, Grandma!" Mazo shouted to her grandmother as Malik picked her up to head to the car, while Brayden grabbed Nate's hand.

"So, where are we going to eat?" Malik asked the group. It was their usual Sunday post-church tradition. They enjoyed eating out and spending time with the kids to wrap up the day.

"Hey, I'll talk to you tomorrow, man. And for you, have a successful and safe trip—I need both my mentor-bosses intact," Rocco said to Brayden and then Malik, shaking their hands. "I'm headed back to the hospital to check on my mom," he added.

Malik and Brayden shook Rocco's hand and hugged briefly, wishing his mom well.

"Keep us posted, Roc. Like we said, if you need anything, let us know," Malik reminded sincerely with a smile. Rocco nodded and headed to his car.

Amina was utterly baffled. She had no idea that Rocco was so closely connected to each of her best friends' children's fathers. What other details had she missed out on last night before she blew up at him in front of his house? She suddenly realized she might have made the biggest mistake by assuming that Rocco could never change.

After he had taken a few steps away, Amina hurried after him, positioning herself in front of him to stop his progress.

"Rocco, wait. Can we talk, please?"

"What do you want? I've got somewhere to be."

"Okay, I can go with you. I'd love to see your mom, too. We can talk on the way."

Rocco lowered his head and sighed deeply.

"Look, it's fine if you want to visit my mom. She'd love that. But I don't want you riding with me."

Amina gasped, taken aback by his cold response. It was so different from anything she had ever experienced from him.

"Roc, just give me a chance to explain—give us a chance, please," she implored.

"What's changed in the last twelve hours? Huh?

Is it that you gave my brother a chance to speak for me—to explain—and you listened?

Or was it seeing people like Brayden and Malik giving me a chance, like I'm someone they respect, unlike you?"

Amina stood speechless, her heart racing, tears growing inside her. Seeing the shift in her expression, Rocco's heart softened—he couldn't bring himself to face the pain in her eyes. He looked away slightly, his voice quiet but final.

"You know... I've worked so hard to get to where I am mentally. It took a great deal of willpower and a lot of prayer. I've come a long way...

You told me last night that you forgave me, but you haven't. You don't trust me, and I can't fault you for that—just like I can't expect you to resolve issues at the same time it took me.

We're all different, and I know you have to do the work for yourself. If not, you'll carry that baggage into your next relationship."

Amina froze; her breath caught in her chest. His words stung, making it sound like he had completely abandoned her and their relationship. She was left speechless.

"Roccorio, what are you saying? What do you mean, my next relationship...?"

"Amina, please," he interrupted, raising his hand to stop her. He needed to get more out. After a deep sigh, filled with sadness and frustration, he continued:

"Without trust, we have nothing—no solid basis to build on. So, I should step back and let you do the work for yourself, not for me. I truly wish you well..."

"Roc?" she whispered, barely able to get the words out, her voice trembling in shock.

"I'm sorry, baby. I gotta go," he said softly, his tone final, as he turned and walked away.

"Rocco!" Amina cried out... "Roc, wait! Wait!"

Brayden stepped in before she could follow him, gently pulling her into an embrace. "Shh..." he murmured as she clung to him, her head resting on his chest, tears pouring.

Malik and Brayden, well aware of the dynamics as Rocco's mentors, understood the weight of the situation.

After securing Mazo in her car seat, Malik felt a deep sense of empathy for both Rocco and Amina. He pulled out his phone and dialed his dad, seeking comfort and guidance for everyone involved, including himself.

After a moment, he called out from the car window, his voice steady despite the weight of the situation.

"Everyone, meet me at my parents' house in an hour for Family Funday." After relaying the message and everyone agreeing, he finished the call with his dad.

"Okay, Dad, I'll be there shortly. Everyone else will meet up in an hour. Thanks so much—and tell Mom the same."

"No problem, son. I'll get the steaks and chicken ready for the grill, and we'll have red potatoes, tossed salad, lemonade, and those *Poppi* sodas you and your sister like. You'll all have a well-balanced meal," Mr. Nelson replied warmly.

Malik chuckled, grateful to be reminded how much he had inherited his dad's love for cooking, especially for others.

CHAPTER 11

Life goes on

Everyone had arrived at the Nelsons' home for Family Funday. They gathered around the beautiful, long, rustic picnic table on the backyard patio, which exuded a clean, intimate vibe. Two hanging fans above provided a cool breeze, while the electric bug lamps posted around the area protected everyone from flying, biting critters and added to the cookout ambiance. See-through plastic cups with tops, napkins, straws, forks, and spoons were strategically placed at the end of the table, with a large cooler of ice sitting beside it on the floor.

"I appreciate how much Mr. Nelson enjoys cooking and how Mama Bria, along with him, makes people feel at home," Heather said as she stepped through the patio door from inside.

Malik stood up, reaching for the platter of wings his mom was carrying right as Heather walked out.

"What's up, man? Where'd you come from?" Malik asked as he placed the platter on the table, then dapping Heather.

"I texted Brayden to see what everybody was doing today. He told me y'all were here after scolding me for not attending church."

"And he should have because you told me you'd be there," Ms. Bria said with a smile.

"I know, Mama, but I overslept."

Ms. Bria looked at her with pursed lips. "Girl, sit your little narrow butt down and eat. How's your mama?"

Malik shook his head, chuckling at his mom's reaction.

"She's doing okay. She had to work today and told me to tell you guys, "Hi."

Mr. Nelson placed a platter of steaks and sausages on the picnic table next to the pitcher of lemonade, ensuring all the food was accounted for. The tossed salad, which Brayden brought out just in time, was the final addition. With everything ready, everyone sat down, chatting and enjoying the meal.

Not even ten minutes later, loud talking could be heard approaching the kitchen patio door. Out came Melanie, Malik's older sister. "No, don't come here. I'll talk to you later, Luke... Uh-uhn! It's only been two weeks... boy, bye!"

Everyone went quiet, listening to her conversation, which was clearly with her husband. She lived just ten minutes away from her parents and had been over more often than usual since kicking her husband out for allegedly cheating.

Melanie immediately scanned the patio and then broke out in a big smile. "Hey, everybody!" she greeted, sitting next to Amina, who had been quiet since the church parking lot scene with Rocco. Malik shook his head as the group greeted Melanie in unison, and the chatter and laughter resumed.

****

About two hours later, everyone was full and content, pitching in to help clean up the patio and kitchen area. Malik stepped away to the side patio to give Zora a heads-up.

"Hello?" she answered on the first ring.

"Hey, how are you? I just wanted to let you know I'll bring babygirl to you shortly."

"I'm good. I'll be here—not going anywhere," she replied.

Malik scoffed softly at her comment, considering elaborating, but decided against it to maintain peace.

"We missed you today—see ya soon," he offered instead, then concluded the call after Zora said, *Okay*.

Zora held the phone until she heard the soft click of the call ending. Little did he know that tears had welled in her eyes just from hearing his voice. She purposely composed herself before he could notice.

As soon as Malik finished the call, he saw his brother-in-law, Lucas, heading toward the backyard.

"Big Luke!" Malik called out, greeting him with a dap and a brotherly hug.

Lucas kissed Mama Bria on the cheek and embraced everyone he knew. Melanie stood with her arms crossed, waiting for him to reach her.

"Lucas, I told you not to come here. We can talk later," she said, frustration clear in her voice.

"Later is now, baby. This is ridiculous!" he shot back, then turned to her parents. "Ma? Pop? I didn't do anything wrong—at least not intentionally," he added, his hands raised in exasperation.

"Don't talk to them! They have nothing to do with this!" Melanie snapped.

The group watched quietly, with Malik and Brayden standing to the side, shaking their heads and chatting.

Standing 6 feet 4 inches tall, Lucas walked up to Melanie, locking eyes with her. "Mel, you're wrong for this," he said softly. "I'm coming home tonight, whether it's the last time or forever. You choose."

With that, he turned and walked away, waving to the group as he exited the backyard. Melanie sighed deeply, lowering her head, conflicted about whether she had taken things too far. She didn't know whether to feel angry or... something else.

"Girl, if you don't go after that man, you may regret it," Ms. Bria scolded...

"Time to stop playing games—you're a married woman with a man who loves you. Your only evidence is seeing a girl in his truck, but you didn't even give him a chance to explain what happened. That's immaturity!"

Melanie let out a frustrated sigh, slightly rolling her eyes. "Okay, Ma, you're doing too much."

"And you're not doing enough to keep your marriage intact!" Ms. Bria shot back.

Amina stood quietly, taking it all in. She couldn't believe the scene unfolding before her—this was a mirror of her situation with Rocco. She, too, had assumed the worst without giving him the chance to explain.

Mr. Nelson walked over to his daughter, wrapping her in a gentle embrace. She leaned her head against his chest, taking a deep breath before releasing a long exhale.

"Baby, listen to your mama," he said softly. "Have you given Lucas the chance to clarify, or did you just assume what you saw was the truth?"

Melanie listened, contemplating his words. She couldn't deny that she was touched by her husband's determination to reconcile, as he had shown up. It showed genuine regret for his actions. But she wanted to make him sweat for a few more days, releasing him from guilt on her terms. She also knew her parents were right.

"Okay, Daddy, I'll speak with him today," she said with a humble nod.

Mr. Nelson kissed Melanie on the forehead, then said goodnight to everyone else before heading inside to relax for the rest of the evening.

Melanie followed suit, hugging everyone before walking to her car, ready to call her husband. "Y'all be good!" she yelled.

"You be good to Luke and let that man come home!" Brayden yelled.

"I'll see. Luke wants some of this 'get-right,' that's all!" Melanie replied with a smirk.

"Man! Don't nobody wanna hear all that!" Malik shouted, his face scrunched up. The entire group burst into laughter, including their mom.

Melanie turned back, sticking her tongue out at her brother, then laughed.

Urban Coffee

When Melanie reached her house, she saw Lucas sitting on the porch swing, swaying patiently.

He was headed back to his grandparents' house, where he'd been staying for almost two weeks after being kicked out.

But something in his wife's eyes and posture led him straight home instead, and his feelings were right.

"I just called you—don't be ignoring my call," Melanie said, stepping onto the porch, waiting for Lucas to respond.

"I knew you were coming. Are you *gonna* open the door or what?" He responded calmly.

"You've had a key the whole time; you could've opened it. It's right there in your hand," she replied, nodding toward the keys.

"Nope. I need *you* to let me in and tell me I can stay since *you* kicked me out for nothing."

"Just because I open it, Luke, it doesn't mean you're staying," she said after unlocking the door.

Lucas followed behind her, threw his keys on the living room table, and sat at the far end of the sectional sofa without uttering a word.

Melanie stood a few feet behind the sofa, her mouth turning up in confusion at his silence.

Lucas adjusted comfortably, leaning to the side with his elbow resting on the sofa's arm, his unwavering gaze fixed on her.

"What? Why are you looking at me like that? Say what you have to say, then leave."

He scoffed, shaking his head. Not wanting to waste more time, Lucas stood up and walked toward her. "Why are you playing games? Tell me to stay, or I'll get my keys and leave. And when I walk out this door this time, no more random calls for quickies to send me back to my grandparents' house. You won't see me for a month or two. I promise you that!" he declared, stepping closer to her—so close she could smell the cinnamon remnants of his breath...

"You know I didn't do anything with that woman," he continued, his voice firm. "She pulled up while I was pumping gas, went to the passenger side of my truck, and hopped in. I got in and told her to get out when I was done. But she wouldn't budge—just laughed, acting stupid... And yeah, I could've gone to her side and made her get out. I know it looked terrible, suspicious even.... But that was before you came out of nowhere, going crazy on me!" Lucas finally explained.

This time, Melanie let him finish the story, unlike at the gas station. Hearing it all now, she felt more at ease deep down. It sounded genuine. Though he could've handled things better, Melanie believed him.

But she wasn't ready to let him off the hook just yet. She stayed silent, arms folded, watching him. Lucas tilted his head in frustration, eyes fixed on her.

"I'm *gonna* make a believer out of you today," he said, his voice laced with frustration. He turned to retrieve his keys from the table.

Melanie, however, thought, *'Not today!* She jumped over the couch in her cute sundress in a flash, snatching the keys before he could reach them. With a swift motion, she climbed back over it, standing there with her arms folded, the keys balled up tightly in her hand.

"Mel, give me my keys," he said, his voice steady but frustrated as he walked toward her with his hand extended.

"No!" she retorted firmly. "We're not done talking."

She quickly pulled her arms away as he reached for the keys and turned her back to him.

He moved closer, wrapping his arms around her waist. A smile tugged at her lips, though she tried to hide it. He knew his wife so well that he sensed the tension had passed, but he still played along with her game.

"For the last time," he murmured in her ear, his breath warm against her skin. "Give me my keys." He kissed her neck, and her breath quickened.

"No..." she breathed out, her pulse quickening, anticipating what would come next. She was ready, but Lucas needed to hear the words from her, because, after everything, he'd been punished for something he hadn't done. He deserved at least that from her.

Lucas slowly withdrew one of his hands from her waist, replacing it around her neck, pulling her back against him with a gentle but firm touch.

"Tell me you want me home," he whispered, his lips brushing her ear as he nipped it lightly.

Melanie couldn't help but set aside her stubbornness, finally saying the words her husband needed to hear. She turned to face him, wrapping her arms around his neck.

"I want you back at home, baby. I'm sorry for being so dramatic."

Lucas was profoundly pleased to hear his wife say those words. He hadn't expected the apology, but hearing it now meant the world to him.

He kissed her lips softly, then pulled back to look at her, his gaze steady and sincere. "Don't ever do that again. I love you, and I fight to stay faithful and make you happy every day. It kills me when you doubt how much I love you."

Melanie was deeply touched by her husband's words. A rush of regret came over her, and she silently vowed to make it up to him in every way she could. The time she'd spent kicking him out would be repaid with double the love and devotion.

Later, they made love and held each other close. The day passed like it usually did—full of love, laughter, and warmth.

Melanie had missed him terribly. She silently repented to God, acknowledging that she had mishandled her marriage and taken it for granted. Eventually, she called her mom to let her know they were okay.

Urban Coffee

Back at the Nelsons, everyone was preparing to go their separate ways, as Monday marked the reset button for the week for most.

As the evening drew to a close, small talk about relationships, loyalty, marriage, and more filled the backyard.

"I don't understand how I'm surrounded by so many good men, and the women in their lives give them so much H-E-double hockey sticks! And I'm struggling to find a good one!" Heather blurted out, causing everyone to burst into laughter.

"This is what I was talking to my son about yesterday," Mr. Nelson said as he returned outside, hearing the chatter and laughter... "So many people put the cart before the horse, and then the whirlwind comes. Brianna didn't dare let me do that to her life," he added, placing his arms around his wife.

Malik looked at his mom, smiling proudly, as he was familiar with their story.

"Mama Bria, you gave Pops a hard time?" Heather asked.

"No, baby, I was trying to keep him from giving me one," she shot back, causing another round of laughter...

"Don't get me wrong, it was tough because look at him—such a handsome and affectionate man," she shared...

I was determined not to mess up so badly that I'd regret it. We had already made a spiritual and emotional connection on our wedding day. But our wedding night was meant for a more mental and physical connection, not before then. Y'all know what I mean... I'm trying not to make my son feel too awkward... his eyes piercing through me!" she chuckled. Everyone laughed.

Malik scoffed, lowering his head. "Thank you, ma," he said lovingly.

"You're welcome, baby," his mom replied, smiling.

"You guys didn't go on dates alone? Brooklyn asked. "How can two people who are attracted to each other get to know one another without spending time dating?"

Mr. Nelson gladly offered his perspective, sharing advice from experience before everyone went their separate ways.

"You get to know each other like you get to know your best girlfriends or guy-friends...

You hang out—preferably in groups—talk, debate, ask questions, and have some memorable fun," he explained.

"Why as a group, though? And is it too late if you've already been intimate?" Amina asked curiously, listening.

"Well, as long as you're living, it's never too late for change or to make things right," Mr. Nelson reassured them.

"And if you bring one or more people along, especially if you've been intimate before, you're less likely to end up at a hotel or your house alone...

"That's if you're truly trying to change the narrative from what society considers the norm—doing what's expected instead of trusting what's right for you and your person," Mr. Nelson said with a shrug.

Ms. Bria smiled at Malik and Brayden. "That's so true. If you don't have the mindset to do things the right way, God's way, you'll still end up in those hotels alone, even after a group date. The two of you have to want to do the right thing. That's the powerful connection and bond you're building. I'm a true witness."

"Mama Bria, why are you smiling at us like that?" Brayden asked, already knowing the answer as he continued to smile.

"You know why; don't play," she laughed.

Malik and Brayden had these talks long before Zora and Brooklyn came into the picture. Their moms had made a pact as best friends before they had children. The agreement was that if they had sons, they would instill the importance of putting God first, treating women with respect, and valuing marriage before starting a family.

"Joy and I were shocked, angry, and happy all at once when we heard y'all were pregnant," Ms. Bria said to Brooklyn, hugging her.

Brooklyn, laughing, buried her face in her hands, resting her head on Mama Bria's shoulder.

Then, out of nowhere, Brayden gently grabbed Brooklyn by the waist from behind, turning her to face him. His voice was steady and sincere.

"It's *gonna* be hard, but we're starting over."

Brooklyn's eyes widened in blissful shock. She stared at him for a few seconds, mouth slightly open, before pulling him into a tight hug, overwhelmed with joy. The sincerity in Brayden's eyes made everything feel right.

Everyone else looked equally stunned—their mouths were wide open, thinking, *'What just happened?'*

Brayden smiled and looked at the group, continuing to hold Brooklyn in his arms, his voice full of emotion.

"All y'all looking crazy, but when I tell you I prayed so much for this—like, for a sign or something! I didn't know how it would show up, but this moment here feels like the answer."

The yard erupted in applause and smiles, and the group always shared the hope that this moment would return for them. It was as if everyone's dream was to see them make it back, to make it right again. But no one was as hopeful as Brooklyn, who was utterly moved by Brayden's words.

She held him tightly, her voice barely above a whisper near his ear, "Thank you, Jesus! We're going to need you, Lord."

Brayden smiled, his arms tightening around her as he murmured, "Amen!"

Malik couldn't help but scoff and shake his head, a sense of happiness flooding him at the thought of his best friend. He had been Brayden's rock, listening to his frustrations and heartache during the tough breakup with Brooklyn.

Suddenly, Malik broke the moment, bursting out with the opening lines of *"Rise Up"* by Andra Day.

His voice was rich with emotion as Brayden and Brooklyn pulled away from their embrace. He dapped Brayden up before pulling him into a quick hug.

"You're broken down and tired...of living life on a merry-go-round..."

Laughter filled the air as everyone was caught off guard by Malik's impromptu performance, which felt perfect for the moment. They all enjoyed his soulful voice. Brayden, never one to miss an opportunity, jumped in with him, doubling the soulfulness.

"And you can't find the fighter...
But I see it in you, so we gonna walk it out...
move mountains... And I'll rise up..."

Although the mini-concert lasted only a minute, it lifted the spirits of everyone present. Once they finished laughing, Malik turned to Brooklyn and hugged her.

"You two are crazy," she chuckled, smiling at their spontaneous outburst.

Malik grinned. "Maybe I'll get a fresh start when I move down the Boulevard, or better yet, in Paris."

"Uh-uhn! Don't do my friend like that!" Brooklyn teased, tapping him on the shoulder as he turned to walk away.

"She left me—more than once—within a twenty-four-hour period. You were there," Malik shot back, grinning.

Brayden scoffed, chuckling at Malik's response. He knew his friend was talking for now, but he was hopeful things would turn in the right direction for him and Zora soon enough.

Malik's mom gave him a warm hug and then motioned for Mazo to follow her into the house, preparing to get her ready so that Malik could take her back home to her mom.

"Take it one day at a time, son," Mr. Nelson advised Malik, his voice steady and reassuring.

We're praying for you two," he added, nodding toward Brayden and Brooklyn before following his wife and Mazo into the house.

Malik smiled and turned to Heather. "I've got your first task," he said, pulling out his wallet and handing her $300.

Heather stepped forward, ready for her first job as his assistant. "I got you, boss man. What do you need?"

"Head to Mel's house and ask her to make the change from the petty cash," Malik instructed, "and tell her to include at least twenty-one-dollar bills. Thanks."

"You got it. I'll be back shortly." Heather headed out with a confident smile.

Meanwhile, Brooklyn was preparing to visit Brayden's house to pick up her watermelon after dropping Amina off at home. It was Brayden's week with their son, and as the primary parent for one week each month, Brayden takes Nate to school before work and picks him up in the afternoons. During the other weeks, they split the convenient co-parenting duties for Brooklyn, whose restaurant schedule wasn't as flexible as Brayden's since he was his own boss.

As they entered the house, passing through the kitchen into the family area, they noticed the front door was already open.

Brayden glanced outside and saw his parents sitting in their car. In contrast, Malik's parents stood next to it, engaged in what appeared to be a serious conversation.

Malik came downstairs, ready to take Mazo home, but he paused when he saw everyone looking out the door.

"What's up?" he asked, his brows furrowing in curiosity.

Before anyone could answer, Ms. Bria spotted Brayden standing in the doorway. She called out, waving for him to bring Malik along. After exchanging glances, they left Mazo and Nate inside with the girls and hurried outside.

As they approached the car, they noticed their moms were smiling. While the sight was reassuring, it only fueled their curiosity about what was happening.

"Do y'all remember us telling you about the oldest family member on my side, Ms. Evadine?" Ms. Bria asked, her eyes twinkling with excitement.

Malik, always one to cut straight to the point, wrapped his arm around his mom's shoulders. "Yes, Ma, we do. What's up? Out with it, Queen."

She chuckled at his impatience, knowing her son never liked drawn-out conversations when something seemed important.

Not long after, another car arrived, parking behind Brayden's parents' car in the driveway. An older woman got out, smiling warmly and hugging everyone.

While Amina played with Nate and Mazo, Brooklyn stayed by the front door, her curiosity piqued by the unfolding scene. She faintly heard Ms. Bria introduce the woman as Banky, Ms. Evadine's daughter.

The conversation with Banky continued for the next thirty minutes, and the emotions were intense. Everyone listened closely, their expressions a mix of surprise and disbelief. Moved by what they were hearing, the husbands made their way to their wives, wrapping their arms around their shoulders in silent support.

As the conversation drew close, the guys could be seen laughing together. Malik, pacing with one hand on his hip and the other on his head, smiled as he walked across the yard.

He and Brayden approached each other, dapped, and then shared a hug with their moms, who were shedding tears of joy.

After about ten more minutes, the tears and hugs started to subside. Still emotional, Bria and Joy sent Banky off with a heartfelt hug and a kiss on the cheek before heading into the house, still holding each other closely. Their eyes glistened with the remnants of tears. Malik and Brayden followed behind, big smiles on their faces. They shook their heads in disbelief at the unexpected turn of events.

Brayden made his way to Brooklyn, who had her arms open. Sensing the weight of his emotions, she welcomed him into a comforting embrace.

"What happened?" she asked anyone who would answer, her voice filled with curiosity as they pulled apart from the hug.

"We'll let them explain it to you," Ms. Bria replied, her smile warm and meaningful.

She, Ms. Joy, and the husbands wrapped everyone in a big hug before heading out in the Nelson's truck for what seemed like official business.

"Mazo, let's go, baby," Malik called to his daughter, who was sitting on the sofa beside Nate, both engrossed in their iPads. "Brayden will fill y'all in," he added, dapping Brayden and Nate before hugging the girls.

Mazo and Nate exchanged little daps and hugs, mimicking their dads, who had done it countless times as best friends.

"Aww, they're too adorable," Amina commented, smiling at the cute moment.

"Lock up for me, man," Malik said to Brayden as he headed outside, strapping Mazo into her car seat before leaving.

He needed time to process everything—what he'd just learned from Banky, the upcoming trip to Paris, and the unresolved feelings from his situation with Zora were a lot.

The twenty-minute drive to Zora's house gave him space to think, even though Mazo's random chatter along the way, which he secretly loved, kept him grounded.

"You have keys to his parents' house?" Amina asked Brayden, her face lighting up at the thought of how close their families were.

"Yeah, he has keys to my parents' house, too. But here's the real—Banky was schooling us on the fact that our moms share the same dad." He got right to it.

"What?!" Brooklyn and Amina both exclaimed simultaneously, their eyes wide and mouths agape.

"Yeah, it's a long story. But that's why our parents left together, heading to the hospital for a blood test. They needed to find out if there was any truth to it and fast."

The girls were stunned, shaking their heads.

Heather came through the front door just then, holding Malik's change. She stopped when she saw the expressions on everyone's faces, sensing the tension in the room.

"What's going on? Where's Malik? I got his change."

Brayden immediately filled her in, and Heather reacted with the same shocked expression as the girls.

Without warning, she ran up to Brayden, jumping into his arms like a child, her legs wrapping around him. He caught her effortlessly, laughing.

Amina scrunched her face, exchanging a look with Brooklyn.

Having heard more about Heather's life struggles, Brooklyn fanned Amina's expression away with a subtle giggle, gesturing for her to calm down.

Heather jumped down from Brayden, clearly excited. "It makes so much sense! I heard rumors about it as a kid, but I never gave it much thought...

Your moms have been best friends since they were little girls, growing up in the same neighborhood in a small town. Both can sing like angels, where you and Malik get your skills!"

Heather was thrilled to see the dynamics of them becoming first cousins, imagining it wouldn't be much different from the close bond they already shared.

After the excitement settled, Heather mentioned heading to Zora's to meet Malik, who had called her. Brayden secured the house, and everyone headed outside to their cars.

"You ready?" Brayden asked Nate, holding out his fist.

"Yes, sir, I'm hungry," Nate replied, giving his dad a fist pound before hopping into the car and strapping himself into the car seat.

"Boy, you're always hungry!" Brooklyn replied, chuckling.

"Do you want me to bring the watermelon to you?" Brayden asked Brooklyn.

"No, I'll come by and get it since I gotta take Amina home first. It looks like it's about to rain soon, too."

"Right. So, make it snappy, sexy," Brayden said, giving Brooklyn a quick kiss on the forehead and a wink.

She blushed, being caught off guard like that.

Amina shook her head and smiled.

"Girl, c'mon. Y'all make me sick!"

They laughed at her before entering their respective cars and going their separate ways.

Urban Coffee

Malik arrived at Zora's after stopping by the Quick-Serv carwash, a stop that his daughter thoroughly enjoyed. He pulled into the driveway and got out, helping Mazo, who had already unbuckled herself from the car seat. He told her to stand in the yard while he retrieved her suitcase from the back of the car.

Just then, Heather pulled up and parked in front of the house. She left her car running as she approached Malik.

Zora, still feeling physically and emotionally sick, was sitting on the back porch, lost in thought. She had heard Malik pull up and rushed inside, then went to the window, where her anger immediately surged when she saw Heather.

She watched them exchange money, then saw Heather hug Malik and give Mazo a high-five before returning to her car.

Zora was heated, so she hurried upstairs to grab her cell phone.

Shortly after, the doorbell rang repeatedly. Malik chuckled, recognizing Mazo's little fingers going at the doorbell, knowing how much it annoyed her mom. It took longer than usual for Zora to answer the door, so Malik knocked as well.

A few seconds later, Zora opened it, and Mazo jumped into her arms.

"Mommy! You missed the family day! You missed it!"

"I know, sweetie. Maybe we can have our own family day," Zora replied as she walked toward the couch, placing her cell phone on the living room table. Malik set Mazo's suitcase on the sofa next to her.

"How are you feeling?" he asked, having received a brief update earlier in the day from Zora's mom, Ms. Shanel.

"I'm good," she answered, tapping her foot on the floor unusually fast.

"Daddy, come help me," Mazo interrupted, grabbing her dad by the finger and pulling him toward the refrigerator. She pointed up at the Teddy Grahams sitting on top of the fridge. "Get that, Daddy—the bear cookies."

Malik chuckled and turned to Zora, asking if it was okay. She nodded, so he retrieved the cookies and returned to the couch. He stood momentarily, preparing to leave, but still concerned about Zora. He couldn't help it—he still loved her.

"You can't even look at me. Why is that?" he asked.

Her foot tapping stopped abruptly.

"Why would you bring that girl to my house?" She briefly glanced at him with her arms folded.

Malik grew tired of her constantly bringing up Heather, especially when she had nothing to do with their current problems. He wanted to get to the heart of what was bothering her.

"Zo, you don't know Heather. This doesn't make sense, and I think you know that."

Zora's arms remained folded, her feet still tapping. She kept glancing between her phone and the window, clearly distracted.

"I don't have to answer you. You made your choice," she muttered, avoiding eye contact.

"What choice is that, Zora?" Malik sighed deeply, frustration lacing his voice. "Since we're on this, we hired Heather as our assistant. That's why she was here giving me money that Mel changed out for my trip in the morning, her first assignment—that's it."

Zora didn't speak, at least not with words. But her breathing quickened, and her nose flared with frustration.

"Look, the mortgage payment—it's in the car. I'll grab it and be on my way," Malik said, annoyance evident in his voice.

As he turned to leave, Zora's phone suddenly rang. She answered it quickly, pressing the speaker button.

"Um...Hello?" she answered, her voice a little hesitant.

"Hey, boo. What's up?" a deep voice asked.

Before Malik stepped outside, he heard the male voice.

He glanced back at Zora, who looked directly at him for the first time since he'd brought their child home.

Um... I'll call you back, Damon," Zora said, quickly ending the call.

Malik scoffed, shaking his head. He turned and walked out the door to his car. Once inside, he grabbed the $2,400 from the glove compartment, still wrapped in a money band. He carried double the mortgage amount, but this time, he counted out $600—half of the exact monthly mortgage payment.

Inside, Zora was pacing in the kitchen when she suddenly stopped at the sound of Malik walking through the door.

He called out for Mazo, and she quickly ran to him from the dining room, where she had been sitting with her iPad and eating her Teddy Grahams. He hugged and kissed her, telling her how much he loved her.

Afterwards, Malik walked toward the kitchen, handed Zora the money, and told her it was his half of the mortgage contribution for their daughter. But before leaving, he had one more thing to address.

"As big as our issues are, did you feel the need to be this cold-hearted? Whatever your goal was, Zora, it worked. I'm done," he said softly, his gaze piercing her soul.

The hurt in Malik's eyes froze Zora in place. She locked eyes with him, unable to move, until he turned away and walked out the door.

At the sound of the door closing, Zora broke down. She sank into the kitchen chair, her head lowered, and cried overwhelmingly. When she finally looked at the money in her hand, panic flowed as she counted it. Suddenly, she grabbed the glass of cider she had been drinking earlier and threw it across the room.

The glass shattered loudly, causing Mazo to shriek and freeze, her eyes wide with shock as she looked at her mom.

Zora rushed to her, embracing her as she slowly sank to the floor. Mazo gently caressed her mom's hair, offering comfort as Zora wept in sorrow, consumed with regret.

"It's okay, Mom," Mazo said softly. "I'll call Daddy back. Don't cry; it's okay. Daddy will make you better."

Zora grabbed her cell phone and called her mom, almost pleading for help. After hearing what happened, Ms. Shanel spoke to her with tight lips.

"You can give it time for you two to cool off tonight, but you better call that man first thing in the morning and tell him what happened to you and his unborn child. It's not fair, Zora! And I pray he forgives you. You need to see the therapist, honey," her mom concluded earnestly.

Later that evening, Ms. Shanel drove over to be with her daughter.

Urban Coffee

It started pouring rain after a while. Brooklyn had already made it to Brayden's house to grab the watermelon he had cut and prepared for her household. Neatly diced and placed in containers for freshness, the rest had been sealed in freezer bags for smoothies.

"I can tell your daddy's a chef. Look how neatly this watermelon is prepared," Brooklyn said, inspecting the fridge and thanking Brayden for taking care of it.

"You're welcome, baby. It was my pleasure," he replied, walking past her to sit on the couch.

He had bathed Nate and tucked him into bed, letting him stay on his iPad a little longer, especially since his mom was stuck there due to the pouring rain. The weather app showed that the rain would settle in less than an hour.

For the last thirty minutes, they had been relaxing and discussing how difficult it would be to shift their relationship away from the physical aspect. They hoped to deepen their mental and spiritual connection, which had already been clear during and after their breakup.

*"A **mental** connection allows for open and effective communication, helping individuals align on similar goals and values and providing a solid foundation to sustain a long-term relationship. During difficult times, a **spiritual** connection offers comfort and guidance because humanity believes in something greater, a higher power."*

"Which is God!" Brooklyn affirmed.

"You better believe it, baby!" Brayden added, and they both chuckled.

Brooklyn had been reading aloud from Google, pointing out what they both agreed was missing in their relationship—the spiritual and mental aspects.

Brayden stood up, grabbed the remote, and played soft jazz. He reached for Brooklyn's hand, and she happily extended hers, allowing him to help her out of the chair. They moved together slowly, in sync, embracing each other, their gazes locked in a genuine love.

“We’ve got a lot of work to do,” Brayden said seriously. She nodded, strongly agreeing.

“Remember what my dad said earlier about praying for these connections with God first because He already knows our desires?”

“Yeah, I was listening. Your dad got deep, too. I enjoyed him,” Brooklyn admitted proudly.

They were thrilled to share this journey, agreeing to work on themselves both together and individually. A family dynamic had already been established with their son, Nate, and marriage was on the horizon as they continued to grow and learn more about each other.

As they danced slowly to the soft music, they shared an intimate kiss and embraced each other tightly. Suddenly, a loud clap of thunder echoed, and Brooklyn, instantly frightened, held on tighter.

“Uh-uh! Maybe God is saying we’re too close,” Brayden said with wide eyes, gently guiding Brooklyn back toward the loveseat and turning off the music.

Brooklyn, still scared, laughed at him as he sat back down on the couch, glancing around. Eventually, he chuckled, too, shaking his head.

“You are so silly,” she said, smiling.

Shortly after, the rain had intensified, sounding like huge droplets pounding on the pavement. Brayden turned off the TV, and they sat silently, listening to the soothing sound of the rain.

Five minutes passed quietly before the doorbell rang.

They both exchanged confused looks, their brows furrowed. Brayden got up to peek out the window before opening the door, and to his surprise, it was Keisha. She was wearing shorts and a tank top, her hair disheveled and eyeliner smeared. Her bloodshot eyes made it clear she had been crying or drinking. She was soaking wet.

"Keisha, what are you doing out here in this weather?" Brayden asked, genuinely concerned and confused.

"I'm pregnant!" Keisha yelled before turning to leave.

Her words hit Brooklyn like a blow to her gut, and she quickly stood up, her hand covering her mouth in shock.

"Keisha! Where are you going?" Brayden called after her, but she didn't look back or say another word. Brayden watched as she walked down the driveway, got into her car, and sped off.

He closed the door, his heart pounding, and turned to Brooklyn. Tears were welling in her eyes, and the weight of the situation hit him hard. Brayden went to embrace Brooklyn, his chest tight with confusion. It felt like a sledgehammer had struck him.

Urban Coffee

Monday Morning 5 a.m.

Malik, preferring to stay productive, woke up early to meditate for 20 minutes, brush his teeth, make coffee, and prepare for his departure. His breakfast consisted of two hard-boiled eggs and three slices of grass-fed bacon. Afterward, he gulped down an entire bottle of spring water—his early morning ritual before any flight.

Mel had already sent over his itinerary, detailing his scheduled Uber ride to the airport, hotel check-in times, internship location details, meetings, and even his downtime.

She had accounted for everything for the next few weeks of his trip, right up to the flight back home. Malik and Brayden had always been able to trust her with all the company plans and agendas—she was indeed a business graduate in every sense.

This morning, Malik wanted to disconnect fully, especially after speaking with his dad the night before. His dad had advised him to try his best to disengage, suggesting he turn off his phone once he settled on the plane. He wanted Malik to focus on wrapping everything up, including closing the deals in Alpine City. Mr. Nelson assured him that Mazo would be well taken care of.

With about fifteen minutes to spare before the Uber arrived, Malik felt he had everything under control—until his cell phone rang.

"Hey, BC, what's up?"

"Good morning. I was checking in before you took off. Have we made any decisions about the project to seal the deal with the coffee café in the city? I know our meeting is a week away, but with everything else going on... I don't know."

Malik sighed deeply before responding.

"Yeah, I know. I desperately need a mental break," he admitted, especially after hearing about Brayden's issue with Keisha late last night.

They had set all these goals, plans, and sacrifices only to have to rewrite them and make more sacrifices, only to see everything fall apart suddenly.

Before Malik's Uber arrived, he and Brayden briefly discussed whether they should continue pursuing other surprise projects. Ultimately, these extra projects contributed to Malik losing his relationship. It was all part of the plan when they eventually decided to turn their house-flipping hobby into a business a couple of years after graduating high school."

Malik and Brayden obtained their Real Estate, Business, and Contractor's licenses before Malik left to pursue his bachelor's and master's degrees in Architecture. Right after, Brayden earned his broker's license to ensure state and legal compliance for their company and to hire real estate agents and contractors in the future.

Given Malik's advanced skills in his field, he connected with industry professionals to complete a building for their company's launch and their dream homes in Alpine City.

Over the past six years, they've worked tirelessly to build Nelson Coleman Realty while also supporting their partners, Zora and Brooklyn, as they pursued their shared dream of owning a coffee shop. This was one of the projects they couldn't share with the girls. It was the ultimate surprise gift.

Malik had already designed the Nelson Coleman building, the coffee café, and the dream homes he and Brayden envisioned sharing with their families in Alpine Crest Villas, a new up-and-coming community in Alpine City, down the Boulevard, fifteen minutes past the city's nightlife.

Some of the additional projects Malik secured were intended to provide the extra funds to build the Urban Coffee Cafe. Hearing the girls' dreams over the years about the urban décor and coffee flavors made it clear that incorporating the café into their realty company's future plans was a no-brainer.

With the realty company and dream homes almost complete, Malik was preparing for his final trip to Japan to complete the architectural internship hours required for his master's degree and architectural licensure. He had planned to spend this last road journey with his family—Mazo and Zora—one of the many surprises to share with her, or so he thought.

After Paris, Japan was supposed to be his last major trip. He had prayed that he and Zora could hold on just a little longer—only a few more months until everything settled. But now, everything felt out of reach, not just with her, but even on Brayden's end. Nothing seemed within grasp anymore.

As Malik finished his call with Brayden, the Uber driver arrived. He gathered his suitcases and carry-on bag, secured his home, and headed to the airport.

Urban Coffee

He arrived at the airport and quickly checked in. With an hour and fifteen minutes to spare before boarding, he decided to grab an iced coffee.

While waiting for his order, his name echoed through the air—a voice he could never forget, though he thought he'd never hear again. Turning, he saw her standing there, even more beautiful than he remembered.

"Malena?" he asked, shocked but happy to see her.

"Hey!" she replied, smiling, her breath quickening.

"I've missed you so much! I can't believe it's you!" Malena confessed as if seeing him again was something she'd been praying for.

Malena is a striking woman of mixed Spanish and African American heritage with a gorgeous smile. Her long, silky, dark brunette hair complemented her 5-foot-9-inch frame perfectly. As a part-time model, she carried herself with an effortless elegance. She looked stunning in her navy blue flight attendant uniform, a full-time job she'd held for five years.

She ran to Malik and embraced him tightly as if she never wanted to let go. He returned the embrace, thankful she had been okay all this time. And for the next thirty minutes, they enjoyed each other's company. Malena, smiling the whole time.

"I'll never forget how you treated me in our relationship... your kisses, the way you held me. You always made sure I was okay. The list goes on and on. I felt so secure with you," she admitted, blushing.

"And then, you left me," he responded playfully.

"No! No! I promise, it wasn't..."

"It's okay, I was just joking," Malik interrupted, his voice soft as he caressed her cheek to calm her.

She gently placed her hand over his, holding it on her face.

Staying true to the humbling spirit he was born with, Malik expressed his appreciation for her sharing her feelings during their two years together. He also ensured she knew their breakup wasn't either of their faults. Her family had to move, and though it was tough, it was a decision Malena's father had to make for his own family.

These two had been high school sweethearts during their junior and senior years, and her parents adored Malik. They caught up as much as possible until Malena's co-workers arrived to fetch her for boarding.

I'll see you when you come on board," Malena said. "I'll be the one helping you find your seat, making sure you're settled and having everything you need."

She kissed him on the cheek before leaving.

Malik scoffed and smiled at her, and she couldn't help but blush. His attentive gaze was always so mesmerizing.

"Okay, thank you," Malik responded. See you soon."

"Girl, he is fine! Who the heck is that?!" one of Malena's flight attendant friends whispered as they walked towards the gate. They all laughed, eager for Malena to spill the tea.

Malik was happy to see her, but his thoughts quickly shifted back to Zora. But just as quickly, the thoughts faded. He knew he needed to disengage, just as his dad had encouraged.

Once he was settled in his seat as promised, he reached for his phone and turned it off—just as Zora's call came through, going straight to voicemail.................. *THE END*.

Urban Coffee II: Picks up with Malik in Paris with his high school sweetheart, Malena. He hadn't spoken to Zora for over a month, leaving her emotionally confused. Struggling with remorse, Zora must reveal painful secrets that could change everything. She's sought therapy in hopes of healing and reconnecting with Malik—will it be enough?

Meanwhile, Brayden and Keisha's drama escalates after her pregnancy is revealed. Keisha's manipulative ways threaten Brayden and Brooklyn's second chance at a future together. Will Brayden return to Keisha, or can his relationship with Brooklyn survive?

Rocco and Amina face new challenges with a third party in the mix, while Devin confronts her past with Chris, a man five years her junior.

As the group navigates love, friendship, and personal growth, a sudden tragedy shakes them to their core.

Urban Coffee II: Explores the complexities of relationships, loss, and self-discovery. Heartache and joy await, leaving readers on the edge of their seats.

About the Author

Denitres B. is a passionate storyteller whose work reflects real-life scenarios and the complexity of human relationships. This book has lived in the depths of my consciousness for a long time, and I am thrilled to have finally completed it. *Urban Coffee: Revised Edition* marks the peak of a 25-year journey, bringing a deeply relatable story to life.

With a background in Business Studies and Social Science, I have spent over 19 years as an administrator in the Technical College System of Georgia and have also become a certified career facilitator.

Apart from storytelling, I enjoy freelance photography, watching suspenseful dramas, and other hobbies that are too numerous to list here. Thank you for joining me on this incredible journey.

Happy reading!

Acknowledgments

To my family, your dedicated love and support have been the backbone of this journey. Your patience, encouragement, and belief in me have kept me grounded and inspired. Thank you for always being there, celebrating the highs, and reassuring me during the lows. Your faith in me has been my greatest motivation.

To my CGTC family, your feedback has been invaluable. Thank you for keeping me on my toes, for your thoughtful critiques, and for always encouraging me to push my boundaries. Your positive reviews when reading samples have helped me stay encouraged when I needed it. I am deeply grateful for your continuous support. *"You know who you are."*

Made in the USA
Columbia, SC
20 September 2025

62139938R00152